A RAVAGED SKIES NOVEL

DECAYED WORLD

DJ COOPER

"In the apocalypse, I think those average, mediocre folks are the ones who are going to live."

—Colson Whitehead

Contents

"FOR THE END OF THE WORLD WAS
LONG AGO, AND ALL WE DWELL
TO-DAY AS CHILDREN OF SOME
SECOND BIRTH, LIKE A STRANGE
PEOPLE LEFT ON EARTH AFTER A
JUDGMENT DAY.
-G K CHESTERTON

Maddie

"Stop." The word muted in Maddie's ear like an ominous whisper, barely audible over the desperate rhythm of her hands pressing against her father's sternum. "Please stop," the disembodied voice said again.

Emily's fingers circled Maddie's wrist, firm but gentle. "Maddie."

She jerked herself away from the grip and pushed harder, ignoring the way her father's ribs yielded beneath her palms. The carpet beneath her knees was sodden with spilled water and her father's bodily fluids, the wool fibers rough against her skin.

"Fifteen compressions, then two breaths," she muttered to herself, trying to remember the exact cadence from her high school lifeguard training. Had it been fifteen or thirty? The panic scattered her thoughts, making the half-remembered certification course blur together. She'd only used CPR once before, on a practice dummy. The training mannequin hadn't felt like this — yielding, cooling flesh beneath her hands.

She bent to deliver rescue breaths, struggling to form a proper seal around her father's mouth. The copper taste of his blood lingered on her lips from the last attempt, mixed with the sour tang of vomit. She counted compressions again, then more breaths. Fifteen more compressions. Two more breaths. She had been a lifeguard in high school, three summers ago. The certification card was still in her wallet, though she'd never needed it until now. CPR worked in movies. It had to work here.

"He's gone, Maddie." Emily's voice cracked. "It's been twenty minutes."

Twenty minutes. The facts scrolled through Maddie's mind like a textbook she had skimmed for an exam: brain damage begins at four minutes without oxygen. Irreversible damage at six minutes. Death at ten.

She kept counting. Thirteen, fourteen, fifteen.

"Maddie." Michael's voice now, from somewhere behind her. "You need to stop."

Her arms burned. Sweat plastered her hair to her forehead, dripped into her eyes and stung. The familiar living room of her childhood home swam before her, the flashlight beams casting grotesque shadows across her father's blue-tinged face. The smell of sickness hung heavy in the air—the sharp, distinctive odor of death was everywhere, clinging to her like a cloying cheap perfume.

Outside, heat pressed against the windows despite the late hour, the July air felt thick and suffocating. Sweat trickled down Maddie's back, her shirt sticking to her skin as the temperature inside the house rose without electricity for cooling. The stifling heat only accelerated the sickness, making the room reek of its subtle grip on the living.

"You need to compress deeper," Emily said softly, her nurse's instincts taking over despite the futility. "At least two inches."

Maddie pressed harder, frustrated at her own inadequacy. The basic CPR from that summer course seemed laughably insufficient now. If only she'd paid attention when her father insisted she take the advanced first aid course instead of the minimum required for lifeguarding. If only she'd gone to nursing school like Hannah instead of business management.

Her father's chest didn't rise with the breaths anymore.

Someone's hand gripped her shoulder, trying to pull her back. Maddie shrugged it off violently.

"Don't touch me!" The words tore from her throat, raw and unfamiliar. "I can still save him!"

"His heart stopped nearly half an hour ago." Emily's professional detachment was crumbling; her eyes shone with unshed tears. "The toxin was too much for his system. We did everything we could."

"We didn't do enough." Maddie's hands kept moving, mechanical, relentless. Compressions that pushed blood through vessels that no longer needed it. A heart that would never restart on its own. "I should've been here sooner. If I'd been here when they first got sick—"

"Madison." Her mother's voice, weak but unmistakable from the sofa across the room. Katherine Foster lifted a trembling hand. "Enough, sweetheart. Let him go."

Maddie's hands froze mid-compression. Her mother hadn't called her Madison since she was twelve—the day she crashed her father's truck into the mailbox. She looked down at his face—the face she'd known all her life—and only a stranger looked back. Skin mottled and waxy. Lips blue-black. Eyes half-open but seeing nothing.

She sat back on her heels, her bloody hands falling limply to her sides.

"Time of death," Emily said quietly, habit more than necessity, "9:47 p.m."

Time of death. Such a clinical phrase. As if her father's life could be reduced to a notation in a chart. As if anything would ever be the same again.

Michael stepped forward, gently pulling a quilt—her mother's favorite, with the patchwork maple leaves—over David Foster's face. The fabric settled like snow, outlining the contours of his nose, his chin, the hollow of his throat.

"I'll help move him," Michael said, his voice low. "We need to…"

He didn't finish the sentence. They all knew what needed to be done. Bodies couldn't stay. Not anymore. Not with the disease spreading.

"Not yet." Maddie's voice was flat, emotionless. "I need a minute."

The others exchanged glances, then quietly withdrew to the kitchen, leaving Maddie alone with her father's body and her mother, who lay shivering under three blankets on the sofa, her skin ashen, her eyes fever-bright as they fixed on Maddie.

"He was proud of you," Katherine whispered. "He kept saying you'd make it back to us."

Maddie couldn't respond. Her throat had closed. A heaviness settled in like concrete hardening in her chest. She reached for her father's hand beneath the quilt. Still warm. The calluses on his palm rough against her fingers—working hands, builder's hands. Hands she should have paid more attention to as they showed her how to fix a leaky faucet, replace a light switch, distinguish between different types of screws.

"Come on, Mads, you never know when you'll need to tell a wood screw from a machine screw," he'd said just last Christmas break, trying to coax her into the store's stockroom to learn inventory.

"Dad, I'm majoring in business, not hardware," she'd

replied, rolling her eyes. *"Besides, when will I ever need to know the difference between galvanized and stainless steel?"*

She squeezed her father's hand now, waiting for the squeeze back that had always been there—when she graduated high school, when she'd left that day for the college tour on the Downeaster with Hannah and Grace.

Nothing. Just flesh, cooling by degrees.

The scent of woodsmoke and pine from his skin was already fading, replaced by the clinical smell of death that no amount of incense or flowers had ever successfully masked at funerals. Soon there would be nothing left of him but memories.

She stood abruptly, her knees protesting after so long on the hard floor. The living room of her home had been transformed in the hours since her arrival. Medical supplies littered the coffee table. The fireplace remained cold despite the stacked wood—nobody had the strength to light it and it was too damn hot anyway. Family photographs watched from the walls, smiling from a time that would never return.

"We need to move him," Emily said, returning to Maddie's side. Her usually neat blonde hair was disheveled, dark circles under her eyes from days without proper sleep. "And your mother needs more intensive care than we can provide here."

"The funeral home," Maddie said, remembering their discussions from earlier. "You said we could set up there."

Emily nodded. "It has running water—they had their own well with a hand pump in the embalming room." She paused wincing then continued, "And more space. James is bringing the wagon now."

"I'll get Mom ready." Maddie's voice was sharper than intended. "She needs to be moved carefully."

Her mother's condition had deteriorated rapidly in the

hours since Maddie had arrived home. What had already been severe symptoms—diarrhea, stomach cramps, dehydration— had progressed despite Emily's intervention. Her skin tented when Maddie pinched it, staying raised instead of bouncing back. Her eyes had sunk into her skull, lips cracked and bleeding.

"Mom?" Maddie kneeled beside the sofa. "We're going to move you to somewhere we can take better care of you, okay?"

Katherine's gaze wandered, unfocused. Her lips moved, but no sound emerged.

"She needs more IV fluids," Maddie said to Emily, who had begun gathering their limited supplies. "Do we have any left?"

"One bag," Emily admitted. "But there might be more at the funeral home. Neal, the director, was something of a prepper according to Beth."

Outside, the creak of wagon wheels and the soft whinny of a horse announced James's arrival. Maddie moved to the window, pushing back the curtain. The night air shimmered with heat, the aurora's glow still visible above the tree line, painting everything in sickly green and purple. James sat at the front of a simple farm wagon, the dappled mare shifting restlessly between the traces. Next to him sat Daniel, rifle across his knees, scanning the darkness.

Even now, they couldn't travel without protection. The world had changed that much.

"They're here," Maddie said, letting the curtain fall back. "Let's get her ready."

Moving her mother was a careful process. They wrapped her in blankets, transferred her to a makeshift stretcher fashioned from an ironing board. Katherine moaned in pain as they lifted her, the sound cutting through Maddie like a physical blow.

"I'm sorry, Mom," she whispered, though she wasn't sure her mother could hear her. "It's going to be okay."

Lies came so easily now.

Her father's body was more difficult—both physically and emotionally. Michael and James wrapped him in a tarp, their movements quick and necessary in the heat. Maddie watched from the porch, the night air offering no relief from the oppressive temperature, as they loaded him into the back of the wagon.

"I'll ride with her," Maddie said as they carefully placed her mother beside her father's shrouded form. The symmetry wasn't lost on her—her parents, side by side in death or near-death, as they had been in life.

She climbed into the wagon, settling on the rough wooden boards. The tarp covering her father's body bulged unnaturally in the weak light. Her mother's face was ghostly pale, her breathing shallow but present. Maddie pulled a woolen blanket higher despite the heat, trying to shield her from the eyes of onlookers.

The wagon jerked forward, wheels grinding against the dry gravel of the driveway. Through the darkness, Maddie could make out other shapes moving along Main Street—shadowy figures heading in the same direction.

"There are other cases," Emily explained, sitting beside her. "At least five more in town. Beth's organizing everyone to bring them to the funeral home."

"It's spreading," Maddie said flatly.

"Yes." Emily's honesty was both brutal and necessary. "And without proper treatment…"

She didn't need to finish the sentence. Without proper treatment, they would die like her father. All of them.

The wagon rolled slowly down Main Street, past dark storefronts she'd known all her life. Foster's Hardware—her father's store—stood on the corner, its windows reflecting the aurora's strange light. How many times had she perched on the counter as a child, watching her father help customers find just the right tool, the right part? How many summer days had she spent stocking shelves, pretending to know the difference between galvanized and stainless steel nails, Phillips and flathead screwdrivers? She'd stacked them where told, arranged inventory by numbers on a sheet, but never truly absorbed the knowledge her father tried to share.

"You know," he'd say, holding up two seemingly identical nails, "this one will rust if you use it outside. This one won't." But she'd been texting friends, thinking about college applications, her mind elsewhere.

Beyond the hardware store, Kristie's Diner showed a faint glow—the only lighted building on the street. Kristie had somehow kept the place running with an old oil stove, serving coffee and whatever food could be scavenged. A gathering place for the living while Maddie headed to a gathering place for the dying.

The funeral home loomed at the end of Main Street, a Victorian monstrosity with a wide front porch. In the heavy darkness, its ornate trim and shuttered windows appeared sinister, unwelcoming. Neal & York Funeral Home, according to the weathered sign. The irony wasn't lost on her—the place where they'd held her grandmother's funeral three years ago would now become both a hospital and a morgue.

Activity swarmed around the entrance. Beth Martin directed people carrying stretchers and supplies, her voice sharp and clear in the stagnant air. Lanterns cast pools of yellow light around the porch, illuminating grim faces and determined movements.

"Bring her inside first," Beth called as their wagon approached. "We've got the main viewing room set up."

The internal geography of the funeral home was familiar to Maddie, though she'd only been there for services. The formal parlor had been transformed—funeral chairs stacked against walls, viewing tables repurposed as patient beds. Someone had lit dozens of candles, their flickering light softening the clinical transformation of the space.

They transferred her mother to an antique fainting couch, its velvet upholstery incongruously elegant amidst the makeshift medical setup. Katherine didn't stir during the move, her condition deteriorating by the minute.

"I need to change her IV," Maddie said, her voice steadier than she felt. She'd watched Emily do it earlier—it didn't look that complicated. Just tubes and needles and saline. "Where are the supplies?"

"Director's office," Beth replied, appearing at her elbow. The police chief had abandoned her uniform, dressed instead in practical cargo pants and a flannel shirt, but the badge still hung from her belt alongside her holster. "Down the hall, first door on the right."

Maddie nodded and headed in that direction, navigating by memory and candlelight. The floor creaked beneath her feet, the elegant wallpaper barely visible in the gloom. The funeral home smelled different than she remembered—dust and disuse mixed with the floral arrangements that had mysteriously survived without water or care, creating a sickly-sweet undertone.

The director's office was untouched, a time capsule from

before. Heavy curtains. Leather-bound appointment book open on the desk. A half-drunk cup of coffee sat on the corner. Maddie pulled open drawers, searching for anything useful. The bottom drawer revealed a cache: IV bags, tubing, antibiotics, analgesics. More than should have been in a funeral home.

"Neal was a prepper," Beth said from the doorway, arms crossed over her chest. "Had a whole conspiracy theory about government collapse. Guess he was right, just for the wrong reasons."

"Is there more?" Maddie asked, gathering supplies with trembling hands.

"Basement's full. Food, water purification, ammunition. We've been keeping it quiet—don't need a riot on our hands."

"My mother's dying," Maddie said bluntly. "We need antibiotics, IV fluids, whatever he has."

Beth studied her, then nodded. "I'm sorry about your dad, Maddie. He was always good to me—gave me credit at the hardware store when I was renovating my place last year." She paused. "I'll help you carry whatever you need upstairs. But we need to be smart about rationing."

Rationing. Another word that had taken on new significance. Before, it meant cutting back on desserts or screen time. Now it meant deciding who lived and who died.

"I understand," Maddie said, though she didn't, not really. If it were up to her, every drop of medicine would go to her mother.

They gathered supplies in silence: IV kits, saline bags, antibiotics, syringes, gauze. Beth helped her carry them to the makeshift ward.

The former viewing room now held eight patients. Her mother, five from town, and two children Maddie recognized from the Thompson farm. All with the same symptoms: severe diarrhea, vomiting, dehydration, fever. Classic cholera presentation, according to Emily, though without lab tests, they couldn't be certain.

Her mother lay nearest the door, her breathing increasingly labored. Maddie knelt beside her, taking her hand. The skin felt like tissue paper, the bones beneath fragile as bird wings.

"Mom? I'm going to change your IV, okay? It'll help you feel better."

Katherine's eyes fluttered open, unfocused. "David?"

Maddie's heart constricted. "It's Maddie, Mom. Dad's…" She couldn't finish.

"I know," Katherine whispered. "I saw them take him away. But he was just here, talking to me."

Hallucinations. A bad sign. Maddie swallowed hard and reached for the IV kit.

The rubber tubing felt tacky against her fingertips as she pulled it. She stared at the connections, suddenly doubting herself. Which went where? The spike? The drip chamber? She'd watched Emily do this, but watching and doing were completely different things.

"Here, let me help," Emily said gently, appearing at her side. She didn't take over completely, but guided Maddie's hands. "You connect this end to the port, like this. Then hang the bag higher—it needs gravity to flow properly."

Maddie nodded, grateful for the assistance yet burning with shame at her own incompetence. She hung the new saline bag from a coat rack someone had repurposed as an IV pole.

"Good," Emily said, uncapping a syringe filled with antibiotics. "Last of the cipro. Let's hope it helps."

Maddie nodded, watching the clear fluid drip into the tube, traveling toward her mother's bloodstream. Too little, too late. The thought came unbidden, unwelcome. She pushed it away.

"I found these in Dad's desk when I got back," she said, pulling a battered notebook from her pocket. The leather cover was worn smooth from handling, the pages dog-eared and stained with various substances. "His notes on water purification, filtering systems. He'd been trying to clean the water but wasn't quite right. If I'd been here sooner..."

"It doesn't matter now," Emily said, her voice flat with exhaustion. "He's gone."

The words hung in the air, undeniable and final.

Maddie flipped through the notebook, her father's familiar handwriting a physical pain in her chest. The pencil marks were smudged in places, but the diagrams were meticulous, each measurement precise. Technical terms leapt from the pages— activated carbon, micron ratings, reverse osmosis—words her father had tried to teach her when she'd reluctantly helped in the store. She remembered shelving water filters, nodding as he explained their purposes, her mind wandering to weekend plans.

Now, staring at these notes, she realized how little she'd absorbed. The diagrams were clear enough, but the terminology was a foreign language. Not for the first time, she wished she'd paid attention when her father spoke about his work with passion in his eyes.

A commotion at the front door pulled her attention. Michael entered, supporting a small figure—Ryan, Daniel's seven-year-old son. The boy's face was ashen, his body limp.

"He started vomiting an hour ago," Michael explained, laying Ryan on an empty fainting couch. "Sarah found him drinking from the creek this morning. Told him not to, but…"

But he was seven years old, and the world made no sense anymore.

Emily moved quickly to examine him, her face grim. "Same symptoms. We need to start rehydration immediately."

Maddie's gaze moved from Ryan to her mother, then to the other patients. Eight people fighting for their lives because of contaminated water. A problem with a solution—one her father had already mapped out in his messy scrawl, if only she could decipher it properly.

She stood, notebook clutched in her hand. "I'm going to try to implement Dad's filtration system. Tonight."

Emily looked up from Ryan's bedside. "Maddie, you need rest. Your father just—"

"Died." She didn't anticipate the harshness of the words, but it didn't change anything. "He died because our water is poisoned," Maddie finished. "And my mother will follow him if we don't fix this. So will Ryan, and who knows how many others." Her voice hardened. "I have to try something. The hardware store has supplies. I just need to figure out exactly what he was working on."

She turned and walked out before anyone could argue, her father's notebook like a talisman in her hand. The night air hit her face, still hot even after sunset. Humidity hung heavy in the air, making each breath feel thick and inadequate. Main Street stretched before her, dark and silent except for a single lantern burning in Kristie's Diner.

Implementation would require supplies from her father's hardware store. Tools. Materials. Knowledge she only partially possessed. She was a business major, not an engineer. She'd never built anything more complicated than a bookshelf, and that had been with her father's guidance every step of the way.

But what choice did she have? Wait for more to die?

Grief and anger coalesced into something hard and sharp inside her chest. There was no time for the luxury of breakdown, no space for the weight of loss. There was only the work that needed doing, even if she wasn't sure she could do it.

She paused, pulling the small leather-bound journal from her bag. The journal Hannah had given her on her birthday. "For documenting our amazing adventures on our way to college," she'd said. Maddie stared at the blank page, then sat on the curb to write by flashlight:

Hannah, I miss you so much right now. Dad died tonight. He never even woke up to say goodbye. I keep thinking that if I'd gotten home sooner, maybe I could have done something. Maybe even saved him. I know you could have. You'd know what to do with his notes, how to build what he designed. I'm terrified I'll mess it up. Mom's really sick too. Everyone is. I'm scared I'm going to lose her too. It feels like the world is just taking everything, one piece at a time. I keep seeing Grace's face when she went under. You feel so far away now in South Portland. When I left I could see your figure getting smaller as I walked away. And now Dad. I don't know if you'll ever read this. I don't even know if you're still alive. But I need to believe you are. I need to believe someone I love is going to survive this. -M

She closed the journal, tucking it back into her bag. The grief would have to wait. There was work to do, knowledge to decipher, skills to learn far too late.

The key to the store waited where it always had—on the hook by the back door. She grabbed it and set off down the street toward Foster's Hardware. Her father's hardware store. A place filled with tools she couldn't name, materials she barely understood, and a chance—perhaps the only one—to save what remained of her world.

Behind her, in the transformed funeral home, her mother fought for every breath. Ahead, the ghost of her father's store—the business he'd built with decades of work, now just another dark building in a dead town.

She gripped his notebook tighter, knuckles white as the tears now rolled freely down her cheeks. She didn't know what she was doing, just that she had to try.

James

The morning air hung heavy with dew as James made his way across the farmyard. Even at this early hour, the July heat promised another scorching day. Insects buzzed in the tall grass beyond the fence line, and somewhere in the distance, a mourning dove called out, its melancholy notes carrying across the fields.

He paused at the well, drawing up a bucket of water. They'd gotten lucky—their deep well remained uncontaminated, unlike the town's water supply. Six more people had fallen ill overnight, according to Michael's report when he'd returned from his shift at the funeral home. That made fourteen cases now, and two deaths. David Foster gone, and old Mrs. Wilkins from the retirement community.

James splashed cold water on his face, the shock of it momentarily clearing the fog of exhaustion. He hadn't slept more than three hours at a stretch in weeks. Neither had Sarah. They'd transformed their peaceful farm into something between a fortress and a refugee camp. Thirteen people now lived on their property, not counting family.

Before heading to the barn, he detoured to the east wing of the farmhouse, where they'd set up a makeshift recovery room for Ryan. His grandson had been one of the first to fall ill after drinking from the creek, despite Sarah's explicit warnings to all the children about using only well water. The boy was on the mend now, though still weak.

James eased open the door to find Ethan sitting beside his cousin's bed, attempting to read aloud from a worn copy of Treasure Island. At ten, Ethan struggled with some of the words, his brow furrowed in concentration.

"'The—cap-tain,' he read haltingly, "…was the ab—abb—'"

"Abomination," James supplied gently.

Both boys looked up, Ryan offering a wan smile from beneath his blankets. His usually rosy cheeks remained pale, but the alertness in his eyes was a welcome improvement from the glassy stare of two days ago.

"Grandpa," Ryan croaked, his voice still rough. "Ethan's reading me pirate stories."

"I can see that." James ruffled Ethan's hair and sat on the edge of the bed. "How are you feeling today, sailor?"

"Better." Ryan shifted, wincing slightly. "Mom says I can maybe get up tomorrow."

"If your fever stays down," James qualified, pressing the back of his hand to the boy's forehead. Still warm, but not burning like before. "You gave us quite a scare, young man."

Ethan closed the book, marking his place with a frayed ribbon. "I told him not to drink from the creek," he said, his voice tinged with the self-importance of a child who'd been proven right. "I told him it was poison."

"You did the right thing trying to warn him," James said. "But we all make mistakes. The important thing is that Ryan's getting better." He turned to his grandson. "No more creek water though, right? Only from the well or what your grandmother boils for you."

Ryan nodded solemnly, his eyes downcast. "I was just really thirsty from playing. The well was too far away."

James noticed the dark circles under Ethan's eyes, the tightness in his small shoulders. The boy had barely left Ryan's side since they'd brought him back from the funeral home, insisting on helping with everything from changing sheets to feeding his cousin broth. Taking on responsibilities far beyond his years.

"You were right, Ethan. Very smart." James squeezed his grandson's shoulder. "But Ryan's going to be fine now, thanks to your mother's care. And yours."

Ethan nodded solemnly, like a miniature adult accepting a professional compliment. It troubled James, seeing childhood slip away so quickly.

"I saw dead people," Ethan said suddenly, his voice flat. "At the funeral place. When Dad took me to bring supplies."

The statement hung in the air, matter-of-fact and chilling.

"Ethan…" James began, unsure how to respond.

"They were just laying there. With sheets over them. But I could see their faces when they moved them." He looked down at his hands. "Mr. Foster was one of them."

James felt his chest tighten. He'd known Michael had taken Ethan to the funeral home—they needed all available hands for deliveries—but hadn't realized what the boy had witnessed.

"That must have been scary," James said carefully.

Ethan shrugged with forced casualness. "I'm not scared. Dad says we have to be strong now." He glanced at Ryan. "Being scared is for babies."

Before James could correct this concerning philosophy, the sound of approaching footsteps drew their attention. Sarah appeared in the doorway, carrying a tray with a bowl of broth and a small slice of cornbread.

"Breakfast for our patient," she announced cheerfully, though James could see the strain behind her smile. "And Ethan, your mother's looking for you. She's back from town and wants to check on that cut on your arm."

Ethan hesitated, looking reluctant to leave his post.

"Go on," James encouraged. "You've been a great help, but Ryan needs to eat now. You can come back after your mother sees you."

With a reluctant nod, Ethan slipped from the room, his small shoulders squared with unnatural rigidity.

Sarah set the tray across Ryan's lap, helping him sit up against the pillows. "Small sips," she instructed gently, handing him the spoon. She turned to James, lowering her voice. "Emily's brought news. Michael found two more cases in the northern part of town."

James nodded grimly. Just what they needed—the illness spreading further.

"I'll speak with her after I check the barn," he said. "I thought I heard something there earlier."

Sarah raised an eyebrow. "Probably just the new cat family. That orange tomcat from the Jenkins place has been hanging around our tabby."

"Maybe." But James's instincts told him otherwise. "I'll just make a quick check."

He left Ryan to Sarah's ministrations and headed back outside. The weight of responsibility pressed down on him with each passing day. They looked to him for answers he didn't have, for security he couldn't guarantee, for food that was stretched thinner with each meal.

He straightened, wiping his face with a handkerchief, and looked out across what had been his retirement project. The vegetable gardens had tripled in size, sprawling across what used to be the east pasture. Daniel and Michael had strung a makeshift fence around the perimeter using wire salvaged from abandoned properties. Beyond that, the remains of the corn crop wilted in the relentless heat, too little rainfall making each ear smaller than it should be.

The distant sound of the barn door creaking pulled his attention. Odd—Sarah wouldn't be collecting eggs for another hour at least. He squinted against the rising sun, watching the barn door swing partially closed again.

His hand moved automatically to his waistband, fingers brushing against the grip of the revolver he now carried everywhere. The gun had been his father's, stored unused in the back of his closet for decades. Now it felt like an extension of his arm, as necessary as his work gloves or pocket knife.

"Sarah?" he called toward the house. No answer. She was tending to Ryan. Emily had been at the funeral home all night with the sick, and Michael remained in town, helping to organize security after rumors of strangers seen on the outskirts.

James moved toward the barn, ears straining for any sound. Another creak of hinges, softer this time. Someone was definitely in there.

He drew the revolver, the weight of it unfamiliar and awkward in his palm. He'd fired it exactly twice since the CME—once to test it, once to kill a rabid fox that had attacked one of their chickens. The idea of using it against a person still felt like something from another world, not the life he'd built over sixty-four years.

"Who's there?" His voice rang out sharper than intended as

he approached the barn door. "I'm armed. Show yourself."

Silence answered him.

He nudged the door with his foot, wincing at the groan of hinges. They'd been meaning to oil them for weeks, but there were always more urgent tasks. Inside, the barn lay in partial darkness, shafts of morning light streaming through gaps in the wooden slats, illuminating dust motes and spider webs.

"Last chance," he called. "Come out now."

A rustling sound came from the back corner near the chicken coop, followed by a hushed voice—too quiet to make out the words. Then a small, terrified whimper.

A child.

James lowered the gun immediately but didn't holster it. "I won't hurt you," he said, softening his tone. "But I need you to come out where I can see you."

More whispers, then movement in the shadows. A figure emerged slowly into a shaft of light—a woman, tall and slender, her clothing dirty and torn. Her hands were raised, open-palmed in surrender, but her chin was lifted in defiance. Her dark eyes assessed him quickly, lingering on the gun.

"Please," she said, her voice hoarse from disuse or thirst. "We don't mean any harm. We just needed somewhere to rest."

"We?" James kept his distance but pointed the gun toward the floor.

The woman turned slightly, nodding into the shadows. "It's okay. Come out."

Two boys emerged, pressing close to the woman's sides. The older one, maybe eleven, positioned himself slightly in front of the younger, a protective stance that spoke volumes. The smaller boy, around eight, clutched what looked like a stuffed dinosaur, its fabric worn and dirty.

James holstered the gun. Children. Hungry, frightened children. Their faces were smudged with dirt, clothes ragged from travel. The woman's arms bore scratches and bruises, her hair pulled back in a tight ponytail, revealing hollow cheeks and exhausted eyes.

"How long have you been here?" James asked, glancing around. He spotted the evidence now—a small pile of belongings tucked behind a hay bale, eggshells scattered near the chicken coop.

"Just since last night." The woman kept one arm around each boy. "We saw the lights from the road but didn't know if it was safe to approach. The barn door was unlocked. I'm sorry—we were just so tired, and the boys…" Her voice cracked slightly.

The older boy spoke up. "We took some eggs. And vegetables from the garden." He pulled himself up straighter. "I can work to pay it back."

James felt something twist in his chest. A boy trying to be a man before his time. How many more children were growing up overnight in this broken world?

"You're safe here," James said, making the decision instantly. "I'm James Thompson. This is my farm."

Relief washed across the woman's face, momentarily softening the hard lines of fear. "Olivia Hawkins. These are my sons, Grayson Junior and Theo." She placed a hand on each boy's shoulder as she named them.

"When did you eat last? A real meal?" James asked, already turning toward the door.

"Two days ago." Olivia hesitated. "We had some jerky yesterday, but I've been saving it."

James nodded. "My wife Sarah is at the house. She'll get you something to eat." He paused, studying them. "Where are you coming from?"

"Portland." Her voice flattened, eyes darting away. "Or what's left of it."

The older boy—Grayson Jr.—pressed closer to his mother, eyes downcast. The younger one, Theo, buried his face against her side.

"And their father?" James kept his voice gentle.

Pain flashed across Olivia's face. "Grayson Senior. He… they took him. When we were trying to leave the city." Her hand tightened on her older son's shoulder. "He made sure we got away. I don't know if he's…" She shook her head sharply, unwilling to finish the sentence in front of her children.

James nodded, understanding. "You can tell me more later. Let's get you to the house first."

He led them across the farmyard, watching as they squinted against the morning sunlight. All three moved with the cautious alertness of prey animals, eyes constantly scanning their surroundings. The younger boy, Theo, stayed pressed against his mother's side, while Grayson Jr. kept looking behind them, checking for threats.

As they approached the house, James spotted a battered pickup truck coming up the long driveway, dust billowing behind it. He recognized it immediately—Frank Wilson's old Ford, one of the few vehicles in town that had survived the CME. What was Frank doing out here so early?

"Wait here a moment," James told Olivia, gesturing to the porch steps. "Let me see what this is about."

Frank pulled up near the barn, killing the engine with a splutter. He climbed out, all smiles and hearty waves, though

James didn't miss the calculating assessment in his eyes as they flicked toward the strangers.

"Morning, James!" Frank called, striding over with his hand extended. His flannel shirt was clean, his beard recently trimmed. Always making an effort to look presentable, was Frank. "Brought you something from town."

He reached into the truck bed and pulled out a large crate. "Some of that corn meal you were asking about last week. Found it in an abandoned pantry during our sweep of the east side properties."

James nodded in thanks, though he couldn't recall asking Frank for corn meal specifically. "Appreciate it, Frank. But you didn't need to drive all the way out here."

Frank grinned, setting the crate down. "No trouble. My boys and I were checking the eastern perimeter anyway. Beth's got us running regular sweeps now." He lowered his voice conspiratorially. "Between you and me, I think we need to expand those patrols. Got a few fellows willing to put in the extra hours. Good men who know how to handle themselves."

James felt a familiar wariness creep up his spine. Frank had been positioning himself as an essential part of community security since the incident at the feed store. Always helpful, always present, but something about his eagerness never sat right.

"Beth's handling the security arrangements," James said neutrally. "Best to coordinate with her."

Frank's smile didn't falter, but something hardened in his eyes. "Course, course. Just offering extra hands. Speaking of which…" He nodded toward Olivia and her boys, who waited nervously on the porch. "New arrivals? Didn't know we were taking in more strays."

The word choice wasn't lost on James. "They came in from Portland. Had a rough time of it."

"Portland, huh?" Frank studied them with renewed interest. "Might be useful. I've been gathering intel on what's happening down there. Mind if I have a word with them later?"

"They need rest first," James said firmly. "And food. Maybe tomorrow."

Frank nodded agreeably, though James could see him filing the information away. "Sure thing. No rush." He glanced around the farm with practiced casualness. "How's the Thompson clan holding up? Heard young Ryan took a bad turn."

"He's recovering," James said, not elaborating.

"Good, good. Nasty business, this water sickness." Frank shook his head in what appeared to be genuine concern. "That's partly why I came by, actually. My crew's been working on a distribution plan for clean water. We've got a system set up in town now. Five gallons per household per day. Figured your brood could use a larger share, what with all the folks you're housing."

James studied him. The offer was helpful—necessary, even—but he couldn't shake the feeling that Frank was building something of his own. A network of obligations and dependencies.

"That's generous, Frank. We're managing with our well for now, but the town certainly needs a system."

"Already implemented," Frank said with evident pride. "Set up collection points at the church and town hall. My boys are keeping order, making sure everyone gets their fair share." His emphasis on "my boys" didn't escape James's notice. "No charge, of course. Just community service."

For now, James thought, but didn't say.

Frank gestured toward the truck, where three men lounged against the tailgate. James recognized Pete from the auto shop and the Grover brothers, Mike and Tommy. All carrying rifles, all watching the farm with too-keen interest.

"Just collecting what others didn't sow," Frank said with a laugh, nodding toward a crate of canned goods visible in the truck bed. "That abandoned Walmart distribution center out by the highway had more than anyone could use. Might as well reap the benefits before it all goes to waste."

Something in his tone made James uneasy. The laugh didn't reach Frank's eyes, and the men by the truck exchanged glances at his words. It seemed like an inside reference, a coded message James wasn't meant to fully understand.

"I should get these folks inside," he said instead, nodding toward the porch where Olivia watched their interaction with visible apprehension.

"Course, course." Frank backed toward his truck. "I'll be in town if you need anything. Oh, and James?" His voice dropped, all pretense of joviality vanishing. "There's talk of strangers scouting our perimeter. Armed men. My boys chased two of them off yesterday. Might want to keep your people close to home."

With that warning—or was it a threat?—Frank climbed back into his truck and pulled away, raising a hand in farewell. The three men piled into the truck bed, rifles across their laps, watching James until they disappeared around the bend.

James watched them go, unease settling in his gut. Frank was becoming a power in town, gathering followers who carried out his bidding with disturbing loyalty. Always helpful, always present when needed, but building something separate from

Beth's official authority. Like that character from the old TV show Daniel used to watch—Poe, was it? The one who smiled to your face while calculating how your resources could serve him.

Sarah met them at the back door, spatula in hand, her gray-streaked hair escaping its bun. Her eyes widened at the sight of the newcomers, but she recovered quickly, her hospitable nature taking over.

"Well, good morning," she said, stepping aside to let them in. "You look like you could use some breakfast."

Olivia hesitated at the threshold. "Ma'am, we're… not clean." She gestured at their dirty clothes, the grime on their skin.

Sarah waved away the concern. "Nothing soap and water won't fix after you've eaten. Come in, come in."

The kitchen was warm and fragrant with the smell of cornbread, one of the few baked goods they could still manage with their dwindling flour supply. James watched as the Hawkins family entered cautiously, taking in the normalcy of the farmhouse kitchen—the checkered curtains, the wooden table, the potted herbs on the windowsill. Theo's eyes grew wide at the sight of food.

"Sit," Sarah instructed, pointing to the table. She shot James a questioning look that he answered with a subtle nod. They'd talk later.

While Sarah served up bowls of oatmeal sweetened with the last of their maple syrup, James stepped onto the porch and pulled the hand radio from his pocket. It was one of four working sets they had, scavenged from the hunting supply store before it was picked clean.

"Thompson to Martin, over." Static crackled as he waited

for Beth to respond.

After a moment: "Martin here. Go ahead, over."

"We've got newcomers at the farm. A woman and two boys from Portland. They're not sick, but I'd like Emily to check them over when she can. The woman might have information about what's happening in the city, over."

A pause. "Understood. Emily's finishing at the funeral home. I'll bring her out myself in about an hour. Any visible weapons or concerns, over?"

James glanced through the window at the small family devouring Sarah's oatmeal, the exhaustion evident in their slumped shoulders. "Negative. Just scared and hungry. They've been hiding in our barn overnight, over."

"Roger that. Martin out."

James pocketed the radio and went back inside, his mind still on Frank's visit and that strange comment about "reaping what others didn't sow." The words themselves seemed innocuous enough, but there was something in Frank's delivery, something in the way his men had reacted, that felt like a veiled message.

As he entered the kitchen, he found Lily and Ryan sitting at the far end of the table. Lily was showing Theo her stuffed elephant, Mr. Trunks, while Ryan watched from his chair, still pale but clearly happy to be out of bed. Sarah must have helped him to the kitchen while James was outside.

"He helps me be brave," Lily was explaining seriously to Theo, who clutched his own stuffed dinosaur. "Especially when things are scary."

"Rex does that too," Theo replied, his voice small but steady. "He kept me safe when the bad men came."

The simple exchange hit James like a physical blow.

Children shouldering fears too heavy for their small frames, finding comfort in worn toys that represented a world already slipping away from them.

"Dad, can I talk to you?" Emily's voice came from the doorway. She looked exhausted, dark circles under her eyes testifying to another sleepless night caring for the ill.

James nodded, following her into the hallway.

"The funeral home is at capacity," she said without preamble. "We're converting the main viewing room to hold more patients. David Foster's gone, and Mrs. Wilkins passed this morning."

"I heard," James said grimly. "Michael mentioned more cases in the northern part of town?"

Emily nodded. "Two more confirmed, three suspected. All with the same symptoms as Ryan had—severe dehydration, diarrhea, vomiting. Classic waterborne infection profile." She lowered her voice. "Beth thinks it might be deliberate."

"Deliberate?" James felt his blood run cold. "You mean someone is poisoning the water?"

"Not poisoning exactly. Contaminating. She found evidence that someone dumped animal carcasses in the watershed above the creek where the town draws water now that the municipal supply is offline." Emily ran a hand through her disheveled hair. "She's investigating, but…"

"But in the meantime, people are dying," James finished. "Christ."

"We need to warn everyone. No creek water, no matter how desperate. Well water only, and even that should be boiled." Emily glanced toward the kitchen. "These new people—the woman and boys—they're from Portland? We need to know what's happening there too."

"I've asked Beth to bring you out to check them over." James hesitated. "Frank was just here. Says he's set up a water distribution system in town."

Something flickered across Emily's face. "I've heard about that. His… crew… is running it. People are already calling them 'The Reapers' in town."

"The Reapers?" James frowned. "Why?"

Emily shrugged. "Something Frank said about 'reaping what others didn't sow' when they brought in supplies last week. It stuck. People whisper it when his group comes around. They're effective, but…" She trailed off.

"But what?"

"Their methods are questionable. Pete Grover broke a man's arm yesterday for trying to take more than his allotted water. Said he was 'making an example.' Beth's worried they're establishing their own authority outside hers."

Before James could respond, the sound of children's laughter—a rare sound these days—drifted from the kitchen. He peered around the corner to see Lily demonstrating how Mr. Trunks could dance, making the stuffed elephant hop across the table while Theo giggled. Ryan watched with a weak smile, and even Grayson Jr. had relaxed enough to lean forward with interest.

For a moment, they looked like what they were—children. Not survivors, not refugees, not premature adults shouldering impossible burdens. Just children, finding joy in a simple game with stuffed animals.

"We have to protect them," James said quietly to Emily. "All of them. Whatever it takes."

Emily's expression softened as she watched the scene. "Yes," she agreed. "Whatever it takes."

The moment of peace was broken by the sound of an approaching engine—Beth's police cruiser coming up the driveway.

Beth

The water sample glowed faintly green in the Mason jar, catching the morning light that streamed through the police station windows. Beth Martin studied it, turning the glass to watch the murky sediment swirl inside. It didn't look dangerous. It didn't look like something that had already killed three people in her town, with eleven more fighting for their lives at Neal & York Funeral Home.

But looks are deceiving these days. Everything was.

"Well?" Robbie Burns hovered at her shoulder, his breath warm against her neck. "What do you think?"

Beth placed the jar on her desk and stepped back. She'd been staring at water samples for two days and was no closer to answers.

"I think it looks like water," she said, frustration edging her voice. "Same as the other six samples. I need a freaking lab, not this—" she gestured at the primitive setup they'd arranged: mason jars, coffee filters, a microscope salvaged from the high school science department.

"Emily seems pretty certain it's cholera," Robbie offered.

"Probably," Beth agreed. "But that doesn't tell us why it's happening now, or how it got into multiple water sources simultaneously." She tapped the jar. "This is from Jenkins Creek, over five miles from the first contamination site. Different watershed entirely."

Robbie adjusted his makeshift deputy's badge—a polished brass shield that Beth had pinned to his chest when Jerry took a bullet to the leg during the feed store standoff. Neither of them mentioned what a farce it was, pretending law enforcement still meant anything.

"You think someone's doing it deliberately." Not a question. Robbie had been a decent handyman before the CME; now he was proving himself a decent investigator, too.

"I know they are." Beth moved to the map spread across the conference table, dotted with red push pins marking contamination sites. "Look at the pattern. These aren't random. They're targeting water sources closest to population centers."

Robbie studied the map, the muscles in his jaw working. He'd lost weight since the collapse, like everyone, but on him it looked good—exposing the angles of his face, hardening him. "Shit."

"Exactly." Beth ran a hand through her short-cropped hair. She hadn't wasted time on haircuts since the world ended. "The question is who. And why."

"Who benefits from making folks sick?" Robbie mused.

"Someone who wants us weakened. Distracted." Beth traced a circle around Cornish with her finger. "After what James told us about the Hawkins family, and those New Guard assholes in Portland… this feels coordinated."

The pre-dawn coffee she'd savored hours ago was long gone from her system. Her head throbbed with fatigue. In the two months since the CME, she'd averaged four hours of sleep a night. The former high school English teacher turned part-time police chief had become, by necessity, a full-time guardian of what remained of their community.

Outside the window, Cornish's Main Street was coming to life. A horse-drawn cart carrying what looked like lumber moved slowly past the station. Two women with baskets headed toward Kristie's Diner, where somehow, miraculously, coffee was still being served. Normal-looking scenes that couldn't hide the wrongness underneath—the silence where cars should be, the wary eyes constantly scanning for threats, the holstered weapons visible on nearly everyone.

Her radio crackled. "Thompson to Martin, over."

Beth grabbed the handheld. "Martin here, go ahead."

"We need to talk." James's voice was tight, controlled. "Found something at the Jenkins Creek crossing. South of town."

"On my way. Over and out." Beth clipped the radio to her belt and reached for her jacket, though the July heat would make it uncomfortable. The weight of the shotgun in the inner pocket was worth the discomfort.

"You need backup?" Robbie asked.

Beth considered it, eyes flicking to the cells where their two prisoners sat. One for stealing medicine, one they'd captured during a skirmish with Sherman's scouts. The second man had refused to talk for three days now, despite increasingly harsh methods. Justice was swift and brutal now. The old Beth would have been horrified. The new Beth didn't have the luxury of principles.

"Stay here," she decided. "Keep an eye on them. I'll radio if I need you."

"You sure? That's Sherman's men's favorite crossing place."

"All the more reason to go check it out." She strapped on her sidearm, checked the magazine. "But keep the frequency open. Anything feels hinky, I'll holler."

Robbie nodded, but worry creased his forehead. There was something between them now, unspoken, undeveloped, but real. A connection forged in survival that neither had time to explore. "Be careful, Chief."

"Always am."

Outside, the heat hit her like a physical force. Late July in Maine wasn't usually this brutal, but climate patterns had shifted subtly since the CME. Hotter days, violent thunderstorms, as if the planet itself was unsettled by humanity's sudden retreat.

The cruiser, one of three vehicles in town that still ran, sat in its privileged parking spot. Most days she traveled on horseback to conserve fuel, but for this, she wanted speed and security. The old Crown Victoria's engine turned over with a reassuring rumble. Pre-1990 electronics, mostly unaffected by the electromagnetic pulse that had fried everything newer.

Beth pulled away from the curb, feeling the familiar weight of the vehicle. Driving had become a strange luxury, almost obscene in its reminder of what they'd lost. She passed Kristie's Diner, slowing as she noticed Frank Wilson holding court at the largest table.

Unlike the last time she'd seen him, he wasn't alone. At least five men surrounded him, each wearing a strip of red fabric somewhere on their person—a bandana around the neck, an armband, a strip tied to a belt loop. Frank's private security force that had materialized seemingly overnight after the CME. She'd overheard people referring to them in hushed tones as "The Reapers," a name that had spread through town after

Frank's offhand comment about "reaping what they didn't sow" when bringing in supplies from abandoned stores.

The name fit their efficient but increasingly brutal methods. Just yesterday, she'd heard how Pete Grover had broken a man's arm for taking more than his allotted water ration—"making an example," he'd called it.

Frank caught her watching and gave a casual wave, his smile never reaching his eyes. One of his men leaned over, whispering something that made the others laugh. Beth filed the observation away for later.

The drive to Jenkins Creek took ten minutes, the road eerily empty. She passed abandoned vehicles, pushed to the roadside in the first days after the CME. A child's bike lay in a ditch, its wheels rusted. A mailbox hung open, unchecked for weeks.

The creek came into view as she rounded the bend, water glittering in the morning sun. James Thompson stood near the bank in conversation with Michael, his son-in-law. Both men carried rifles slung across their backs—standard practice now, even during daylight. More surprising was the presence of Ethan, Michael and Emily's thirteen-year-old son, squatting at the water's edge with a stick in hand.

Beth parked the cruiser and approached them, boots crunching on gravel. Her hand rested instinctively on her sidearm, a habit formed long before the collapse but honed to instinct now.

"Morning." James's weathered face was grim. Despite the heat, he wore long sleeves, the fabric dark with sweat at the collar and armpits. "Thanks for coming so quick."

"What have we got?" Beth asked, eyes already scanning the surroundings.

Michael nodded toward the creek bank. "Show her."

"Ethan, step back now," James said firmly. The boy reluctantly moved away from the water, his expression far too serious for a child his age.

"I found it," Ethan announced, staring up at Beth with a mixture of pride and apprehension. "Dad and Grandpa were looking in the wrong spot."

Beth noted the way Michael's jaw tightened at his son's pronouncement. "That so?" she asked the boy.

Ethan nodded, a jerky, forceful movement. "I saw something green under the water. They were looking downstream." He pointed with his stick. "It's there, behind the rocks. Something shoved in between."

James led her to the edge of the creek, pointing to a spot upstream where the water narrowed between two large rocks. "Michael spotted it during patrol this morning."

"Actually, I spotted it," Ethan corrected, earning a sharp look from his father.

At first, Beth saw nothing unusual—just the creek burbling over smooth stones, the water clear enough to see the pebbled bottom. Then James reached down with a stick and nudged something half-submerged near the bank.

A small device bobbed to the surface, roughly the size of a coffee can. Dark green, camouflaged to blend with the creek bed, with a slow drip coming from a valve near the bottom.

"What the hell?" Beth crouched for a closer look, careful not to touch it. "Is that—"

"Some kind of time-release container," Michael confirmed.

Beth's mouth went dry. "You're sure?"

"Positive." Michael's expression was hard. "Whoever

placed it knew what they were doing. It's weighted to stay in place even during higher water flow, positioned at a natural collection point, and camouflaged. This isn't amateur hour."

"Have you opened it?"

James shook his head. "Thought you'd want to see it first. Could be rigged somehow."

"Is it a bomb?" Ethan asked, his voice small but steady, the question so incongruous coming from a child.

Michael placed a protective hand on his son's shoulder. "No, buddy. But it's dangerous in a different way."

Beth weighed the risks. "Let's remove it. Carefully. I want to know what's inside."

"Can I help?" Ethan asked eagerly, stepping forward.

"Absolutely not," Michael said sharply. "You're already not supposed to be here. We agreed you'd stay at the lookout point."

The boy's face flushed. "But I found it! I should get to help!"

"Ethan," James said, his tone gentler but no less firm, "what do we say about roles in an emergency?"

The boy's shoulders slumped. "Everyone has a job. Mine is to watch and report, not engage."

"That's right." Beth noticed how Ethan parroted the words—clearly a lesson that had been repeated often. "And you did your job perfectly. You spotted something dangerous. That's good work."

Ethan brightened slightly at her praise, but the frustration remained evident in his stance—a child desperate to prove himself in an adult world.

Between the three adults, they managed to extract the

device from the creek bed using branches to avoid direct contact. Up close, the craftsmanship was even more disturbing. It was intentionally releasing whatever it was that was contained directly into the water.

"We should take it back to the station," Beth said. "I don't want to risk opening it here."

Michael looked doubtful. "If it's biological, we need to be careful."

"The damage is already done," Beth pointed out grimly. "Whatever was in there has been leaking into our water supply for days."

They wrapped the device in James's bandana and placed it carefully in the trunk of the cruiser. Beth felt the weight of what they'd found settling in her stomach like lead. This wasn't just contamination; it was an attack.

"You need to check the other branches, especially the smaller little feeder streams," she told James and Michael. "Every water source on the map. If there are more of these, we need to find them. Now."

"We're on it," James assured her. "Daniel's organizing search parties from the farm. We'll cover everything within five miles."

Beth nodded, already calculating next steps. "I'll have Robbie alert everyone in town to boil water, no exceptions. And we need to question the prisoners again."

"You think they know something?" Michael asked.

"One of them has to." Beth's jaw tightened. "And I'm going to find out what."

"Can I come with you?" Ethan asked, his eyes suddenly alight with interest. "I could help with the interrogation."

The question sent a chill through Beth—the eagerness in the boy's voice, the casual way he used the word "interrogation," as if it were a game rather than a grim necessity.

Michael's face darkened. "Absolutely not. You're going straight back to the farm with your grandfather." He turned to James. "I'll join the search parties after I drop him off."

Ethan's face contorted in anger and disappointment. "But Dad—"

"This isn't a discussion," Michael cut him off. "This is exactly why I didn't want you coming along."

The boy fell silent, but the mulish set of his jaw promised further rebellion. Beth recognized the look—the same one she'd seen on teenagers caught shoplifting before the collapse, a dangerous cocktail of defiance and wounded pride.

"Ethan," she said, crouching to his eye level, "I need your help with something important."

Suspicion replaced anger in his eyes. "What kind of help?"

"The other kids at the farm—especially the younger ones—will be scared when they hear about this. They'll need someone strong to look out for them, someone who understands what's happening but can keep them calm."

The boy considered this, clearly weighing whether she was patronizing him. "Like a junior deputy?"

Beth nodded seriously. "Exactly like that. Intelligence gathering and civilian protection."

The terms, military and official-sounding, seemed to satisfy him. Ethan straightened his shoulders. "I can do that."

"Good man." She rose, catching Michael's grateful look over the boy's head. "I'll see you at the council meeting tonight."

The drive back to the station was a blur, her mind racing through implications. This wasn't opportunistic crime or desperate scavenging. This was strategic. Calculated. The work of someone who understood how to bring a community to its knees.

When she pulled up to the station, Robbie was waiting outside, expression tense. "We've got a situation."

Beth's hand moved to her weapon. "What kind of situation?"

"Frank Wilson." Robbie lowered his voice. "One of the Grover boys saw him meeting with strangers at the old logging road, exchanged something. When Frank spotted him watching, he threatened him."

Beth thought of Frank waving to her earlier, surrounded by his red-banded followers. "When?"

"About an hour ago. Kid just came in, scared shitless."

"Where's Frank now?"

"Kristie says he's still at the diner with his crew."

Beth made her decision. "Get the device from my trunk. Carefully. Bag it and lock it in the evidence room. Then keep an eye on our guests." She nodded toward the cells inside. "I need to talk to our Sherman friend first. Then I'll have a chat with Frank."

"Want me to come along?"

"No. Better if he doesn't feel cornered." Beth checked her sidearm again, a gesture that had become as automatic as breathing. "But be ready if I call."

Inside, Beth headed straight for the holding cells. The station had only two—more than enough for Cornish in the before times. The first held Ned Pratt, caught stealing antibiotics from the makeshift clinic. The second contained a man who'd only identified himself as Cooper, captured three days ago during a skirmish with what they believed were Sherman's scouts.

Cooper sat on the narrow cot, back against the wall, watching her approach with cold, assessing eyes. Unlike Ned, who looked haggard and remorseful, Cooper maintained an air of patient confidence—a man simply waiting for the game to change in his favor.

"Found something interesting today," Beth said, unlocking his cell door and stepping inside. She remained standing, forcing him to look up at her. "A water contamination device. Know anything about that?"

Cooper's expression didn't change. "Sounds serious."

"Three dead so far. Eleven sick, including a seven-year-old boy." Beth kept her voice calm, controlled. "That makes this biological warfare. War crimes territory."

A flicker of something—not quite concern, but awareness—crossed his features. "Sorry to hear that."

"I think you know more than you're saying." Beth moved closer. "And I think it's time you started talking."

Cooper shrugged. "Got nothing to say."

Beth studied him—the set of his shoulders, the careful neutrality of his expression. This wasn't their first conversation. For three days, they'd gone through this dance, his silence more unyielding with each attempt. The traditional methods weren't working. And they were running out of time.

"Robbie," she called, not taking her eyes off Cooper. "Bring me the kit from my desk drawer."

Robbie appeared a moment later, holding a small leather case. His eyes widened slightly when he realized which kit she meant, but he handed it over without comment.

"Give us some privacy," Beth said quietly. "And turn off the recording equipment."

"Beth…" Robbie hesitated. "You sure about this?"

"I'm sure." Her voice left no room for argument. "Make sure no one interrupts us."

Alone with Cooper, Beth unzipped the leather case, laying out its contents methodically on the small table. Pliers. A hunting knife. Antiseptic. Gauze. The tools weren't chosen for their efficacy in extracting information—they were what she had available. But the psychological impact of their careful arrangement was calculating.

"Last chance to talk to me like a civilized person," she said.

Cooper's eyes fixed on the implements, a barely perceptible tightening around his mouth the only indication of concern. "Is this what passes for civilization now?"

"You tell me." Beth picked up the knife, turning it so the blade caught the light. "Your people are poisoning our water. Children are dying. How civilized is that?"

Something shifted in Cooper's expression. "Not my call."

"But you knew about it." Beth leaned closer. "Who placed the devices? How many more are there? What's in them?"

Cooper maintained his silence, but sweat beaded on his upper lip now.

"I used to be an English teacher," Beth said conversationally, testing the knife's edge with her thumb. "Did you know that? Taught high school for twelve years before becoming part-time police chief. Never even fired my weapon outside the range until the collapse." She met his eyes. "I used to tell my students about Macbeth—how once you wade into blood, it becomes easier to keep going. Turns out Shakespeare knew what he was talking about."

She set the knife down, picking up the pliers instead. "I don't want to do this, Cooper. But I have fourteen people fighting for their lives because of whatever you and your friends put in our water. I need to know what it is, how to treat it, and how to find the rest of the devices."

Cooper's jaw clenched. "I'm just a scout. I don't know the details."

"But you know something." Beth moved with sudden speed, grabbing his hand and forcing it palm-down on the table. She positioned the pliers over his pinky finger. "Start talking, or I start breaking."

Outside the door, she heard footsteps approaching, then a hushed argument—Robbie warning someone away. Then another voice, younger, insistent. Ethan. The boy must have followed them back to the station instead of going to the farm.

Cooper must have heard it too. His eyes flicked toward the door. "Got kids listening? That the kind of example you want to set?"

The question hit its mark. For a moment, Beth hesitated, the ethical lines she was crossing suddenly stark in her mind. She'd been a teacher—dedicated her life to nurturing young minds, to modeling moral behavior. Now she was about to torture a man while a child might be watching.

But that same child might die if the water contamination continued. Ryan Thompson might die. More families might lose parents, children, grandparents to this calculated attack.

"Last chance," she said, voice hardening.

When Cooper remained silent, she applied pressure to the pliers. He gasped, then clamped his mouth shut.

"The devices," she demanded. "How many?"

"I don't know exactly," he ground out.

"Guess."

"Six, maybe eight." His breath came in short bursts. "Different watersheds."

"What's in them?"

"Some kind of bacterial culture. Concentrated. I don't know the details."

"Who placed them?"

Cooper hesitated, and Beth increased the pressure. A small crack sounded as the bone began to give.

"Specialists," he gasped. "Four-man team. In and out three nights ago."

"And Sherman? Where is he now?"

"Temporary base. Old military installation north of Portland." Cooper's face was white with pain. "Gathering forces. Planning to move within the week."

"Move where? To attack Cornish?"

"Among others. You're first on the list because of the resistance last time."

Beth released the pressure slightly but kept the pliers in place. "How many men?"

"Thirty-five, maybe forty now." Cooper was talking faster now, the words tumbling out. "Plus alliances with smaller groups. Weapons from the National Guard armory. Tactical equipment."

"These specialists who placed the devices—they still around?"

Cooper hesitated again, calculation returning to his eyes

despite the pain. Beth saw the moment he decided to lie. "No. They went back south."

She increased pressure again, eliciting a cry of pain. "Truth."

"Shit! Alright—two stayed behind. Monitoring the devices."

"Where?"

"Cabin. Old fire watch station on Ridge Mountain." His eyes locked on hers, hatred burning through the pain. "You're dead, you know that? All of you. Sherman doesn't leave witnesses."

Beth released his hand, her own trembling slightly with the enormity of what she'd just done—and what she'd learned. "We'll see about that."

As she gathered the tools and returned them to the leather case, Cooper cradled his injured hand, watching her with newfound wariness. "You're no better than us now."

The accusation hit her like a physical blow because she'd been thinking the same thing. Where was the line between protection and becoming the very thing she was fighting? She'd just tortured a man for information. What would she do tomorrow? What would she sanction next week?

"The difference," she said finally, "is that I'm not targeting children."

As she turned to leave, Cooper's voice stopped her. "Your boy. The one outside. What's his name?"

The implied threat turned Beth's blood to ice. She spun back, drawing her weapon in one fluid motion, pressing it against Cooper's temple before conscious thought caught up to the action.

"Don't," she said, the word barely audible. "Don't even think about it."

Cooper smiled despite the gun barrel against his skin. "Just making conversation."

Something snapped inside Beth—the accumulated stress, fear, and moral compromise of the past two months crystallizing into a single, terrible moment of clarity. Her finger tightened on the trigger.

Cooper's eyes widened as he realized he'd miscalculated. "Hey, wait—"

The gunshot was deafening in the confined space of the cell. Cooper slumped sideways, a spray of red staining the wall behind him. Beth stood frozen, the echo of the shot still ringing in her ears, the smell of cordite sharp in her nostrils.

The cell door burst open. Robbie stood there, his own weapon drawn, eyes wide with shock. "Beth! What—"

She lowered her gun slowly, her hand steady despite the chaos in her mind. "He threatened Ethan."

Robbie holstered his weapon, concern replacing shock as he took in her expression. "You okay?"

"No." The honesty surprised her. "But it doesn't matter. We need to move fast. Cooper confirmed the water contamination is deliberate. Sherman's operating out of a military installation north of Portland, planning to move on Cornish within the week."

"Dammit," Robbie breathed. "How many?"

"Thirty-five to forty, plus allies. And they have two specialists monitoring the devices from the old fire watch station on Ridge Mountain." She brushed past him, striding toward her office. "We need to convene the town council immediately. And send a team to that cabin."

"Beth," Robbie caught her arm. "You just shot a prisoner. We need to talk about that."

"Later," she said sharply. "Right now, we need to—"

Her words cut off as she spotted Ethan standing in the hallway, eyes wide and face pale. From his position, he couldn't have seen into the cell, but the gunshot would have been unmistakable. The boy stared at her with a mixture of fear and fascination that made her stomach turn.

"Ethan," she said, forcing her voice to remain calm. "You're supposed to be at the farm."

"I wanted to help." His eyes darted toward the cell behind her. "Did you… did you shoot him?"

Beth exchanged a glance with Robbie, who subtly moved to block the view into the cell. "Ethan, this isn't a place for children right now. Where's your father?"

"Searching for more of those water things with Grandpa." Ethan took a step closer, his curiosity overwhelming caution. "Was he one of Sherman's men? Did he tell you about the poison?"

Before Beth could answer, the station door banged open, and Frank Wilson strode in, flanked by two of his red-banded followers. His confident smile faltered slightly at the tableau before him—Beth with gun still in hand, Robbie blocking a cell doorway, Ethan standing wide-eyed in the hallway.

"Sounds like I missed something interesting," Frank observed, gaze flicking between them.

"Frank." Beth holstered her weapon with deliberate calm. "Perfect timing. I was just about to come find you."

"Oh?" His eyes narrowed slightly.

"Robbie," Beth said, not taking her eyes off Frank, "take

Ethan back to the farm. Now. Tell them I'll be there shortly with updates."

"But—" Ethan began to protest.

"That wasn't a request," Beth said, steel in her voice. "Go with Robbie. Now."

The boy looked like he might argue further, but something in her expression must have convinced him of the futility. With a reluctant nod, he allowed Robbie to guide him toward the door.

As they passed Frank, one of his men—Pete Grover, sporting a red bandana around his neck—blocked their path. "What happened to the prisoner?"

"None of your business," Robbie replied tersely. "Move."

Pete looked to Frank, who nodded almost imperceptibly. The man stepped aside, but his eyes followed Ethan with unsettling interest.

Once Robbie and Ethan were gone, Beth turned her full attention to Frank. "We need to talk."

"Sounds serious." Frank glanced toward the cell. "Your prisoner have an accident?"

"He confirmed what we suspected," Beth said, ignoring the implied question. "The water contamination is deliberate. Part of Sherman's planned attack on Cornish."

Frank's expression shifted from casual interest to focused attention. "When?"

"Within the week. His forces are gathering at a military installation north of Portland." Beth studied his reaction carefully. "Tommy Grover mentioned seeing you with strangers at the logging road this morning."

A flicker of annoyance crossed Frank's features. "Kid

should mind his own business."

"This is my business, Frank." Beth stepped closer. "Anything affecting the security of this town is my business. So I'll ask directly: who were you meeting with?"

Frank's men tensed, hands drifting toward concealed weapons. The atmosphere in the station charged instantly with potential violence.

"Easy," Frank said, his voice level. "Let's not do anything hasty." He spread his hands in a gesture of openness. "I've been establishing communication with other survivors. Groups in neighboring towns, isolated homesteads. Building a network."

"Without informing me." Beth kept her own hands relaxed but ready. "That's not how we agreed to operate."

"With respect, Chief, the situation's evolving faster than your traditional methods can handle." Frank's smile returned, smooth and practiced. "My boys—The Reapers, as people have taken to calling them—they're just trying to help. We're all on the same side here."

The deliberate use of the nickname confirmed Beth's suspicions—Frank was embracing the identity his group had acquired, using it to build their mystique.

"If we're on the same side," Beth countered, "then you'll share all intelligence you've gathered and coordinate your 'boys' through proper channels."

Frank studied her for a long moment. "I heard what happened in there," he said finally, nodding toward the cell. "Old Beth Martin would never have done that. But maybe new Beth Martin understands what it takes to survive now." He leaned closer. "My Reapers understand too. They've been saying for weeks we need harsher measures against Sherman's people. Sounds like you're finally catching up."

The implication hung in the air—that she was becoming more like him, embracing the brutal pragmatism his group represented.

"I did what was necessary," Beth said carefully. "Nothing more."

"Of course." Frank's smile widened. "That's all any of us are doing. What's necessary." He glanced at his watch. "Town council meeting tonight?"

"Six o'clock. James's farm."

"We'll be there." Frank turned to leave, then paused. "One more thing. I've been meaning to tell you—we found another contamination device yesterday. Near the reservoir."

Beth stared at him. "And you didn't report it?"

Frank shrugged. "My boys handled it. Just reaping what others sowed, as I like to say." His smile didn't reach his eyes. "See you tonight, Chief."

After they left, Beth stood motionless in the silent station. Blood pounded in her ears. She'd tortured a man for information, then killed him. Lost control in a way she'd never believed possible. And somewhere along the way, she'd started down a path that looked disturbingly similar to Frank's—justifying increasingly extreme actions in the name of protection.

The worst part was that she couldn't see an alternative. Not with Sherman's forces gathering, not with water sources poisoned, not with children's lives at stake.

She moved to her desk and sank into the chair, suddenly exhausted. The photograph of her and her father at her academy graduation stared back at her—both in uniform, both smiling with the certainty of those who believed in justice and order. What would he think of her now?

The answer came unbidden: He would have done the same. To protect the town, to protect the innocent, to protect the children—he would have crossed the same lines.

Hannah

Hannah Mitchell stood at her bedroom window, watching the ember-flecked darkness beyond the neighborhood barricade. The makeshift wall, constructed from overturned cars, shipping pallets, and corrugated metal, still held. A monument to suburban determination that had transformed Crestview Lane from a quiet South Portland cul-de-sac into something approaching a fortress.

Tonight, the barricade wouldn't be enough.

She counted four separate fires beyond their perimeter, orange flames licking at the night sky, casting grotesque shadows across abandoned homes. To the east, where the Pattersons had tried to establish their own safe zone, a column of black smoke rose, blotting out stars. The screams stopped about half an hour ago, but lingered in her mind.

Her fingers closed around the binoculars, cool metal against her skin. The night air drifting through the open window carried the acrid scent of burning plastic along with something heavier, something worse—burning flesh. Hannah had spent enough time in the anatomy lab to recognize the smell. It clung to her nostrils, coating the back of her throat.

She forced herself to scan methodically through the binoculars, cataloging details with clinical precision. Something she'd learned, a skill from the early medical school classes, now repurposed for survival. Movement near the Henderson place. Flashlight beams darting through the darkness. At least six distinct light sources, moving with purpose. Not the chaotic looting they'd witnessed in the early days after the CME, but something organized. Methodical.

"Hannah?" Her mother's voice, deliberately soft, from the bedroom doorway. Rebecca Mitchell's hair, usually neatly coiffed, hung limp around her pale face. Dark hollows beneath her eyes mapped the chronic sleep deprivation. "Your father wants everyone downstairs. Now."

Hannah lowered the binoculars. "They've reached the Henderson place. Six, maybe eight of them. Moving fast."

Her mother's expression tightened. "How long?"

"Twenty minutes. Maybe less."

Rebecca nodded, information absorbed and processed. Hannah's analytical nature came from her mother, a high school physics teacher who approached even apocalyptic collapse with scientific detachment. "Bring your pack. And Hannah—"

"Mom—"

"I know." Rebecca's hand trembled slightly against the doorframe. "Grab what you can carry. Jake's already loading the cart."

Hannah turned back to the window for one final survey. The flashlight beams had converged on the Henderson house. A piercing scream cut through the night, distinctly female. Mrs. Henderson. Hannah's hands convulsed around the binoculars. Eight weeks ago, Julia Henderson had hosted a neighborhood barbecue, proudly showing off her spring garden and complaining good-naturedly about her husband's obsession with his vintage Mustang.

She lowered the binoculars, unable to watch what came

next. In the street below, she could see her father and fourteen-year-old brother moving silently in the darkness, loading their delivery cart—a heavy-duty garden cart with reinforced wheels that her father had modified with a motorcycle cargo cover. Their planned escape vehicle. It had seemed almost comical during drills. Now it represented their only hope.

Hannah moved with practiced efficiency, retrieving her pack from beneath the bed—a hiking backpack containing clothes, basic medical supplies, water purification tablets, and her most precious possessions: a dog-eared medical text, a journal from Maddie, and a photograph of her family from before. She added her stethoscope and the small medical kit that was required equipment for classes.

The memory of Maddie squeezed her heart—their tearful separation when she left Portsmouth, Maddie continuing north to Cornish while Hannah stayed with her family in South Portland. Sometimes, in the rare quiet moments between emergencies, Hannah found herself wondering if her friend had made it home. If any place could still be called home.

A soft double-tap on the wall—her father's signal. Hannah slung the pack over her shoulders and crept down the stairs, avoiding the third step with its telltale creak. Their colonial-style house felt like a tomb. Curtains drawn tight, furniture pushed against doors and windows. Almost suffocating in the inability to just live.

In the kitchen, her father stood reviewing a hand-drawn map spread across the center island. Thomas Mitchell, a civil engineering professor who had once designed infrastructure improvements for Portland, had transformed into their community's defense coordinator. His beard, more salt than pepper now, couldn't hide the gaunt angles of his face.

"Henderson's is gone," he said without preamble, not

looking up from the map. "The Pattersons too."

"I saw the smoke," Hannah confirmed.

Thomas traced a route on the map with his index finger. "We take the utility access behind Maple Street, follow the creek bed to the old rail line, then head north through the conservation land." His finger stopped at a small X. "There's a hunting cabin here. Josh Warren stayed there last fall. Says it's isolated, well-stocked. If we move now, we can be there by dawn."

Hannah studied the route. "That's at least eight miles. Jake can't—"

"I can make it," her brother interrupted from the doorway. Jake's reedy adolescent frame seemed weighted down by the pack on his shoulders, but his jaw was set with determination. Acne still dotted his forehead—an incongruously normal teenage concern amid collapse. "I've been practicing with the cart. I can handle it."

Their mother entered behind him, her own pack secured, a rifle slung across her back. Rebecca Mitchell, who had once boycotted a supermarket for selling hunting magazines near the checkout, now moved with the practiced comfort of someone who had spent hours at the makeshift neighborhood firing range.

"The Washburns?" Hannah asked. Elderly neighbors who had sheltered with them for the past week after their own home became structurally compromised during a storm.

Her father's expression hardened. "Not coming."

"What? But Mrs. Washburn can barely walk without—"

"Their choice," her mother cut in sharply. "They feel they'd slow us down."

The unspoken reality hung in the air, the Washburns had

chosen to stay behind rather than burden a family they knew would sacrifice their own safety to help them. A sacrifice that would likely cost four lives instead of two.

Hannah felt sick. "We can't just—"

"We can," her father said quietly. "We have to." He rolled up the map, securing it with a rubber band. "They've made their decision. We need to honor it by surviving."

Another scream pierced the night, closer now. The Newton place, just one street over. Hannah flinched.

"It's time," Thomas said.

The family moved silently through the darkened house to the cellar door. For three weeks, they'd been reinforcing this escape route—removing fence panels behind the property, marking a path with reflective tacks visible only with their UV flashlight, calculating exact distances and travel times. Theoretical preparation for a scenario they'd prayed would never materialize.

Hannah's father moved first, easing open the cellar bulkhead that led to their backyard. The night air rushed in, heavy with smoke and summer heat. He scanned with the UV light, checking for movement, before gesturing them forward.

The garden cart waited, loaded with supplies and covered with black fabric to eliminate reflection. Jake took position between the handles as they'd practiced, his narrow shoulders squared with resolve.

Thomas crouched before him. "Remember—slow and steady. Follow exactly ten paces behind me. Stop when I stop. Move when I move." He gripped Jake's shoulder. "You can do this."

Jake nodded, swallowing hard.

They moved like shadows across the now familiar yard.

Past the vegetable garden that had sustained them after the grocery stores emptied.

Hannah kept her eyes fixed on her mother's back, counting steps in her head. Thirty paces to the property line. Fifteen more to the gap in the Rogers' fence. Twenty to the drainage culvert that would shield them from view.

A gunshot cracked the night, sharp and definitive, from the direction of their house. Hannah flinched, nearly stumbling. The Washburns. Her mind filled the narrative gaps. Discovery, confrontation, resolution. The merciful explanation was that Mr. Washburn had taken matters into his own hands. The alternative—

She refused to complete the thought.

They reached the culvert, crouching in its concrete shelter. Water trickled around their ankles, cold despite July's heat. Thomas peered out, using the mirror-on-a-stick contraption he'd fashioned from a dental implement and a telescoping radio antenna.

"Clear to the tree line," he whispered. "But we need to move fast. They're working house to house now."

Hannah glanced back toward their home. From this vantage point, she could see figures moving on their street—black silhouettes against the ambient glow of distant fires. Methodical searchers examining each house. A window shattered somewhere, followed by laughter.

Her father tapped her arm, reclaiming her attention. He pointed to a dense stand of maples fifty yards ahead. Their next cover point. Hannah nodded, understanding the silent command.

They moved in practiced formation—Thomas first, then Rebecca, Hannah, and finally Jake pushing the cart. The soft squeak of its right wheel seemed thunderous in the quiet night, though Hannah knew it was barely audible beyond a few feet.

Halfway to the trees, a shout rang out behind them.

"THERE! BY THE CREEK!"

Hannah's head snapped around. A figure stood atop the Newtons' garage, pointing in their direction. The beam of a powerful flashlight swept toward them, not quite reaching their position but closing fast.

"RUN!" her father barked, abandoning stealth.

They broke into a sprint, abandoning their careful formation. Jake struggled with the suddenly unwieldy cart, its contents shifting and rattling. Hannah dropped back to help him, grabbing one handle and pulling alongside her brother.

"Leave it!" her mother shouted.

"No!" Jake's voice cracked with strain. "Our supplies—"

The flashlight beam found them, harsh white light freezing them in its glare. A triumphant whoop followed.

"Got movement! Four of them!"

Hannah's father appeared beside them, shoving them forward. "The trees. NOW."

They abandoned the path, crashing through underbrush, the cart bouncing violently over uneven ground. Hannah felt branches whipping her face, catching in her hair. Behind them, voices called to each other, organizing pursuit.

"Sullivan, take the left! Morgan, cut through the other yard!"

Coordinated. Practiced. These weren't opportunistic looters but a trained unit. Hannah's medical brain cataloged the implications as though she were performing triage. Tactical experience, organizational hierarchy, equipment resources.

Terrifying conclusions.

They reached the trees, plunging into darkness. Her father pulled them deeper into the woods, away from their planned route, improvising in response to discovery. The cart snagged on roots and fallen branches, slowing their progress dramatically. After five minutes of brutal progress, Thomas halted them with a raised hand.

"Listen," he whispered.

Hannah strained to hear past her own ragged breathing and pounding heartbeat. Voices in the distance, moving parallel to their position. Flashlight beams sweeping methodically through the trees. The pursuers had split up, attempting to flank them.

"They're herding us," her father said, voice tight with realization. "They've done this before."

Hannah's blood ran cold. Not just pursuit but strategy. These people knew exactly how to drive fleeing families into predetermined kill zones.

Rebecca unslung her rifle. "How many rounds do we have?"

"Not enough," Thomas replied grimly. "We need to separate."

"No." The word escaped Hannah automatically, visceral rejection of the idea.

Her father gripped her shoulders. "The cart's too slow, too noisy. They're tracking it." His eyes, reflecting pinpricks of distant flashlights, were steady on hers. "You and Jake head northeast toward the conservation land. Your mother and I will draw them south."

"Dad, we can't—"

"Hannah." Her mother's voice cut through her protest.

"You're the navigator. You know the rally point." Rebecca pressed something into her hand—the UV flashlight with its nearly invisible beam. "Get your brother there. We'll find you."

The lie hung between them, recognized but unchallenged. Hannah felt tears burning behind her eyes but forced them back. Tears were a luxury for the old world.

Jake looked from his parents to Hannah, fourteen-year-old comprehension dawning on his face. "No. We stay together. That's the rule."

"New rule," their father said gently. "Adapt and survive." He began quickly transferring essential supplies from the cart to their packs. Water. Ammunition. Medical kit. Food concentrates. "Travel light, move fast. No fires, no open ground until you reach the cabin."

Hannah stood frozen, unable to process the rapid dissolution of their careful plans. A nearby shout jolted her back to immediacy.

"They're close," her mother warned, scanning the darkness. She thrust the rifle into Hannah's hands. "Take this. You remember what you learned?"

Hannah nodded mechanically. The few weeks of crash-course firearms training at the neighborhood range. Stance. Breath control. Sight picture. Squeeze, don't pull.

"I can't leave you unarmed," she protested.

Thomas drew a pistol from his waistband. "We're covered. Now go."

Flashlight beams grew closer, converging on their position. No more time for debate or goodbyes. Hannah grabbed Jake's arm, pulling him away from the cart, away from their parents.

"We'll find you," she promised, the words hollow even as she spoke them.

Her mother's face softened for just a moment. "We know you will." She touched Hannah's cheek once, a gesture so tender it hurt. "Now run."

Hannah pulled Jake deeper into the woods, away from the approaching lights. Behind them, their father began noisily moving the cart in the opposite direction, deliberately drawing attention.

"Hey!" Thomas shouted into the darkness. "Over here, you bastards!"

The pursuit shifted immediately, flashlight beams swinging toward the sound. Hannah and Jake crouched behind a fallen oak, watching as their parents became the decoys in a desperate gambit.

"We can't leave them," Jake whispered, his voice breaking.

Hannah's arm tightened around her brother's shoulders. "We have to." The words searing in her throat. "It's what they want. It's how we survive."

They watched in helpless silence as their parents disappeared into the darkness, pursuers converging from multiple directions. Hannah counted at least eight flashlight beams in pursuit. She tried not to think about what would happen when they caught up.

"This way," she whispered when the pursuit had moved far enough away. She oriented herself using the distant glow of burning buildings, calculating their position relative to the planned escape route. "Warren Woods is not that far off."

Jake didn't move. "What if—"

"No what-ifs," Hannah cut him off sharply. "Just survival. One step at a time." She softened her tone with effort. "That's what Dad would say, right?"

This reached him. Jake nodded, wiping his face with a

grimy sleeve. "One step at a time."

They moved through the midnight forest like ghosts, Hannah leading with the UV flashlight that cast its nearly invisible beam only she and Jake could see with their attuned night vision. Every sense strained for signs of pursuit. Every rustle of leaves or snap of twigs froze them in their tracks.

An hour passed. Then another. The distant fires of South Portland receded behind them as they pushed northwest. No sounds of pursuit. No gunshots. Hannah refused to interpret this absence, focusing instead on navigation. The conservation land should be just ahead—acres of protected forest that backed up against a highway overpass where they should be able to get to the other side of the highway. If they could reach it before dawn, they'd have cover for the most dangerous part of their journey.

The trees began to thin, revealing a ribbon of open ground—Payne Road—that they would need to cross. Hannah halted at the forest edge, studying the exposed terrain. Fifty yards of moonlit vulnerability before the safety of the far tree line.

"We wait," she decided. "Watch for five minutes before crossing."

Jake nodded, crouching beside her. In the faint moonlight, his face looked much younger than fourteen. A child thrust into circumstances no child should face. Hannah felt a surge of protective fury. Not that long ago his biggest concern had been making the freshman baseball team.

"Do you think—" he began.

Hannah shushed him with a finger to her lips, ears catching a distant sound. Voices. Male. Approaching from the south. She pulled Jake lower behind a tangle of mountain laurel.

Two men emerged from the treeline sixty yards to their left, moving with the confidence of those who believed themselves alone. They wore what looked like tactical gear—dark clothing, equipment vests, weapons slung across their chests. One carried a handheld radio that crackled with intermittent static.

"—confirmed four targets but only caught the two," a voice reported through the static. "Still searching for the others."

Hannah's breath caught. The two. Her parents.

The taller man lifted the radio. "What condition are the captures in?"

A pause, then: "Female is intact. Orders are to bring her back. Male resisted. He's done."

Jake made a strangled sound beside her. Hannah clamped her hand over his mouth, her own heart shattering inside her chest. She understood the clinical euphemism. Done. Her father was dead. Her mother…she forced herself not to complete the thought.

"Any word on the other targets?" the second man asked.

"Heading northeast according to Sullivan. Probably trying for the highway."

"That's our sweep zone anyway. We'll find them."

"Orders are to take them alive if possible. Sherman wants information about Cornish."

Hannah froze. Cornish. Maddie's hometown. The very place they were headed.

"Roger that. Will advise if we make contact."

The men moved across the road with practiced efficiency, disappearing into the trees on the far side. Hannah remained motionless, mind racing. They knew about Cornish. They were specifically gathering intelligence about it. Which meant Maddie and the others there were also targets.

Beside her, Jake shook with silent sobs, his body curled around the knowledge they'd just received. Hannah wanted nothing more than to comfort him, to share in his grief, but survival demanded compartmentalization. Mourn later. Survive now.

"We need to move," she whispered when the men had been gone for ten minutes. "Different direction. They're sweeping northeast, we're going northwest."

Jake looked up, face streaked with tears and dirt. "But what about the cabin?"

"It's compromised. They might know where we're headed." It didn't matter, they needed to get there. "There's a road up ahead that goes under the highway. We can stay off the main roads until we get outside of Gorham then pick up route 25 above their search grid."

"And Mom?" Jake's voice cracked.

The question had no good answer. Their mother was alive but captured. Attempting a rescue with their limited resources would be suicide.

"We get to safety first," Hannah said, the words like ground glass in her throat knowing it was likely she wouldn't survive. "Then we plan. One step at a time, remember?"

Jake didn't respond, but he stood when she pulled him up, followed when she led him in their new direction. The weight of what they'd just heard—their father dead, mother captured, hunters searching specifically for them—seemed to physically press him toward the earth.

They traveled in silence for another hour, making a wide arc around any populated areas, staying as deep into the wooded areas as possible. Dawn was approaching, the sky lightening to charcoal at the edges. Soon they would lose the cover of darkness. Hannah had no good solution for daylight travel, but stopping wasn't an option either.

"Listen," Jake whispered suddenly, freezing in place.

Hannah stopped, head tilted. At first, she heard nothing but the pre-dawn stirring of birds. Then—an engine. Not the rumble of a car or truck, but the higher-pitched whine of an ATV.

"Down," she ordered, pulling Jake into a shallow depression beneath a fallen pine alongside the road.

The sound grew louder, approaching from the east—directly from the area they had avoided. Hannah pulled branches over their position, creating rudimentary camouflage. Jake pressed against her side, his breathing shallow and controlled. They'd practiced this drill too, though never with such stakes.

The ATV appeared through the trees behind them, moving slowly along what must have been a game trail. A single rider, male, scanning the forest floor methodically. Looking for tracks. Looking for them.

Hannah felt Jake tense beside her as the vehicle approached within thirty yards of their hiding place. She squeezed his arm in silent warning. The rider paused, cutting the engine, listening. For an excruciating minute, the only sound was the rustle of leaves in the early morning breeze.

The man dismounted, rifle in hand. "I know you're out here," he called, voice carrying in the quiet forest. "Making it harder on yourselves just means making it harder on your mother when we do find you."

Jake's muscles bunched beneath Hannah's restraining hand. She dug her fingers into his arm, a silent plea.

"Sherman's got plans for Cornish," the man continued conversationally, moving in a slow circle around his vehicle.

"Your friends up there won't even see us coming. But you could help them, you know. Tell us what defenses they have, what resources. Make it easier for everyone."

Hannah's mind raced. These people knew who they were, knew their connection to Cornish, but somehow believed they knew something.

The man moved closer to their position, following some instinct or sign Hannah couldn't identify. Twenty yards. Fifteen. His boots crunched on fallen pine needles.

"Your mother's waiting," he said. "Wouldn't want to keep her waiting too long. These aren't men with much patience."

Ten yards. Hannah's hand closed around the grip of the rifle hidden beneath her body. She'd fired it exactly twelve times during practice sessions. Never at a living target. Never with intent to kill.

"Last chance to make this easy," the man called, now close enough that Hannah could see dirt caked in the treads of his boots. "Three… two…"

A branch snapped somewhere to their left. The man swung toward the sound, weapon raised. "Got you," he said with satisfaction, moving away from their hiding place toward the noise.

Hannah didn't hesitate. She raised the rifle, bracing it against the fallen tree trunk, and sighted on the man's back as he moved away. Stance. Breath control. Sight picture. Her finger found the trigger.

Squeeze, don't pull.

The shot cracked through the dawn stillness, deafening in the quiet forest. The man jerked, stumbled, but didn't fall. Hannah worked the bolt, chambering another round. Her second shot went wide as the man dove for cover.

"Run!" she shouted to Jake, pushing him away from their position. "Head west! Go!"

Jake scrambled away as Hannah fired again, forcing the man to keep his head down. She ejected the spent casing, chambered another round. Four left. Had to make them count.

The man returned fire, bullets thudding into the tree trunk above her. Hannah rolled to a new position, spotting him behind the ATV. She aimed for the vehicle's gas tank, remembering her father's lessons about creating distractions.

The bullet punctured metal with a dull ping. No explosion like in movies, just a steady stream of fuel spilling onto forest duff. Hannah fired once more, aiming lower, hoping for a spark from the engine block.

Nothing. Two rounds left.

The man must have realized her intention. He abandoned the ATV, moving in a crouching run toward better cover. Hannah tracked him through the rifle sight, leading slightly as they'd had taught her. This time when she fired, the man went down, clutching his leg.

Hannah didn't wait to see more. She rolled away from her position, running in a crouch toward where Jake had disappeared. Behind her, the wounded man shouted into his radio.

"Contact! Targets are armed! Need backup in sector seven!"

She found Jake two hundred yards west, crouched behind a massive oak, eyes wide with shock. "Did you—"

"He's alive. We need to move. Now." Hannah grabbed his arm, pulling him deeper into the forest. "Others will be coming."

They ran without regard for noise or tracks, pure survival

instinct driving them forward. The rising sun filtered through the trees, casting long shadows across their path. Day had broken, and with it, their slim chance of invisible passage.

After twenty minutes of hard running, Hannah called a halt. They needed to assess, to plan. Jake collapsed against a tree trunk, chest heaving with exertion and adrenaline crash. Hannah checked their position using landmarks and the rising sun.T

"The traffic circle is 202 and 112 if we follow 112 it'll take us to 25 just past Gorham." she calculated. "If we keep moving west, we'll reach it within the hour."

"Then what?" Jake asked, voice hollow. "Where do we go?"

Hannah had been avoiding this question. Their carefully mapped route to the hunting cabin was now deadly. Their parents—she pushed away the thought, focusing on immediate survival.

"Northwest," she decided. "Toward Cornish. We have to warn them." And find Maddie, she added silently.

"That's probably twenty miles."

"One step at a time." Hannah unslung her pack, extracting a water bottle. "Drink. Small sips."

Jake obeyed mechanically. "Will they kill Mom when they can't find us?"

The question Hannah had been dreading. She considered lying, offering false comfort. But her brother deserved truth, however brutal.

"I don't know," she admitted. "But she's valuable to them for information. And as bait." She squeezed his shoulder. "Mom's smart. She'll find a way to survive until we can find help."

Jake nodded, needing to believe it as much as Hannah did. They rested for exactly five minutes by Hannah's watch, then shouldered their packs and continued.

The distant sound of ATV engines followed them, sometimes fading, sometimes growing closer, as the search grid expanded. Hannah kept them moving steadily, angling slightly northwest, avoiding roads and open ground where they might be spotted.

By mid-morning, the trees began to thin. Through the branches, Hannah caught glimpses of route 25. What they found was a graveyard of abandoned vehicles.

"We'll follow it from the treeline," she decided. "Less chance of being spotted than if we walk on the roadway."

Jake nodded, conserving energy by speaking only when necessary. He'd retreated into himself since hearing about their parents, moving on autopilot. Hannah recognized the signs of shock but had no time or resources to address it. Survival first, then grief. Then revenge.

They kept moving, keeping within the tree cover while using the roadway as a navigation guide. The elevated roadbed gave Hannah occasional vantage points to scan for pursuit, though the scattered vehicles provided potential hiding places for watchers as well.

During one such pause, sheltered behind a roadside pine, Jake clutched her arm suddenly. "Listen."

Hannah froze, straining to hear past the whisper of wind through needles. Voices. Multiple speakers, male, coming from further down the road. She eased forward, pulling Jake with her into a better observation position.

Four men stood beside a military-style truck parked amid the abandoned civilian vehicles. The hood was up, two of them working on the engine while the others stood guard. All were armed with rifles similar to those carried by their pursuers in the forest.

"Same group?" Jake whispered.

Hannah studied them, noting the similar tactical clothing, weapons, and organized behavior. "Probably. Different unit."

As they watched, one of the men opened the truck's rear compartment and withdrew something that made Hannah's blood freeze. A handheld device with a small satellite dish attachment—communications equipment far beyond what isolated survivor groups should possess.

The man extended the antenna and began speaking into a handset. Though too distant to hear his words, Hannah could see him pointing up the road, toward Cornish. Another man unfolded a map on the truck's hood, all four gathering around it.

"They're planning something," she whispered. "Coordinating."

Jake's eyes narrowed. "For Cornish?"

"Seems likely." Hannah's mind raced through implications. "We need to get closer. Hear what they're saying."

"That's crazy," Jake protested. "If they see us—"

"Then we need to make sure they don't."

Hannah studied the surroundings. "Stay here," she instructed Jake. "If anything happens, run north and don't stop."

"No." His voice held a newfound hardness. "I'm coming with you." He met her gaze directly. "Dad's gone. Mom's captured. I'm not losing you too."

Hannah recognized the futility of argument. "Fine. But you

stay behind me. Do exactly as I say. If I tell you to run, you run. Promise me."

Jake nodded grimly.

They circled wide through the forest, crossing the road a quarter-mile back where a fallen tree provided cover for their passage. Approaching from the opposite side, they used abandoned cars as stepping stones, moving silently toward the concrete barrier near the truck.

Hannah could hear voices now, though still indistinct. She led Jake to a position directly opposite the truck, the three-foot concrete barrier between them and discovery. If they raised their heads above it, they would be immediately visible to the men on the other side.

"—main force moves in three days," one man was saying, voice now clear. "Sherman wants that farm compound taken intact. Resources prioritized."

"What about the town itself?" another asked.

"Secondary objective. Control the farm, you control the food. Town falls afterward."

Hannah and Jake exchanged glances. The Thompson farm. They had to be talking about the Thompson farm where Maddie was headed.

"How many we thinking?" A third voice, deeper than the others.

"Full strike team. Forty, minimum. Coordinated from multiple vectors. Should be over in hours."

"And our job?"

"Advance scouts. Confirm defenses, identify key targets, locate water supplies."

Hannah's fists clenched. The water contamination in South

Portland had started just before the attacks. If they were planning the same for Cornish…

"Timeline's accelerated after that incident with the prisoners," the first man said. "One of them escaped, heading north. Sherman doesn't want to risk them reaching Cornish with a warning."

"That prisoner from the Henderson place? The one who killed Morgan?"

Hannah froze. The Henderson place. Mrs. Henderson, whose scream she'd heard just before fleeing. They were talking about someone who had escaped their group—someone potentially heading toward Cornish as a warning.

"Yeah, woman put up one hell of a fight. Got loose during transport, killed a guard. Sherman's pissed. Wants her found yesterday."

"What about the other captures from last night? That woman and the dead guy?"

Jake tensed beside her. Hannah gripped his arm, warning him to remain silent.

"Being processed at base. Woman knows something about Cornish defenses. Sherman's personally handling that interrogation."

Bile rose in Hannah's throat. She forced it down, focusing on the intelligence being revealed. Location. Timeline. Force strength. Tactics. Information that could save lives if they could get it to Cornish.

The sound of an approaching engine cut the conversation short. The men quickly folded their map, closing the truck hood.

"That'll be the advance team," one said. "Let's move."

Hannah pulled Jake lower behind the barrier as a convoy of

three vehicles approached—two ATVs and another truck. As they pulled alongside, she caught fragments of new conversation.

"—nearly had them at the creek crossing, but they split up."

"Any sign since?"

"Blood trail heading west. One of them's wounded. Can't have gotten far."

Hannah's hand moved unconsciously to her rifle. They were still hunting them, still tracking.

"Sherman wants all units on search pattern. Priority is the Mitchell kids." The man who spoke wore some kind of insignia on his shoulder that marked him as a leader. "They have a connection to Cornish."

Jake's breathing quickened beside her. Hannah squeezed his arm, silently urging calm.

"We sweep the highway corridor next," the leader continued. "Teams of four, half-mile spacing. They may be heading north. Some cabin—we box them in."

Orders were distributed quickly, efficiently. Within minutes, the group had reorganized into smaller units and departed, spreading out back toward the interstate. The original truck remained, two men staying behind as a communications relay point.

Hannah pulled Jake back the way they'd come, moving silently until they were safely within the forest cover again.

"They're hunting us specifically," Jake whispered, fear evident in his voice.

Hannah nodded grimly. "They know who we are. The good part is, that they think we're heading north." She checked her watch. "And they're planning to attack the Thompson farm in three days."

"We'll never make it to Cornish on foot in time," Jake said. "Not with them searching for us."

"Ah, yes but searching for the cabin. The thing is we need to get to Cornish before they figure it out."

Hannah stared at the road, mind racing through options. They needed transportation. They needed to move faster than pursuing teams could track them. They needed a miracle.

As if in answer, her eyes landed on an abandoned motorcycle lodged in the drainage ditch beside the road. A dirt bike, its frame dented but largely intact. The kind of vehicle that could navigate around the automotive graveyards blocking major roads. The kind that might still run after a CME if it was old enough.

"Wait here," she instructed Jake.

"Hannah—"

"Two minutes. Count them."

She darted toward the motorcycle before he could protest further, keeping low and using abandoned cars as cover. The dirt bike was half-buried in mud from recent rains, its handlebars twisted at an odd angle. Hannah examined it quickly, looking for the manufacturing date stamped on the frame. A 1988 Honda XR200R. Old enough to have survived the CME.

She dug it out with her hands, mud caking beneath her fingernails as she worked frantically. The bike was damaged but not destroyed—bent handlebars, cracked fender, but the engine and frame appeared intact.

Two minutes stretched to five as Hannah struggled to free the motorcycle from the ditch. Finally, she managed to drag it onto level ground, checking the gas tank with a quick shake.

Not empty, though impossible to tell how much fuel remained. The battery would be dead after sitting for weeks, but if the magneto was still functioning, she might be able to bump-start it.

Hannah pushed the bike back toward Jake's position, staying low and using abandoned vehicles for cover. Her brother's eyes widened as she approached.

"Are you serious?" he whispered.

"It's our only chance," Hannah replied, voice tight with urgency. "Those search teams won't be on the wrong track for long. We need to move fast and unpredictably."

Jake studied the motorcycle dubiously. "Can you even get it started?"

"Maybe." Hannah surveyed their position. The forest sloped gently downward for about fifty yards before leveling out—perfect for a bump-start attempt. "I need you to help me push it to build speed, then I'll pop the clutch."

Jake nodded, moving to position himself beside the bike. "What if it's too loud? They'll hear us for miles."

"Then we outrun them." Hannah's voice held more confidence than she felt. "The reason that truck is sitting is the road is too clogged for vehicles. You saw them moving them. This bike can go where their trucks and ATVs can't."

They pushed the motorcycle to the edge of the forest, Hannah watching for any sign of the search teams. The two men at the communications truck were still visible in the distance, but their attention was focused northward, away from Hannah and Jake's position.

"On three," Hannah instructed, straddling the bike and affixing her pack to the handlebars. "Push as hard as you can, then jump on behind me when I tell you."

Jake positioned himself behind the motorcycle, hands on the rear rack. Hannah put the bike in neutral, working the clutch and testing the throttle. The cables were stiff but functional.

"One… two… three!"

Jake pushed with all his strength as Hannah steered the bike down the gentle slope. The momentum built quickly, the motorcycle rolling faster as gravity assisted their efforts. At the bottom of the slope, Hannah dropped into second gear and released the clutch.

The engine stuttered, coughed—then roared to life with a sound that seemed to shake the forest. Hannah gunned the throttle, the bike lurching forward.

"NOW!" she shouted.

Jake sprinted alongside, grabbing her outstretched hand and swinging himself onto the back of the seat as the motorcycle accelerated. His arms wrapped tightly around her waist as Hannah opened the throttle further, the bike bouncing over uneven ground.

Behind them, shouts erupted from the highway. The communications team had heard the engine and were already running toward vehicles.

Hannah drove deeper into the forest, navigating between trees, using the motorcycle's agility to their advantage. The engine's roar seemed impossibly loud in the quiet woodland, announcing their position to anyone within miles. But speed now outweighed stealth. They needed distance more than concealment.

"Which way?" Jake shouted against her ear.

Hannah oriented herself using the sun's position. "Northwest! We'll parallel the road but stay off it for now!"

The motorcycle bucked and jolted over fallen branches and

uneven terrain, but Hannah kept it upright through sheer determination. Behind them, the whine of ATV engines rose and fell as search teams changed direction, homing in on the motorcycle's distinctive sound.

They burst from the forest onto a narrow maintenance road—packed dirt with gravel shoulders, likely used by utility crews. Hannah turned north, opening the throttle fully. The motorcycle responded admirably, accelerating down the straight stretch despite its damaged condition.

For ten minutes they raced as fast as the small engine would go, the road twisting through woodland and occasional clearings. Hannah hunched low over the handlebars, Jake pressed against her back. The engine's pitch fluctuated worryingly, but maintained power. Behind them, the sounds of pursuit faded, then disappeared entirely.

"I think we lost them!" Jake shouted over the engine noise.

Hannah didn't respond, focusing on the road ahead. They'd gained temporary advantage through speed and unpredictability, but the motorcycle's noise meant their general direction was obvious. Search teams would spread out, establish roadblocks, attempt to funnel them into containment zones.

The road crested a small rise, offering momentary visibility across the landscape. Hannah slowed slightly, assessing their options. To the northwest, forested hills rolled toward distant mountains. To the northeast, cleared farmland stretched toward what had once been suburban development. The road was visible as a black ribbon cutting north through both territories, parts of it clogged with abandoned vehicles.

"We need to get off this road," Hannah decided, turning the bike toward a game trail that angled northwest into deeper forest. "Too predictable."

The trail narrowed as they entered denser woodland, branches whipping at their arms and faces. Hannah slowed by necessity, navigating between trees and over exposed roots. The motorcycle's engine grumbled its protest at the rough treatment.

"Hannah," Jake's voice was tense against her ear. "Gas."

She glanced down at the fuel gauge, needle hovering just above empty. Another resource to carefully manage. Another countdown timer on their survival.

"We'll find more," she assured him, though the promise felt hollow. Siphoning fuel would mean approaching abandoned vehicles on major roads—exactly where Sherman's people would be watching.

The trail widened as it descended into a shallow valley. A stream glittered between mossy banks, the water clear and inviting after hours of flight. Hannah steered toward it, cutting the engine as they approached.

The sudden silence was almost disorienting after the constant growl of the motorcycle. Birds resumed their calls overhead. The stream burbled over smooth stones. Deceptively peaceful.

"Ten-minute rest," Hannah announced, dismounting stiffly. "We get the water purified and drink, refill water bottles, check the map, then move."

Jake collapsed beside the stream, cupping water toward his mouth with trembling hands that Hannah smacked away handing him the lifestraw and water bottle. The adrenaline crash was hitting him hard, his fourteen-year-old body pushed beyond reasonable limits. Hannah felt it too—a bone-deep weariness that made every movement deliberate, conscious.

She retrieved the map from her pack, orienting it using the stream and surrounding landmarks. If her calculations were correct, they'd covered nearly five miles since escaping the search teams a significant head start on foot pursuers, though vehicles could close that gap quickly.

"Where are we?" Jake asked, moving to look over her shoulder.

Hannah pointed to their approximate position. "Here. About maybe ten miles from Cornish." Her finger traced potential routes. "If we follow this watershed, we eventually hit the Saco River. From there, we can follow it to within a mile or so of Cornish, but first we will have to get across it. I think here in Limington we can cross," she said, pointing to the map.

Jake studied the map silently, absorbing the enormity of distance still to cover. "How much gas do you think we have left?"

Hannah shook her head. "We might have ten miles. Fifteen if we're lucky and keep to flat terrain." She folded the map carefully. "We'll need to find more."

"Or abandon the bike and continue on foot," Jake suggested.

"Last resort." Hannah glanced at her brother's exhausted face. "We need the speed."

She moved to examine the motorcycle more thoroughly now that immediate pursuit had faded. The damaged handlebar made steering difficult but manageable. The real concern was fuel. Without it, their transportation advantage evaporated.

"Hannah," Jake called quietly from the stream edge. "Look."

She joined him, following his gesture to the muddy bank. Footprints—fresh ones, made within hours—crossed the stream from east to west. Multiple sets, at least four distinct patterns. Boot treads, similar to those worn by their pursuers.

"They've been through here," Jake whispered unnecessarily.

Hannah studied the tracks, noting their direction. Not pursuing them specifically. These had been made before their flight, but moving purposefully through the territory. Another team, positioned ahead of them rather than behind.

"They're everywhere," she realized aloud. "This isn't just about us. They're establishing a presence across the entire region."

Jake looked up sharply. "Surrounding Cornish?"

"Preparing for their attack." Hannah traced the footprints with her eyes, following their path up the opposite bank and into the trees. "Advance teams, like they said. Mapping routes, identifying resources." She straightened, decision made. "We need to parallel their path but stay north of it. Use their own route planning to our advantage."

They rested ten minutes as she'd said they would, then prepared to move. The motorcycle started more easily this time, its engine settling into a rough but steady rhythm. Hannah steered more carefully now, balancing speed against fuel conservation, constantly scanning for signs of pursuit or advance teams.

They followed game trails and logging roads where possible, avoiding open ground and major thoroughfares. The sun climbed toward noon, then began its slow descent westward. Hours passed with no sign of active pursuit, though twice they diverted course after spotting what appeared to be scout positions on elevated terrain.

The gas gauge dropped steadily despite Hannah's conservative operation. By mid-afternoon, the needle rested firmly on empty, the engine surviving on whatever fuel remained in the lines and carburetor.

"We need to find gas," Jake stated the obvious as they coasted down a gentle slope, engine straining.

Hannah nodded grimly. "There's a small town marked on the map about three miles northwest. Crossroads with a general store and gas station."

"You think there's anything left?"

"Doubt it. But there might be abandoned vehicles we can siphon from." Hannah didn't mention the obvious risk—that such a location would be a natural checkpoint for Sherman's forces. The danger was self-evident.

The motorcycle's engine coughed once, twice, then died completely as they crested the next rise. Hannah let momentum carry them as far as possible before the bike slowed to a stop. Jake dismounted first, stretching his cramped legs while Hannah examined their position.

From their elevated vantage point, she could see the small town in the distance—a cluster of buildings surrounding a crossroads, exactly as the map had indicated. No movement was visible, but that meant nothing at this distance.

"We walk from here," she decided. "Hide the bike in case we find fuel."

They pushed the motorcycle into dense underbrush, covering it with branches and leaves. Even if they found fuel, Hannah wasn't certain they should risk the noise of the engine again. But eliminating options seemed foolish when so few remained.

With the rifle slung across her back and her pack secured, Hannah led Jake toward the distant buildings. They moved cautiously through the forest edge, stopping frequently to listen and observe. The town showed no signs of life as they approached—no smoke from chimneys, no movement between buildings.

"Looks abandoned," Jake whispered as they crouched at the forest edge, studying the settlement from two hundred yards away.

Hannah wasn't convinced. "Maybe. Or maybe they're just being careful." She pointed to a small gas station at the crossroads. "That's our target. But we observe for thirty minutes first."

They settled into position, using binoculars to study every aspect of the apparently deserted town. The gas station stood at the intersection, its pumps useless without electricity but potentially harboring fuel in underground tanks. Several vehicles sat abandoned in its small parking lot, including a pickup truck and two sedans.

"Nothing's moving," Jake said after twenty minutes of observation. "No smoke. No lights. I think it really is abandoned."

Hannah remained cautious. "We approach from the west, using those buildings as cover. In and out in five minutes. Fuel only, no scavenging."

Jake nodded, understanding the priority. They circled wide, approaching the town from downwind in case dogs or other sentries might catch their scent. The back side of the general store provided cover for their final approach, its loading dock offering a sheltered vantage point.

"Stay here," Hannah instructed her brother. "Watch my back. One whistle if you see anything suspicious, two for immediate danger."

"I should come with you," Jake protested.

"One of us needs to maintain a lookout." Hannah

transferred her water bottle to Jake's pack, lightening her load. "Five minutes. That's it."

Before he could argue further, Hannah slipped away, moving in a crouching run between buildings. The silence of the town pressed against her ears, broken only by the creaking of unstable structures and the distant call of a hawk. Every doorway, every window, seemed to watch her passage.

She reached the gas station without incident, ducking behind a rusted Subaru in its lot. The building appeared untouched, its windows intact, door closed. Unlike many structures she'd seen since the collapse, it showed no signs of looting or forced entry.

Too pristine. Warning bells sounded in Hannah's mind.

She studied the vehicles in the lot more carefully. The pickup truck—an older Ford with faded blue paint—had its driver's door slightly ajar. A perfect siphon target, but the open door suggested previous scavenging. The sedans were newer models, likely rendered useless by the CME.

Hannah moved to the pickup, approaching from the rear quarter panel. The truck's bed contained miscellaneous items—a tarp, some bungee cords, a crushed soda can. She peered cautiously through the windows. Empty interior, keys dangling from the ignition. The gas gauge on the dashboard rested just above a quarter-tank.

She retrieved a length of rubber tubing from her pack—part of their prepared bug-out equipment—and started to position herself beside the truck's fuel port. Something made her pause, some instinct or perception below conscious thought. Hannah crouched lower, examining the ground beneath the vehicle.

Fresh oil spots. Not the weathered stains of a long-abandoned vehicle, but the glossy wetness of recent operation.

Hannah froze, senses suddenly hyperalert. The truck hadn't been sitting idle for two months. Someone had driven it recently. Very recently.

She backed away slowly, eyes sweeping the gas station building with new scrutiny. The untouched appearance, the functioning vehicle, the keys left conveniently in the ignition—all wrong for a truly abandoned location.

A trap.

Hannah retreated behind the Subaru again, pulse hammering in her throat. The entire setup screamed ambush—a staging area disguised as abandoned, with bait for desperate travelers. She needed to get back to Jake immediately, to retreat before whoever monitored this location returned.

She began moving toward the general store where she'd left her brother, staying low and using abandoned vehicles for cover. Halfway there, a metallic click froze her in place—the distinctive sound of a rifle safety being disengaged.

"That's far enough," a woman's voice called from behind the gas station. "Hands where I can see them."

Hannah's mind raced through options, calculating her position relative to cover, the distance to Jake's hiding place, the single round remaining in her rifle. No good choices presented themselves.

Slowly, she raised her hands, keeping her rifle slung across her back. "I'm just passing through," she called. "Looking for fuel."

"Aren't we all."

The speaker emerged from behind the gas station—a woman in her fifties, short gray hair cropped close to her scalp, rifle held competently but not aggressively. She wore what appeared to be a park ranger's uniform, though the insignia had been removed.

"You're young to be traveling alone," the woman observed, keeping a cautious distance.

"I'm not alone," Hannah replied, honesty seeming the safer option given Jake's hidden position.

The woman's expression remained neutral. "Your companion can come out too. We don't hurt kids here."

Hannah hesitated, weighing risks and alternatives. If this woman intended harm, Jake's position remained their only advantage. But if she truly offered help, refusing cooperation might escalate the situation unnecessarily.

Before Hannah could decide, Jake emerged from behind the general store, hands raised, mirroring her posture. He'd made the decision for them.

"Smart boy," the woman said, lowering her rifle slightly but not completely. "Now, where are you two headed in such a hurry that you didn't think to announce yourselves?"

"North," Hannah answered cautiously.

"Everybody's heading north these days." The woman studied them with narrowed eyes. "Running from something? Or someone?"

Jake opened his mouth to answer, but Hannah cut him off. "Just looking for somewhere safer."

The woman snorted. "Aren't we all." She gestured with her rifle toward the general store. "Come on then. You look half-starved, and Ellen's got stew on."

Hannah didn't move. "Who are you?"

"Park service. Or was. Name's Diane." The woman's expression softened slightly. "We're just survivors, same as you. Got about fifteen of us holed up here, keeping an eye on the crossroads."

"Waiting for travelers to rob?" Hannah couldn't keep the suspicion from her voice.

Diane laughed, a surprisingly genuine sound. "If that was our game, you'd already be trussed up or worse. No, we watch for a different kind of visitor these days." Her expression hardened. "Military types. Moving in groups. Taking what they want and who they want."

Hannah exchanged a glance with Jake, silent communication passing between them. "Sherman's people," she said.

Diane's posture changed instantly, rifle coming back to ready position. "You with them?"

"God, no." Hannah fought to keep her voice steady. "They attacked our community. South Portland. Killed our father. Took our mother." The words felt strange, spoken aloud for the first time. Making it real.

Diane studied them for a long moment, then slowly lowered her weapon. "Come inside," she said finally. "You need to talk to Marcus. He's been tracking their movements for a while."

Hannah hesitated only briefly before nodding. Information about Sherman's operations might be worth the risk of trusting strangers. She moved to Jake's side, placing a protective arm around his shoulders as they followed Diane toward the general store.

"What about fuel?" she asked as they walked. "Our bike's hidden in the woods. We need to reach Cornish."

Diane glanced back sharply. "Cornish? That where you're headed?"

"We have friends there. And Sherman's planning to attack

it in three days. We heard them talking." Hannah met the older woman's gaze directly. "We need to warn them."

Diane's pace quickened. "Then you definitely need to talk to Marcus. And yes, we can spare fuel—though traveling by motorcycle isn't the safest choice with Sherman's patrols everywhere."

The general store's windows had been covered with plywood from the inside, explaining its abandoned appearance from outside. Diane knocked a specific pattern on the back door—three short, two long—before opening it and ushering them inside.

The store's interior had been transformed into a functional living space. Shelves created room divisions, sleeping pallets arranged along walls, a woodstove in what had been the deli section providing heat for cooking. About a dozen people moved about the space, all looking up as Hannah and Jake entered.

"Found these two scouting the gas station," Diane announced. "They've got information about Sherman. Where's Marcus?"

A tall Black man rose from a chair near the woodstove, notebook in hand. Gray threaded his close-cropped hair and beard, and he moved with the slight limp of an old injury. "Right here. What kind of information?"

Hannah stepped forward. "Attack plans. Timetable. Force strength. And they're specifically targeting Cornish—the Thompson farm in particular."

Marcus gestured them toward the woodstove, where an older woman stirred a pot of something that smelled miraculous after hours of hunger. "Sit. Eat. Then tell me everything, detail by detail."

For the next hour, Hannah and Jake recounted their experiences—the attack on South Portland, their parents' fate, the overheard conversations about Sherman's plans. They omitted nothing, including their connection to Maddie in Cornish and their desperate need to warn the community.

Marcus listened without interruption, occasionally making notations in his book. When they finished, he studied his maps spread across what had once been the checkout counter.

"This matches our intelligence," he confirmed grimly. "We've been tracking Sherman's expansion for weeks. Originally thought Portland was his only target, but he's getting bolder, extending his reach."

"You have to help us get to Cornish," Hannah pressed. "They need to prepare."

Marcus exchanged glances with Diane and several others. "We've been avoiding direct confrontation. We're observers, not fighters."

"Then give us fuel. Let us go." Hannah leaned forward, intensifying her argument. "Sherman's not just taking territory. He's building something. A network. Communications equipment, coordinated units, strategic resource seizure. Where do you think he'll look next?"

The room fell silent, the implications settling heavily on everyone present. Finally, Marcus nodded.

"We'll help you," he decided. "Not just with fuel, but with transport. Motorcycle's too exposed, too noisy. We've got a better option."

He led them to a back storage room where, incredibly, an aluminum canoe rested on sawhorses. Hannah stared at it, momentarily confused.

"The Saco River runs about a half-mile west of here,"

Marcus explained. "Passing within a mile of Cornish. Bit of a fast current to go against this time of year. You could make it if you push hard."

Hannah's mind raced through the possibilities. The river would allow silent travel. Sherman's forces seemed focused on roads and established routes. Waterways might be less heavily monitored.

"We haven't spotted patrols on the river itself," Diane added, reading her thoughts. "They're watching bridges, major crossings. But stick to the edge where the current isn't so strong, travel at night when possible, you should slip right through their net."

Hope…that fragile, dangerous emotion Hannah had been suppressing flickered tentatively in her chest. "You'd give us a canoe? Just like that?"

Marcus smiled grimly. "Not 'just like that.' Information exchange. You tell us everything you know about Sherman's operations. We tell you what we've observed. And if—when—you reach Cornish, you tell them about us. Tell them there are other communities organizing. Watching. Preparing."

Hannah nodded solemnly. "Consider it done."

That evening, while Jake rested, Hannah pored over maps with Marcus and his group. They marked known patrol locations, observer posts, suspected supply caches. She described the communications equipment she'd seen, the command structure she'd observed. Every detail might mean survival for someone down the line.

"You should sleep," Diane advised as midnight approached. "River journey's arduous even with a current, going against it is far more difficult."

Hannah knew she was right, but sleep seemed impossible

with her mother's fate unknown and her father's death still a raw wound. Every time she closed her eyes, she saw the flashlight beams searching through trees, heard the radio transmission confirming her father was "done."

"I keep thinking about my mom," she admitted quietly. "What they're doing to her. What she's enduring."

Diane's weathered hand covered Hannah's. "Your mother made her choice. The same choice any parent would make. Honor it by surviving."

Hannah nodded, throat too tight for words. She moved to the sleeping pallet assigned to her, lying beside Jake's already sleeping form. Her brother's face, relaxed in sleep, looked painfully young. She pressed her knuckles against her mouth to stifle the sob building in her chest.

Survive first. Mourn later. Warn Cornish. Find Maddie. One step at a time.

Dawn came too quickly, gray light filtering through cracks in the plywood coverings. Marcus's group moved with practiced efficiency, preparing the canoe, loading it with supplies—food, water, a small medical kit, even a handheld radio with twice the range of any they'd previously owned.

"It's got a scrambled channel," Marcus explained, showing Hannah the settings. "We monitor continuously. If you run into trouble, broadcast your position. We might not be able to help directly, but we can gather intelligence, maybe create diversions."

The canoe was transported to the river by four of Marcus's strongest people, Hannah and Jake following with Diane. The morning mist hung over the water, providing additional concealment as they prepared to launch.

"Stay in the brush along the river's edge whenever

possible," Diane instructed as they loaded the last supplies. "Current's fastest in the center, and you'll be harder to spot from overpasses and such. There's a railroad bridge a few miles north—major patrol point."

Hannah memorized the instructions, committing key landmarks to memory. Marcus passed her a sealed waterproof packet.

"Map of the river with landmarks," he explained. "And everything we know about Sherman's operations. Get it to whoever's in charge."

Hannah secured the packet in her inner jacket pocket. "Thank you," she said simply. "For everything."

Diane helped them position the canoe at the river's edge. "Remember, these people—Sherman's troops—they're not just opportunistic raiders. They have a plan, purpose, logistics. They're thinking long-term."

"We'll remember," Hannah assured her, stepping carefully into the canoe's bow. Jake took the stern position, paddle gripped in white-knuckled hands.

As they pushed off from the bank, the current immediately caught them, pulling them downstream. Hannah dug her paddle into the water, establishing steering control. Jake matched her rhythm after a few awkward strokes, the canoe finding its smooth, swift course up along the banks of the Saco River.

Hannah looked back once to see Diane and Marcus watching from the shore, already growing small with distance. Unlikely allies in a world where every encounter carried potential death. She raised her paddle briefly in salute before returning to the rhythm of forward motion.

The river wound northward, trees crowding the banks on either side. The morning mist began burning off as the sun climbed higher, illuminating a landscape simultaneously familiar and foreign. The natural world continued unchanged while human civilization crumbled around it.

Hannah focused on the paddle's rhythm, on the pull of water and the canoe's response. Behind her, Jake maintained steady, increasingly confident strokes. Neither spoke for the first hour, conserving energy and processing all they'd learned.

"Do you think we'll make it in time?" Jake finally asked, voice carrying easily over the water.

Hannah considered the question seriously. More river miles to cover than overland. Sherman's forces preparing from multiple vectors. A community unaware of specific threats.

"Yes," she said firmly, refusing to entertain the alternative. "We'll make it."

The canoe shot forward as if propelled by her determination, cutting through the water toward Cornish. Behind them, South Portland burned. Hannah dug her paddle deeper, pulling harder against the current.

Ethan

Ethan Thompson knew what dead people looked like. He'd seen four of them now, not counting the ones on TV from before. Dead people didn't look asleep like everyone said. They looked empty, like somebody took all the important parts and left just the outside behind.

Mr. Foster was the worst. His face turned the color of the blueberries, and his mouth hung open like he was trying to say something important that nobody would ever hear. Ethan hadn't meant to look, but curiosity pushed him forward when the adults pulled back the sheet. The memory stayed stuck in his head like a burr on his sock.

Now, sitting cross-legged beside Ryan's bed, Ethan tried not to think about whether his cousin would end up like Mr. Foster. The room smelled like rubbing alcohol, mixed with something sour that reminded him of the time milk spoiled in their refrigerator after the lights went out. Sweat beaded on Ryan's forehead despite the cool cloth Aunt Jessica kept replacing.

"Are you listening, Ryan?" Ethan asked, holding the comic book higher so the pictures faced his cousin. "This is the part where Batman figures out the Riddler's clues."

Ryan's eyes remained closed, his breathing quick and shallow. He looked smaller than his seven years, lost in the too-large bed with its patchwork of mismatched blankets. Three days ago, he'd been running through the cornfield playing hide-and-seek. Now he couldn't even sit up.

"Batman's smart," Ethan continued, determined to finish the story even if Ryan couldn't hear him. "He looks for patterns. That's what Dad says is important—looking for patterns so you can guess what happens next."

The bedroom door creaked open, and Aunt Jessica stepped in, carrying a fresh basin of water. Her face looked pinched and tired, dark circles under her eyes like smudged pencil marks. She smiled when she saw Ethan, but it was her grown-up smile ,one that didn't reach her eyes.

"How's our patient?" she asked, sitting carefully on the edge of the bed. Her broken ankle, wrapped in an improvised cast of cardboard and strips of bed sheet, stretched out awkwardly before her.

"I'm reading him Batman," Ethan said. "He likes the pictures with the fighting."

Aunt Jessica nodded, dipping a cloth in the fresh water and wringing it out. "That's very thoughtful of you, Ethan. I'm sure it helps him feel better."

Ethan watched her place the cool cloth on Ryan's forehead, noting how her hands trembled slightly. Grown-ups' hands weren't supposed to shake. They were supposed to be steady, like when Dad showed him how to hold a hammer or Mom checked his temperature.

"He's going to get better, right?" Ethan asked, the question escaping before he could trap it behind his teeth.

Aunt Jessica's hands stilled. "Of course he is. Your mom is taking excellent care of him."

But Ethan caught the flicker in her eyes—the same look his dad got when Ethan asked if Grandpa's truck would ever work again. Adults thought kids couldn't tell when they were lying, but Ethan could. Little lies had a different feel than big ones. This was a big one.

"I should go help Grandpa," Ethan said, carefully closing the comic book.

Aunt Jessica nodded, relief crossing her face. "That's a good idea. Just don't go beyond the fence line, okay? Your father's very clear about that rule."

"I know the rules," Ethan said, trying to sound like he always followed them.

Outside, the July heat hit him like opening an oven door. Sweat immediately prickled along his scalp as he stepped off the porch into the farmyard. The world had a strange, hazy quality through the shimmer of heat rising from the ground. Sophia, his twelve-year-old sister, was hanging laundry on the line with Lily helping by handing her clothespins from a basket. The smaller girl's stuffed elephant, Mr. Trunks, sat propped against the basket like he was supervising.

Ethan avoided them, heading instead toward the barn where he could hear the rhythmic pounding of a hammer. Inside, the relative coolness washed over him, along with the familiar smells of hay, manure, and sawdust. Grandpa James and Dad were reinforcing the side door, adding heavy cross beams to the already sturdy structure.

"Hand me that box of three-inch nails," his dad said to Grandpa without looking up. The muscles in his forearms flexed as he drove another nail through the thick wood. Sweat darkened his shirt between his shoulder blades.

Ethan stepped forward. "I can get them."

Both men turned, surprise registering on their faces.

"Thought you were reading to Ryan," Grandpa said, his weathered face creasing with concern. "Everything okay?"

"Aunt Jessica's with him now," Ethan said with a half-shrug. "I wanted to help out here instead."

Dad and Grandpa exchanged one of those grown-up looks that meant they were having a silent conversation. Ethan hated those looks.

"Sure, buddy," Dad finally said. "The nails are on the workbench over there. Bring the whole box."

Ethan retrieved the nails, proud that he knew exactly which ones were the three-inch without having to ask. He'd been paying attention these past weeks. Three-inch nails for framing. Two-inch for general woodworking. Roofing nails had wide heads. Finishing nails had barely any heads at all.

"Why are you making the door stronger?" Ethan asked as he handed over the box. "Is it because of those men Beth was talking about? Sherman's men?"

Dad's hammer paused mid-swing. Another look passed between the adults, this one sharper, more concerned.

"Just precautions," Grandpa said carefully. "Like tying your shoes before a race."

"But we're not racing," Ethan pointed out, logic overcoming his desire to seem agreeable. "We're hiding."

Dad set down his hammer and crouched to Ethan's level, his knees cracking like kindling. "We're not hiding, buddy. We're preparing. There's a difference."

"What's the difference?"

"Hiding means you're scared and don't have a plan. Preparing means you're smart and ready for whatever comes next." Dad's hand settled on Ethan's shoulder, heavy and warm. "And we are very prepared."

Ethan nodded, though unconvinced. He'd heard the whispered conversations in the kitchen late at night when they thought he was asleep. He'd seen Beth's face when she told Grandpa about the water device they'd found. And he'd watched how the adults started moving medicines and food into the storm cellar, labeling it "inventory organization" when it was clearly much more.

"Can I help?" Ethan asked.

Dad hesitated, then nodded. "You can sort these screws by size." He pointed to a jumbled pile on the workbench. "We'll need them organized for the next project."

It wasn't real work. Just busy work to keep him occupied, but Ethan didn't complain. At least they weren't sending him to play with the younger kids or collect eggs from the chicken coop again. He settled on an overturned bucket and began separating the screws into piles, listening carefully to the adults' conversation.

"Michael, we need to talk about evacuation routes," Grandpa said quietly, hammering another nail into place. "Beth confirmed this morning that those devices were deliberate contamination."

Dad grunted as he lifted a heavy beam into position. "The cellar can hold everyone for three days, maybe four, with tight rationing. But if they cut off access to the well..."

"We'd need to move to the hunting cabin. The problem is getting everyone there safely with Ryan and Jessica's conditions." Grandpa wiped sweat from his forehead with his sleeve. "And I'm concerned about Frank's intentions. His 'boys' are positioning themselves at every strategic point in town."

"You think he's working with Sherman?" Dad asked, his voice dropping even lower.

Ethan strained to hear, pretending to focus on his sorting.

"I don't know," Grandpa admitted. "But I don't trust his timing. Showing up at first light, offering help we didn't ask for. Knowing details about the farm that Beth hadn't shared publicly."

Ethan's fingers worked mechanically, sorting screws while his mind pieced together fragments of information. Frank was the man with the red cloth tied to his arm who'd come to the farm yesterday. The man whose smile looked more like a smirk, who'd stared at Ethan too long when Grandpa introduced them. Ethan didn't like the way Frank looked at the farm, like he was counting things in his head.

A shadow fell across the barn entrance, and Ethan looked up to see Grayson Jr. standing in the doorway. The older boy's presence surprised him—Grayson usually stuck close to his mother and brother, suspicious of everyone else. His dark eyes scanned the barn's interior before settling on Ethan.

"Your mom's looking for you," Grayson said, his voice carrying across the space. "Something about cleaning up for lunch."

Dad and Grandpa paused their work, turning toward the newcomer.

"Thanks for letting us know, Grayson," Grandpa said warmly. "Ethan, you should go wash up. We'll finish here."

Ethan hesitated, reluctant to leave just as the conversation was getting interesting. "I'm not done sorting—"

"It's fine," Dad cut him off. "Go on now."

With no choice but to obey, Ethan carefully set aside his piles of screws and followed Grayson out of the barn. The older boy moved with a cautious awareness that reminded Ethan of the half-wild cats that lived in the back field—always watching, always ready to bolt at the first sign of danger.

"Your mom's not really looking for me, is she?" Ethan asked when they were out of earshot of the barn.

Grayson shrugged, glancing back over his shoulder. "No. But I wanted to talk to you."

Curious now, Ethan followed as Grayson led him toward the old oak tree at the edge of the farmyard, its massive branches providing a rare patch of shade in the relentless heat.

"What did you want to talk about?" Ethan asked, settling cross-legged in the cooler grass beneath the tree.

Grayson remained standing, shifting his weight from foot to foot. "Those men your grandfather was talking about. Sherman's men. I've seen them before."

Ethan's eyes widened. "You have?"

"In Portland. They took over everything. Started with just helping out, offering protection. Then they took control of the food, the water, the weapons." Grayson's voice had a hollow quality. "My dad tried to stand up to them. That's why we had to run."

A chill ran through Ethan despite the heat. "What happened to your dad?"

Grayson's face hardened. "They took him. We got away, but they took him." He picked at the bark of the oak tree, peeling off a strip with his fingernail. "Your mom's a nurse, right?"

Ethan nodded.

"And your dad was in the military?"

"Yeah, Army. They deployed him three times before I was even born.

Grayson seemed to be weighing his next words carefully. "That's why Sherman wants this place. It's not just the food or the land. It's the skills. They take people too. The ones with useful skills."

The implications sank in slowly. Mom was the only medical professional for miles. Dad knew tactics and security. Grandpa understood farming and community organization. Grandma Sarah knew how to preserve food and stretch supplies.

"Did you tell the grown-ups this?" Ethan asked.

"My mom told your grandfather some of it. But they don't really listen to kids." Grayson finally sat down, pulling his knees to his chest. "That's why I wanted to talk to you. We should be ready."

"Ready for what?"

"To fight. Or to run." Grayson's gaze was steady, older than his years. "Adults are going to try to protect us, send us somewhere 'safe' if trouble comes. But nowhere's really safe anymore."

Ethan thought about this, turning the concept over in his mind. It made a cold kind of sense. Grown-ups spent so much time trying to shield kids from bad things that they sometimes missed the obvious—that the bad things would find them anyway.

"What should we do?" Ethan asked, leaning forward.

"Know the escape routes. Have a pack ready with essentials. Learn where they hide the important stuff." Grayson ticked the points off on his fingers. "Most importantly, watch everything. Adults miss things because they're so busy dealing with their own problems."

"Like what?"

"Like that guy with the red band," Grayson said. "Frank. He came back early this morning when everyone was still asleep. I saw him from the window. He was looking at your water well, writing something in a little notebook."

Alarm shot through Ethan. "Did you tell anyone?"

Grayson shook his head. "Who'd believe me? I'm just some kid."

Before Ethan could respond, a high, panicked shout came from the direction of the house. Both boys jumped to their feet, instinctively moving toward the sound. Sophia stood on the porch, frantically waving.

"Ethan! Come quick! It's Ryan!"

His heart lurching into his throat, Ethan broke into a run, Grayson close behind. They pounded across the farmyard, dust kicking up beneath their sneakers. As they reached the porch, Ethan saw Mom emerge from the house, medical bag in hand, her face set in lines of grim determination.

"What's happening?" Ethan gasped.

"Mom said Ryan's fever spiked," Sophia explained, her voice trembling. "He started shaking all over. Aunt Jessica is with him, but Mom says it's bad this time."

Ethan started to follow his mom inside, but she turned and blocked his path with an outstretched arm.

"Not now, Ethan," she said firmly. "I need space to work."

"But I want to help!" The words burst from him, desperate and raw.

Mom's expression softened briefly. "The best help you can give is keeping the younger kids calm and away from Ryan's room. Can you do that for me?"

It was busy work again. Keeping him out of the way—but the urgency in his mother's voice left no room for argument. Ethan nodded reluctantly.

"Good boy," she said, already turning back toward Ryan's room. "Sophia, I need you to get more clean cloths from the laundry line. And find your grandmother—tell her we need more of the willow bark tea."

As his mom disappeared down the hallway, Ethan stood frozen on the porch, uncertainty washing over him. Through the open window, he could hear Ryan's labored breathing and Aunt Jessica's muffled sobs. The sounds tightened something in his chest, making it hard to draw a full breath.

"Come on," Grayson said quietly, tugging at Ethan's sleeve. "We should find the little kids like your mom said."

Ethan nodded mechanically, allowing himself to be led away from the house. They found Lily and Theo, Grayson's younger brother, near the chicken coop, taking turns tossing feed to the hens while Mr. Trunks the stuffed elephant supervised from a fence post.

"Mom wants us all to stay out here for a while," Ethan said, trying to sound normal. "We could play a game or something."

Lily looked up, instantly alert to the strain in his voice. "Is Ryan okay?"

"Mom's taking care of him," Ethan replied, avoiding a direct answer. "He needs quiet to rest, that's all."

Lily's lower lip trembled. "He's getting worse, isn't he? Like Mr. Foster did."

The comparison sent a spike of fear through Ethan's gut. "No! Ryan's younger and stronger. Mom says that makes a difference."

"But what if—"

"Let's play Sentries," Ethan interrupted, desperate to change the subject. "Like Dad taught us. We each take a direction and watch for anything unusual. It's important practice."

Theo's eyes lit up. "Like real guards? Can I have a weapon?"

"No weapons," Ethan and Grayson said simultaneously.

"But we can use these," Grayson added, picking up four straight sticks from near the coop. "They're guard staffs. Very important tools for sentries."

The younger children accepted this compromise eagerly, and soon Ethan had organized them into a patrol pattern around the chicken coop, each assigned a compass direction to monitor. As they settled into their game, he found himself automatically scanning the farm's perimeter, noting potential weaknesses, escape routes, and shelter points just as he and Grayson were discussing.

His mind went back to what Grayson saw. Frank had been examining the well. Writing notes. Ethan remembered the water contamination device they found, how the adults spoke of it in hushed, worried tones.

The thought made Ethan's stomach twist. He needed to tell someone. Dad, Grandpa, anyone, but they wouldn't believe him based only on Grayson's word. They'd pat his head and tell him not to worry, that the grown-ups would handle everything.

"Ethan!" Lily's voice broke through his thoughts. "Someone's coming!"

He turned sharply, following her pointing finger toward the main road. A plume of dust rose in the distance, marking the approach of a vehicle. Few working vehicles remained after the CME, which narrowed the possibilities significantly.

"Grayson, take the little ones to the barn," Ethan ordered, decision made in an instant. "Use the back entrance where Dad and Grandpa were working. Stay there until I come get you."

To his surprise, Grayson didn't argue, just nodded and gathered Theo and Lily with quiet efficiency. "What about you?"

"I'm going to see who it is," Ethan said, sounding braver than he felt. "I'll be careful."

As the others headed for the barn, Ethan ran toward the house, intent on warning the adults. He burst through the back door just as Grandpa emerged from Ryan's room, his face gray with worry.

"Ethan, I told you to stay—"

"Someone's coming," Ethan interrupted, pointing toward the front of the house.

Grandpa's expression shifted instantly from concern to alertness. He moved to the window, pushing aside the curtain to peer out at the approaching dust cloud.

"Go tell your father," he said, voice tight. "He's in the workshop. Then get to the cellar and stay there. Quickly now."

Ethan hesitated. "But Ryan—"

"Is stable for now," Grandpa cut him off. "Go, Ethan. That's an order."

Recognizing the tone that brooked no argument, Ethan nodded and dashed back outside. Instead of heading directly to the workshop where Dad maintained their limited arsenal, he detoured toward the driveway, determined to see who approached before sounding the alarm.

He crouched behind the large hydrangea bush at the edge of the front yard, its blue flowers providing reasonable cover while allowing him to see the road. The vehicle drew closer—an old pickup truck with a faded blue paint job. Ethan's heart hammered against his ribs as he recognized the red strip of cloth tied to the antenna. It was Frank Wilson.

Maddie

The leather-bound notebook sat open on the counter; its margins crowded with her father's precise handwriting. Diagrams filled the pages—intricate schematics for water filtration systems drawn with the careful hand of someone who understood exactly how each component connected to the next. Maddie stared at the technical drawings, trying to make sense of the tangle of lines, arrows, and annotations.

"PVC male adapter, one-inch… activated carbon pre-filter with micron rating…" She traced the words with her finger, frustration building as she encountered term after term that meant nothing to her. "What the hell is a backflow prevention valve?"

Three days had passed since her father's death. Three days of grief and guilt compounded by urgent necessity. The water contamination that had killed David Foster was spreading, affecting more people every day. Her mother's condition had worsened overnight, and the limited antibiotics Emily had were running out.

Maddie rubbed her eyes, gritty from exhaustion and poor light. The hardware store—Foster's Hardware, her father's pride and joy—stood dark except for the camping lantern on the counter. Power remained a memory, like so many comforts of the old world. The store had become her refuge, workshop, and now her greatest challenge.

"You did this a thousand times," she whispered to herself, flipping through pages of increasingly complex designs. "You grew up in this store. You should know this."

But the truth mocked her from every incomprehensible diagram. She'd spent her childhood here without absorbing any of it. While her father patiently explained the difference between galvanized and stainless steel, she'd been texting friends under the counter. When he'd demonstrated how to replace a faucet, she'd been mentally rehearsing excuses to leave early for a party. All those lessons, all that knowledge offered freely—and she'd let it slide away, certain she'd never need it.

"Stupid," she muttered, slamming the notebook closed. "So stupid."

The sound echoed through the empty store, bouncing off shelves stocked with items she could name but couldn't fully explain. Pipe fittings. Valves. Tools whose specific purposes remained mysteries. Her father had known every item, understood its function, its application. Had tried to teach her.

She moved to his office at the back of the store, the small space that had been command central for Foster's Hardware for over twenty years. More notebooks lined the shelves, each labeled in his methodical hand. *Inventory 2023. Special Orders. Plumbing Repairs. Electrical Code Updates.*

Cardboard boxes filled one corner, hastily packed when she'd vacated the house two days ago. Family photos. Tools. The handmade quilts her mother crafted back when there was time for hobbies. She'd grabbed whatever seemed important, unable to dwell in the house where her father had died.

Behind the desk, a jumbled pile of blueprints and technical

manuals threatened to topple from their precarious stack. And there, poking from beneath a water-stained catalog, the edge of a notebook she hadn't seen before. Newer than the others, its blue cover unmarked by years of handling.

Maddie tugged it free, surprised by its weight. The first page bore a single title in her father's bold script: *Emergency Water Filtration & Purification Systems.*

Her heart skipped. Her father had been preparing for this—not for the specific disaster, perhaps, but for the possibility of something. She knew he was always inventing ways for people to need hardware items. Did he worry about water or simply want to make another sale?

She turned the page with reverent care. Unlike the other notebooks with their cryptic shorthand and technical jargon, this one began with something different:

For Maddie, when she's ready to learn. Start with the basics.

Tears blurred her vision, hot and sudden. She blinked them away, unwilling to risk a single drop on the precious pages. The next sheets contained simplified diagrams, each component labeled not just with technical terms but with explanations.

Activated carbon: Works like a sponge for chemicals and some bacteria. Think of it as millions of tiny caves that trap the bad stuff.

Micron filter: The smaller the micron rating, the finer the filtration. 5 micron catches dirt and sediment. 1 micron catches most bacteria.

Ceramic filter: The workhorse. Water passes through tiny pores in the ceramic material, leaving contaminants behind.

The ache in her chest threatened to overwhelm her. She swallowed hard against it, forcing herself to focus on the gift she'd been given—a roadmap through her own ignorance. Page after page of information distilled specifically for her learning style.

She knew he'd planned for her to take over, even though she had other thoughts. The way he outlined not only the items and what they do, but also so many ways to use them. Oddly, most of the builds were survival centered. It made her question if he'd planned for such things.

The slam of the store's front door jerked her from contemplation. Maddie instinctively reached for the hunting knife she'd started carrying, moving quickly from the office to the main floor.

"Hello? Anyone here?" A woman's voice called.

Maddie recognized it instantly. "Back here, Jessica."

Jessica Thompson navigated carefully through the darkened aisles, the beam of her flashlight sweeping across shelves. Daniel's wife moved awkwardly with her broken ankle supported by a makeshift cast and crutches fashioned from tree branches. Despite her injury, she'd insisted on coming into town when Emily had mentioned Maddie's struggle.

"This place is even darker than I remember," Jessica said, making her way to the counter where Maddie stood. "How can you see anything?"

"You get used to it," Maddie replied, though in truth, she'd developed a pounding headache from squinting at diagrams in poor light. "How's Ryan?"

Jessica's expression tightened. "Still feverish, but Emily thinks he turned a corner this morning. Taking food again, at least." She gestured to Maddie's work area, the notebooks and scattered components. "James wanted me to check in. See if we could coordinate efforts."

Maddie felt a flush of embarrassment heat her cheeks. The Thompson farm had clean well water, but outlying families depended on creeks or shallow wells now proven dangerous. She'd promised filtration systems days ago, yet had nothing to show but confusion and false starts.

"I haven't made much progress," she admitted. "Dad's designs are more complicated than I realized."

Jessica nodded, setting her crutches aside to examine the notebooks. "Daniel mentioned your father had been experimenting with advanced systems." She picked up a PVC pipe fitting, turning it in her hands with comfortable familiarity. "What specifically are you stuck on?"

Maddie hesitated, pride warring with necessity. "Everything," she confessed finally. "I can't even identify half the components he mentions. I know they're somewhere in the store, but…"

"But there are thousands of parts, and hardware stores don't exactly come with a search function anymore," Jessica finished wryly. She studied the diagrams, nodding to herself. "I'm no expert, but I renovated our first apartment before the kids came along. Plumbing was always my favorite—logical, orderly."

"You understand this?" Maddie asked, hope flickering.

"Some of it." Jessica tapped the notebook. "This looks like a multi-stage filtration system. Sediment trap first, then activated carbon, then the ceramic filter elements." She looked up. "Let's start with identifying the basic pieces. I'll help you find them in the store."

For the next hour, Jessica patiently guided Maddie through the inventory, translating technical terms into practical descriptions.

"This is a male adapter," Jessica explained, holding up a

threaded fitting. "See how the threads are on the outside? Female adapters have threads on the inside. They receive the male end."

"That actually makes sense," Maddie said, examining the piece. "Dad tried to explain this when I was sixteen. I remember rolling my eyes and thinking I'd never need to know plumbing terms."

Jessica laughed softly. "I thought the same about changing tires until I got a flat on a country road in a thunderstorm."

They moved through the store, Jessica identifying components, while Maddie created an inventory list. With each item, memories surfaced. Her father showing a customer this exact valve, explaining flow rates and pressure ratings while Maddie pretended to organize receipts, mentally elsewhere.

"I should have paid attention," she blurted, the words escaping before she could stop them. "He tried so hard to teach me, and I just... I didn't care."

Jessica paused, compassion softening her features. "You couldn't have known, Maddie."

"But that's just it—he did know. Not about the CME specifically, but that someday this knowledge would matter." Maddie gestured to the notebook. "He was preparing for a crisis while I was planning my marketing major and thinking about which parties to attend." Bitterness crept into her voice. "Now he's gone, and people are dying because I can't build what he designed."

"People aren't dying because of you," Jessica said firmly. "They're dying because someone deliberately contaminated our water. Big difference."

Maddie didn't respond, unconvinced. They worked in silence for several minutes, the only sounds their footsteps and the occasional clink of components being sorted.

"How's your mother?" Jessica asked finally.

The question sent fresh pain through Maddie's chest. "Worse today. Emily says the antibiotics aren't working as well as they should. Her systems are too depleted from the initial illness."

"I'm sorry," Jessica said quietly. "You have to have faith. She's a fighter."

Maddie nodded, not trusting her voice. Her mother had deteriorated rapidly over the past twenty-four hours, skin waxen, breath labored. The same progression her father followed.

"That's why I need to make this work," she said after a moment, gesturing to the notebooks and components. "Clean water might not save her, but it could save Ryan and the others. It's what Dad was trying to do."

"Let's try to build a prototype," Jessica suggested. "Nothing fancy—just a basic single-stage filter to make sure we understand the concept. I understand a little about plumbing but this is a bit more and I think we can both benefit."

They gathered the necessary components: a five-gallon bucket, PVC pipe fittings, a package of activated carbon Maddie found in the water treatment aisle, and several sizes of mesh filters.

"Your father's design is elegant," Jessica observed, studying the diagram again. "But complex. We should start simpler. Just a gravity-fed carbon filter. Once we get that working, we can add the ceramic elements and pre-filters."

Maddie nodded, relief washing through her at having a concrete starting point.

Outside, the July sun began its descent, casting long

shadows through the store's windows. Time was running short—for her mother, for Ryan, for everyone dependent on contaminated water sources.

The first test was a spectacular failure.

"I don't understand," Maddie said, staring at the murky liquid dripping from their makeshift filter. "It looks worse than when we started."

Jessica frowned, examining the connection points. "The seal isn't tight here," she said, pointing to where the PVC pipe met the bucket. "And I think we need finer mesh. This is letting too many particles through."

Frustration burned in Maddie's throat. Such a simple thing—cleaning water—and she couldn't even manage that. Meanwhile, her mother lay dying from contamination these filters were supposed to prevent.

"It's getting late," Jessica said gently. "I should get back to the farm before dark. Daniel worries."

Guilt joined frustration. Jessica had spent hours helping her, and they'd produced nothing but dirty water and wasted materials.

"I'm sorry for wasting your time," Maddie said, not meeting Jessica's eyes.

"You didn't." Jessica gathered her crutches, wincing as she adjusted her weight. "We learned what doesn't work. That's progress." She nodded toward the prototype. "We can try a food-grade silicone sealant for the connections. And layer the filtration media. Tomorrow we'll start with coarse sand on top, then finer sand, then the carbon."

Maddie wrote down the suggestions in her notebook. "Thank you. For everything."

"James wants to know when we think we might have

working units," Jessica said carefully. "No pressure, but the farm well can only support so many people. We need solutions for the outlying families."

The weight of responsibility pressed down on Maddie's shoulders. "Do you think we can do this?"

Jessica nodded. "One step at a time."

Maddie glanced around the store, seeing it with fresh eyes. Jessica had noticed her cot in the office. The back room had cabinets and she'd set up a propane stove.

"Have you been staying here?" Jessica asked.

Maddie looked down, saying, "I couldn't stay in the house. Not after…"

"Do you need anything?"

"No, I'm okay. Plus I'm close to Mom. If she gets better—"

Jessica cut her off, "When! When she gets better."

"When," Maddie said with a small smile. "When she gets better, I'm going to move us fully over here."

After Jessica left, Maddie cleaned up their failed experiment, mentally cataloging each mistake. Wrong sealant. Mesh too coarse. Carbon not properly prepared. Incorrect flow rate. Little details her father would have known instinctively from years of experience.

She needed to visit her mother. The funeral home was at the other end of Main Street, a fifteen-minute walk that felt longer each day as her mother's condition deteriorated. Gathering her coat and the hunting knife, Maddie locked the store's front door and set out into the early evening.

Cornish had changed dramatically in the weeks since the CME. Main Street, once bustling with tourists and locals, now stood eerily quiet. Abandoned cars lined the curbs, some pushed aside to clear lanes for the few working vehicles and horse-drawn carts. Windows were boarded up, doors reinforced. The only building showing consistent activity was Kristie's Diner, where the resourceful owner had converted to wood-fire cooking and become a community hub.

The sun hung low over the western hills, casting the town in amber light that belied the desperation simmering beneath the surface. Maddie walked quickly, eyes scanning her surroundings with the new situational awareness everyone had developed. A figure moved between buildings ahead—one of Frank Wilson's men, red band tied around his arm. She adjusted her course to avoid him, unease prickling along her spine.

Neal & York Funeral Home loomed at the end of the street, its Victorian architecture gothic and imposing in the fading light. The building that had once hosted somber ceremonies now served as Cornish's makeshift hospital, its formal viewing rooms converted to treatment wards for the water-sick.

Emily Thompson met her at the door, her medical bag slung over one shoulder, exhaustion evident in the dark circles beneath her eyes.

"How is she?" Maddie asked, the question automatic by now.

Emily's hesitation told her everything. "She's holding on," Emily said finally. "But not responding to the antibiotics as well as I'd hoped."

Maddie swallowed hard. "Can I see her?"

"Of course." Emily led her through the main viewing room, now filled with makeshift beds. Every cot was occupied, the sick ranging from elderly to heartbreakingly young. Ryan Thompson had been moved back to the farm once he'd stabilized, but others had taken his place. The air smelled of antiseptic and illness, the quiet moans of the suffering providing a constant soundtrack.

Her mother lay in what had once been the funeral director's office, afforded privacy by virtue of her relationship to Maddie and her worsening condition. Katherine Foster's skin had taken on the waxy pallor Maddie recognized from her father's final hours. Her breathing came in shallow gasps, each inhalation a visible struggle.

"Mom?" Maddie said softly, taking her mother's hand. The skin felt paper-thin, bones prominent beneath. "It's me."

Katherine's eyes fluttered open, unfocused at first, then finding Maddie's face. Recognition sparked briefly. "Madison," she whispered, using Maddie's full name as she only did in moments of gravity.

"I'm here." Maddie forced a smile, though her heart was cracking beneath her ribs. "How are you feeling today?"

"Better," her mother lied, the word barely audible. Her gaze drifted past Maddie to the empty space beside her. "Your father was here earlier."

Ice flooded Maddie's veins. The same hallucination her father had experienced before the end. "Was he?"

"Telling me not to worry." Katherine's fingers twitched against Maddie's palm. "Said he'd found the problem with the water. Fixed it."

Tears burned behind Maddie's eyes. "That sounds like Dad."

"You're working at the store," her mother said, the statement somewhere between question and observation.

"Yes." Maddie stroked her mother's hair back from her forehead, the strands damp with sweat despite the room's coolness. "Using Dad's designs to make water filters."

A ghost of a smile touched Katherine's lips. "He always said you'd take over someday."

"I should have paid more attention," Maddie confessed, the words escaping on a shaky breath. "He tried to teach me everything, and I just… didn't listen."

"You weren't ready then." Her mother's eyes drifted closed, energy flagging. "You are now."

Emily appeared in the doorway, a fresh IV bag in hand. "We need to change her fluids," she said quietly.

Maddie nodded, giving her mother's hand a final squeeze. "I'll be back tomorrow, Mom. I promise."

Her mother didn't respond, already drifting back into the restless sleep that claimed her more frequently now. Maddie stood, legs unsteady beneath her.

"How long?" she asked Emily once they were in the hallway, the question barely a whisper.

Emily's professional demeanor cracked, compassion and exhaustion showing through. "Days. Maybe less. I'm sorry, Maddie. We're giving her everything we have, but…"

"But it's not enough," Maddie finished. The same words she'd repeated to herself about her own efforts with the filtration systems. Never enough. Always too late.

"You should prepare yourself," Emily said gently. "And decide what you want to do afterward. We can't…" She hesitated. "The traditional funeral services aren't possible anymore. We need to make decisions quickly when the time comes."

The clinical reality of death in this new world hit Maddie with fresh force. No funeral home services. No cemetery plots being maintained. Just quick, practical handling of bodies to prevent further disease.

"I understand," she said, though the words strained in her throat. "Thank you for everything you're doing, Emily."

Outside, dusk had deepened to true darkness, the night sky brilliant with stars unmarred by light pollution. Maddie stood on the funeral home steps, momentarily paralyzed by grief and responsibility. The weight of her mother's impending death collided with the urgent need to create working filtration systems, leaving her breathless with the impossibility of both tasks.

One step at a time, she told herself, echoing Jessica's words from earlier. One connection at a time.

The walk back to the hardware store passed in a blur of swirling thoughts and half-formed plans. By the time she reached the familiar storefront, the decision had crystallized into certainty.

With Jessica's suggestions fresh in her mind, Maddie disassembled the filtration bucket entirely, examining each component with critical eyes. Where had they gone wrong? What assumptions had they made?

The answer came to her as she studied her father's diagrams again: they'd rushed. Skipped steps. Tried to solve the complicated problem before mastering the fundamentals.

Start with the basics.

Maddie retrieved a clean five-gallon bucket from the janitorial section and began again. This time, she worked methodically through each stage, referencing her father's notes constantly. The hole for the spigot needed to be precisely measured, not estimated. The layers of filtration media had to be arranged in the correct sequence. The activated carbon required preparation—rinsing to remove dust, then proper packing to prevent channeling.

Midnight came and went as she worked, fatigue pushed aside by determination. Outside, Cornish slept beneath the starlit sky, unaware of her solitary efforts in the darkened store.

Finally, near dawn, Maddie stepped back to examine her creation. The filtration system looked crude compared to her father's designs, but every connection was secure, every component properly prepared. She retrieved a jar of creek water she'd collected earlier—visibly cloudy with sediment and possible contaminants.

Heart pounding, she poured the water into the top of the filter and waited. The liquid percolated slowly through the layers of sand, carbon, and ceramic, driven by nothing more complicated than gravity. Minutes passed. Then, from the spigot at the bottom, the first drops emerged.

Clear. Completely, perfectly clear.

Maddie caught the filtered water in a clean glass, holding it up to her lantern. No visible particles. No cloudiness. She brought it to her nose, detecting only the faint mineral scent of clean water.

She'd done it. Created a functional filter with her own hands but she needed Emily to confirm it was free from contamination.

The enormity of the accomplishment crashed over her, bringing with it a wave of exhaustion so profound that her knees nearly buckled. She sank onto a nearby stool, still clutching the glass of filtered water.

Hannah

"I'll take the first watch," Jake offered, voice rough with unshed tears.

Hannah shook her head. "I need you rested. You'll take second shift." She saw him about to protest and added, "I won't be able to sleep anyway."

This truth he accepted, nodding before curling beside their packs on the riverbank, under the tarp stretched between a couple of trees, his adolescent frame somehow looking smaller in the darkness. Hannah positioned herself at the water's edge, rifle across her knees, field of fire clear through the gap in their blind.

The forest settled around them, night creatures resuming their activities after the disturbance of their landing. Insects chirped and whirred. An owl called from nearby, answered by another farther off. The familiar symphony of woodland night that had once seemed peaceful on camping trips now carried potential threats in every unexpected pause or crescendo.

Hannah focused on practicalities, mentally inventorying their supplies. Three packs, each containing water, supplies and food, that would get them to Cornish, if tightly rationed. First aid supplies divided between them in case of separation. Ammunition for the rifle—twenty-seven rounds remaining. Maps, compass, her father's multi-tool, water purification tablets. The handcrafted fishing kit Jake had assembled. Their mother's medications while packing them. All carefully split between the three packs. Two were personal packs they'd run with if they had to and the third filled with consumable supplies that could either be ditched or shifted to the other two.

She thought of her parents, especially her father. Without their sacrifice, they would be dead or captured. She couldn't help but wonder about her mother.

The thought brought unwelcome moisture to her eyes. Hannah blinked it away, focusing on the darkness beyond their shelter. Mourning was a luxury they couldn't afford, not with miles still to cover and dangers everywhere.

Their plan had been clear. Simple…head up the Saco River to Cornish, where Hannah hoped to find Maddie.

Maddie. The name conjured her friend's face, their tearful parting in Portsmouth. She couldn't help but wonder about her. Had she made it? Was she safe, or had she encountered similar horrors on her journey?

Hannah's thoughts circled through these questions, keeping sleep at bay as effectively as caffeine.

Four hours later, the eastern sky began to lighten imperceptibly, black giving way to the deepest blue. Hannah checked her watch—time to wake Jake for his shift. She turned toward the shelter's interior where her brother slept fitfully, arms wrapped protectively around his pack, his face troubled even in sleep.

Before she could wake him, a twig snapped in the forest ahead.

Hannah froze, rifle raised, every sense suddenly hyperalert. The sound had been close—thirty yards at most, too heavy for a small animal. She eased deeper into the shadow of their blind, reducing her silhouette while maintaining visibility outward.

Movement flickered between trees—a human figure moving cautiously through the underbrush. Then another behind it. Low voices carried on the still morning air, too indistinct to make out words but clearly human.

Hannah's finger settled beside the trigger guard, ready to move if necessary. She counted four separate figures now, moving in a loose formation that suggested training or at least coordination. Not Sherman's men. There was no tactical gear visible in the pre-dawn light, and their movements were too hesitant, too cautious. Local survivors, perhaps, or refugees like themselves.

Still, she took no chances. Shifting her position silently, she placed herself between the approaching group and the shelter where her brother slept. The rifle's familiar weight steadied her, though the prospect of using it against other humans still felt surreal.

The strangers drew closer, their hushed conversation becoming audible.

"—said there's a stream somewhere around here," a male voice whispered. "I can hear it. We need to refill before moving on."

"Not sure I trust his directions," a woman replied. "Nothing's been where he said it would be."

"We don't have much choice," a third voice added. "The containers are almost empty."

Hannah analyzed their speech patterns, their movements, the little she could discern of their appearance in the dim light. Not organized raiders. Just survivors, like them, moving through uncertain terrain.

Still, she waited, watching as they passed within twenty

yards of the shelter without noticing it. Their exhaustion was evident in the slump of shoulders, the dragging of feet. A group of six—three men, two women, and what appeared to be a teenage girl, all carrying small packs and improvised weapons.

Only when they had passed well beyond the shelter did Hannah relax marginally, easing her finger completely away from the trigger. She debated waking Jake but decided against it. The strangers were headed toward the river, but away from their position. No immediate threat.

An hour later, as the forest gradually brightened with dawn, Hannah heard them returning, their footsteps heavier with the weight of filled water containers. This time, they passed even closer to the shelter, and Hannah tensed again, rifle ready.

"Did Portland look like that when you left?" one man asked another, voice carrying clearly in the morning stillness.

"Worse," came the reply. "The fires had reached the peninsula by then. Those New Guard bastards were using them to drive people where they wanted them."

Hannah's pulse quickened. Portland. The New Guard. The same forces that had attacked South Portland, that had taken her father.

"You think they'll come this far north?" the woman asked, fear evident in her voice.

"They're already expanding," the man replied grimly. "Sherman's got scouts as far as Gray, according to that guy at the gas station. Planning something big, he said."

The name sent ice through Hannah's veins. Sherman. The name she'd heard shouted during the attack, the leader whose men had destroyed their community.

"We should warn them," Jake's voice came suddenly from beside her, making her jump. He had awakened silently, moving to her side without her noticing.

Hannah hesitated, calculating risks against potential information. These people had knowledge that could help them—routes to avoid, threats to be aware of. But revealing themselves carried its own dangers.

Decision made, she nodded to Jake before raising her voice. "Hold there," she called, keeping the rifle visible but not directly aimed. "We don't want trouble."

The group froze, shock evident in their sudden stillness. Hands moved toward weapons but stopped when they registered the rifle in Hannah's hands.

"We're just passing through," the lead man called back, slowly raising his hands to shoulder height. "No quarrel with you folks."

"You mentioned Portland," Hannah said, remaining behind the partial concealment of their blind. "And Sherman."

The group exchanged glances, tension visible in their postures. Finally, the man who had spoken about Portland stepped forward slightly.

"You from there?" he asked cautiously.

"South Portland," Hannah replied. "Our neighborhood was hit two nights ago."

Recognition and sympathy crossed the man's weathered face. "Oh Lord, hit Deering three days before that. We barely got out."

Hannah and Jake exchanged glances. Slowly, keeping the rifle ready but lowered, Hannah emerged from the shelter. Jake followed, positioning himself to watch both the strangers and the surrounding forest.

"I'm Hannah," she offered, not giving their last name.

"This is my brother."

"Neil," the man replied. "This is my wife Carla, our daughter Zoe. The others are Manuel, Violet, and Lonny. We were neighbors before…" He trailed off, gesturing vaguely to encompass everything that had happened.

"You mentioned Sherman," Hannah pressed. "What do you know about him?"

Neil's expression darkened. "Buncha no good scum. Started gathering followers right after the CME, offering protection in exchange for obedience. Took over the Portland police headquarters, then started expanding outward, neighborhood by neighborhood. We heard from a guy passing through that he got run out of some place early on and set off on some kind of vendetta."

"They're organized," Manuel added, a tall fat man with graying temples. "Not like most of the gangs. They have communication equipment, vehicles that still run, actual tactics."

"And they're moving north," Hannah said, connecting their information with what she'd overheard during their escape.

Neil nodded grimly. "Setting up outposts, securing resources. We heard they've got some kind of base north of Portland now. Military installation, maybe the National Guard armory."

The implications settled heavily on Hannah's shoulders. Not just random raiders, but an expanding force, now armed with military organization and equipment. A threat that wouldn't dissipate with distance and time.

"Where are you headed?" Carla asked, her arm protectively around her daughter's shoulders. The girl—Zoe—looked about Jake's age, dark circles under her eyes speaking to sleepless nights and constant vigilance.

"Northwest," Hannah replied vaguely. "We have family there."

Another half-truth. Maddie wasn't a blood relative, but was as close to family as anyone outside their immediate circle. Closer now, perhaps, with her father gone and her mother's situation still unknown.

"We're aiming for New Hampshire," Neil said. "Lonny has people in North Conway who were living off-grid even before. Might be safer there, further from Sherman's expansion."

Hannah nodded, understanding their logic. Distance from Sherman's base would provide some security, though how far his reach extended remained unknown.

Her look filled with sorrow and loss and Neil approached cautiously. "I'm sorry," he said simply. "We've all lost someone."

Hannah nodded, throat too tight for words.

"The South Portland attack," Manuel said hesitantly. "Was it like Deering? House to house?"

"Yes." Hannah forced herself to focus, to share information that might help others. "They surrounded the neighborhood first, cut off escape routes. Then moved in systematically, marking houses they'd cleared."

Neil and Manuel exchanged glances. "Same pattern," Manuel confirmed. "They're getting more efficient each time."

"They took some people alive," Hannah continued, the memories sharp-edged and painful. "Women mostly. Young men with certain skills. Our mother. The rest..." She didn't need to finish.

"Witnesses from Deering said they're building something,"

Carla added quietly. "Not just taking over, but creating infrastructure. Supply chains. Communication networks."

"For what purpose?" Jake asked, voicing the question Hannah had been turning over in her mind.

Neil shrugged. "Power? Resources? Who knows anymore. The old rules are gone."

The conversation paused as they all absorbed this stark reality.

"We should move on," Neil said finally. "Still have ground to cover before nightfall."

Hannah nodded, calculating their own timeline. "We need to break camp too."

An awkward moment followed as both groups recognized the crossroads before them—continue separately or join forces. Hannah weighed the options quickly. The strangers had useful information and additional resources, but also made them a larger, more visible target. Two people could move quietly; eight would leave a trail even a novice could follow.

Neil seemed to reach the same conclusion. "Different directions," he said, nodding toward the northwest where Hannah had indicated they were headed. "Safer that way. Smaller groups attract less attention."

"But we should share what we know," Manuel added. "Routes, threats, safe zones."

"One more thing," Neil said as they prepared to part ways. "There's a group operating northeast of here, along the Saco River. Different from Sherman's people. They're helping refugees, maintaining some kind of warning system."

"Allies?" Hannah asked skeptically.

"Not sure," Neil admitted. "But not enemies either, from

what we heard. If you cross the Saco, might be worth looking for them."

Hannah filed the information away—potentially useful, though she'd reserve judgment until seeing evidence firsthand. Trust had become a luxury few could afford.

As the strangers gathered their supplies, Zoe approached Hannah hesitantly. The teenage girl pulled something from her pocket—a small packet wrapped in foil.

Hannah stared at the small package, unexpectedly touched by the gesture, and suddenly felt guilty. They had packs filled with food and supplies and the young girl had just offered them a tiny packet of what little food they had.

Zoe nodded, eyes far older than her years. "We all lose people," she said, echoing her father's words. "But we keep going anyway."

The simple truth of this statement struck Hannah with surprising force. The world had collapsed around them in ways no one could have predicted. But they were still moving, still breathing, still fighting forward one step at a time.

The strangers departed heading northwest, along a small deer trail and an ache built in Hannah's chest.

"We need to move too," Hannah said, meeting Jake's eyes.

Hannah studied him for a moment, her fourteen-year-old brother now carrying responsibilities no child should bear, yet handling them with a steadiness that made her chest ache with pride and grief simultaneously.

"You heard them talking about Sherman," she said quietly.

Jake's expression hardened. "We need to warn the Thompsons. Warn Maddie."

"Yes." Hannah checked her rifle one last time before

slinging it across her back. "But we need to be alive to do that."

They gathered their supplies efficiently, erasing signs of their presence from the shelter. As they prepared to leave, Hannah squeezed the small foil packet.

James

The morning sun had barely crested the eastern tree line when James heard the first shouts. He set down his coffee mug—a chipped ceramic relic with "World's Best Grandpa" faded from too many washings—and moved swiftly to the kitchen window. In the farmyard below, Michael sprinted toward the north pasture where three of the younger children were feeding the chickens. But it wasn't the children who drew James's eye—it was the unmistakable figure of Ethan running in the opposite direction, toward something at the edge of the property.

"Damn it," James muttered, already moving. He grabbed his rifle from its place by the door—a habit that had become as automatic as putting on shoes—and crossed the kitchen in four long strides. On the back porch, he paused only long enough to confirm his suspicion. Ethan was headed directly for the northern fence line where they'd spotted movement yesterday.

"Ethan!" Michael's shout carried across the yard, urgent and sharp. "Get back here! NOW!"

But the boy either didn't hear or chose to ignore his father's command. He disappeared into the tall grass beyond the mowed perimeter, clutching something that gleamed dully in the morning light.

James took the porch steps two at a time, his knees

protesting the impact. Age was the enemy he couldn't shoot or outsmart, a fact that frustrated him daily now that physical strength had become currency in this new world.

"What's happening?" Sarah appeared at the screen door behind him, dish towel still in hand.

"Ethan," James replied, the single word conveying everything his wife needed to know. "Get Daniel. Tell him to bring the radio."

He didn't wait for her response, instead setting off across the yard at a pace that balanced urgency against the practical need to conserve energy. Michael had already changed direction, now pursuing his son toward the fence line. James cut diagonally across the vegetable garden, taking the most direct route while scanning the trees beyond their property. Movement flickered between the trunks—more than one person, moving parallel to their fence.

A high, piercing whistle cut through the morning air—the alert signal they'd established weeks ago. James's head snapped toward the source: Grayson Jr. stood atop the old stump near the chicken coop, pointing urgently toward the same spot where Ethan had disappeared.

"Three men!" the boy shouted, his young voice cracking with tension. "Armed! Just beyond the north fence!"

James's blood ran cold. Ethan was running directly toward armed strangers—strangers who could easily be Sherman's scouts, or worse.

He broke into a full run, no longer concerned with conserving energy. As he passed the chicken coop, he barked orders at Grayson. "Get inside! Take the others with you! Storm cellar! Now!"

The boy nodded sharply and jumped down, already

gathering the younger children who stood frozen near the coop, eyes wide with confusion and fear. James registered their faces briefly. Lily clutching Mr. Trunks with white-knuckled fingers, Theo looking torn between following Grayson's lead and running after Ethan, his new friend.

"GO!" James shouted when they hesitated, and that broke their paralysis. Grayson herded them toward the house, using the same calm efficiency that had impressed James since the boy's arrival.

Ahead, Michael had reached the edge of the tall grass. James watched him pause for just a moment before plunging in after his son, disappearing from view except for the occasional movement of grass tips marking his progress.

James's lungs burned as he pushed himself harder. Behind him, he heard the farmhouse door slam, followed by Daniel's voice calling instructions to others. Good. The security practicing was being implemented. But the tight knot in his stomach didn't loosen—too many variables, too many potential threats converging at once.

He reached the edge of the tall grass just as a gunshot cracked through the morning stillness.

A single shot. Then silence.

James froze, every muscle tensing as he strained to hear something, anything that would tell him what was happening beyond his line of sight. The tall grass swayed gently in the morning breeze, indifferent to human drama. Twenty yards in, he could see where Michael had pushed through, creating a narrow path.

"Michael?" he called, voice pitched to carry without shouting. "Ethan?"

Nothing. Then—

"Stay back!" Michael's voice, tight with strain. "Armed men at the fence! Ethan's down!"

The words hit James like physical blows. Ethan down. What did that mean? Injured? Caught? Or something worse?

The strategic part of his brain—the part that had kept them alive in spite of this societal collapse. He recognized the possible trap. Lure family members out one by one, pick them off at the perimeter. Classic ambush technique.

But this was Ethan. His grandson.

James made his decision in a heartbeat. He dropped to a crouch and moved into the grass, using Michael's path but staying low, rifle ready. The stalks brushed against his face and arms as he advanced, each step measured and deliberate despite the screaming urgency in his chest. Fifteen yards. Ten. He could hear voices now—multiple speakers, words indistinct but tones clear. Argument. Tension. Negotiation?

He paused, listening intently. Michael's voice, pitched lower than usual. A stranger's response, clipped and hostile. Another voice telling someone to shut up. And then, miraculously, Ethan's voice—breathless, high with fear, but unmistakably alive.

James moved forward again, more quickly now. Five more yards brought him to a small clearing in the grass where the scene revealed itself in fragments: Michael kneeling, one arm around Ethan who sat on the ground, pale-faced but visibly unharmed. Beyond them, the fence line, and on the other side, three men wearing mismatched clothing but uniformly grim expressions. One held a rifle pointed skyward—the source of the warning shot, James guessed. Another clutched his hand to his chest, blood seeping between his fingers.

"—totally uncalled for," the injured man was saying, voice

tight with pain. "Little psycho slashed me with a goddamn knife."

"After you grabbed him," Michael countered, his body positioned to shield Ethan. "What did you expect?"

James stepped fully into the clearing, rifle not aimed directly at the men but angled for quick deployment if needed. "Problem here?"

All heads turned toward him. Relief washed across Michael's face, followed by a flash of embarrassment. A father caught in a situation he couldn't fully control. The three strangers tensed, the one with the rifle adjusting his stance subtly.

"Grandpa," Ethan's voice quavered slightly. "I saw them scouting our fence. They had wire cutters."

James took in the scene more fully now. Sure enough, a pair of heavy-duty cutters lay in the grass on the opposite side of the fence. The three men wore no identifying markers—not Sherman's people, then, or at least not obviously so. Just opportunists, probably.

"You're trespassing," James said flatly, addressing the strangers.

The apparent leader—a tall man with a scraggly beard and calculating eyes, gave a smile that didn't reach his eyes. "Free country, last time I checked. Just passing through."

"With wire cutters?" James nodded toward the tool. "Planning a bit of fence modification as you 'passed through'?"

The man shrugged, not bothering to deny it. "Times are tough. Heard you folks had a nice setup here. Thought maybe you could share some resources."

"We share with those who ask," James replied evenly. "Not those who sneak around cutting fences."

The injured man spat on the ground. "Your insane kid slashed me! Cut deep, too. That's assault, old man."

"Approaching a minor with wire cutters at our property line? That's attempted breaking and entering at minimum," Michael countered. "Attempted kidnapping if we're feeling formal about it."

James kept his attention on the leader, recognizing him as the real threat. The injured man was in pain, angry, but contained for now. The third one, the youngest of the group, barely out of his teens from the looks of him, seemed nervous, eyes constantly darting between James's rifle and something in the trees behind them.

"Look," the leader said, spreading his hands in a conciliatory gesture that didn't match his watchful eyes. "Misunderstanding, that's all. We didn't realize kids would be out here unsupervised."

"He wasn't unsupervised," James replied coldly. "He was on family property, and you were trespassing. Still are." He nodded toward the trees. "How many more of you back there?"

A flicker of surprise crossed the leader's face, quickly controlled, but visible. James had guessed correctly. These three weren't alone.

"Don't know what you're talking about," the man replied, but his eyes gave him away, darting briefly toward the woods.

The sound of multiple people moving through the grass behind James announced the arrival of reinforcements. Daniel emerged first, then Robbie Burns, both carrying rifles. Two more of their neighbors followed, forming a loose semicircle. Six armed defenders now faced the three trespassers.

"Everything alright, Dad?" Daniel asked, not taking his eyes off the strangers.

"Caught these gentlemen about to do some unauthorized landscaping," James replied. "They were just leaving. In the direction they came from." He emphasized the last point, making it clear they wouldn't be permitted to continue along the farm's perimeter.

The leader assessed the changed odds, something calculating and cold moving behind his eyes. For a moment, James thought he might try something anyway. Then he nodded sharply.

"We'll be on our way, then. No harm intended."

"Your friend needs medical attention," James nodded toward the injured man, whose sleeve was now soaked with blood from Ethan's defensive slash. He pulled a clean bandana from his pocket and tossed it over the fence. "Pressure bandage until you can clean it properly."

The gesture wasn't kindness—not entirely. It was a demonstration. We have resources. We have organization. We're not defenseless.

The leader caught the bandana and passed it to his injured companion without comment. The younger man gathered up the wire cutters, shoving them into a backpack with nervous movements.

"This isn't over," the injured man muttered, wrapping the bandana around his bleeding hand. "Little bastard cut me deep."

"It's over," James stated firmly. "Don't come back. Next time won't be a warning shot."

The three men backed away slowly, disappearing into the trees. Only when they were completely out of sight did James lower his rifle slightly. He turned to Ethan, keeping his voice level with effort.

"Are you hurt?"

Ethan shook his head, eyes huge in his pale face. "I'm okay. He just grabbed my arm. I remembered what Dad taught me about using whatever you have as a weapon." He looked down at the folding knife still clutched in his hand—one of Michael's, James recognized, definitely not something Ethan was permitted to carry.

Michael had noticed too. His face tightened as he gently took the knife from his son's fingers. "We'll discuss where you got this later," he said quietly. "Right now, I'm just glad you're safe. But Ethan—" his voice sharpened, "—what were you thinking, running toward strangers at the fence? You broke at least three safety protocols."

Ethan's shoulders hunched. "I saw them from the chicken coop. Grayson said they had wire cutters. I thought I could stop them before they cut through." His voice dropped to a whisper. "I wanted to help."

James sighed, the adrenaline ebbing and leaving behind a weary clarity. The boy had been reckless, yes—but his intentions had been protective. Heroic, even, in a misguided way. The new world was forcing children like Ethan to grow up too quickly, taking on responsibilities beyond their years while simultaneously lacking the judgment that came with experience.

"Inside, all of you," he decided. "The others in town need to know about this. If these three are scouting our defenses, others will follow."

As they trudged back through the tall grass toward the farmhouse, Michael kept Ethan close by his side. The boy moved with the shellshocked slowness of someone coming down from an adrenaline spike, his earlier bravado deflated.

"I just wanted to protect everyone," Ethan said suddenly,

voice small. "Like Dad does. Like you do," He said, glancing up at James.

James rested a hand on his grandson's shoulder, feeling the bird-like delicacy of bones beneath his palm. So fragile, despite the boy's conviction of his own toughness.

"I know," he said gently. "But being brave also means being smart about the risks you take. Those men could have—" He stopped himself. No need to plant specific fears in the boy's mind. "They could have hurt you. And that would hurt all of us."

Ethan nodded, but something in his eyes told James the message wasn't fully absorbed. The boy's worldview was shifting, taking on the harder edges of their new reality, developing its own internal logic that might not align with adult perspectives.

The farmyard came into view, no longer the peaceful scene of early morning chores. Sarah stood on the porch, rifle in hand, while Jessica kept watch from an upstairs window. The younger children were nowhere to be seen—safely in the storm cellar, James presumed, following his instruction.

James felt a surge of pride mingled with sorrow. This wasn't the life he'd wanted for them—especially not for the children—but they were rising to meet it with remarkable resilience.

"Get Ethan inside," James told Michael quietly. "He needs to process what happened."

Michael nodded, guiding his son toward the house with a protective hand on his back. James turned to Daniel and Robbie.

"I want a full perimeter check. Those three weren't alone. There are others in the woods. And they were too interested in our setup to be random scavengers."

"Sherman's scouts?" Daniel suggested grimly.

"Possibly. Or Frank's people testing our defenses." James glanced toward the road, where dust from a vehicle hung in the morning air. Speak of the devil. "Either way, I want four-person patrols until further notice. No one is to be alone, not even to check the chicken coop."

As the men dispersed to organize the patrol groups, James headed toward the house. He needed to update Beth via radio, warn her about potential scouts in the area. But first, he needed to check on Ryan. The boy's fever had stabilized overnight, but he remained weak, unable to leave his bed.

Just as he reached the porch steps, a truck appeared at the end of their long driveway. A blue pickup with red fabric tied to the antenna. Frank Wilson's vehicle. The coincidence sent a chill through James's spine. Three scouts at their northern perimeter, and now Frank arrives unannounced, minutes after the confrontation.

Sarah joined him on the porch, her eyes tracking the approaching truck. "Convenient timing," she remarked, echoing his thoughts.

"Very." James didn't bother hiding the suspicion in his voice. "Let's see what story he brings today."

The truck pulled up to the farmyard gate, an outer barrier they'd constructed across the driveway, and stopped. Frank emerged alone, hands raised in a gesture of friendly greeting that felt increasingly theatrical with each visit.

"Heard there was some excitement up this way," he called, approaching the gate with the casual confidence of someone who expected to be welcomed. "Thought I'd check if you folks needed any assistance."

James kept his expression neutral as he walked down to

meet Frank at the gate. "How exactly did you hear about something that happened less than ten minutes ago?"

Frank's smile didn't waver, but something flickered in his eyes, a recalculation. "One of my boys was running a patrol along the south road. Said he heard a gunshot from this direction."

Another convenient explanation. James filed it away with growing certainty that Frank was connected to the morning's events, though the exact nature of that connection remained unclear.

"Just a warning shot," James replied, deliberately vague. "Nothing we couldn't handle."

Frank's gaze moved past him, scanning the farmyard where patrol groups were now forming, weapons checked, assignments distributed. "Looks like you're mobilizing for more than a simple warning shot."

"Precautions," James said shortly. He made no move to open the gate.

The unspoken message hung between them: Frank wasn't being invited in today. The other man's smile tightened almost imperceptibly.

"Offering my team's services," Frank persisted. "We've got twenty men armed and ready. Could help secure your perimeter, run counter-surveillance on those woods." He nodded toward the northern tree line. "I'd wager, whoever it was, wasn't just some random scavengers probing your defenses."

The statement confirmed James's suspicion that Frank knew far more about the morning's events than he should. Either his patrols were more extensive than acknowledged, or he had some connection to the trespassers themselves.

"You know how it is, people start spreading out in search of space. We've got it covered," James replied with a subtle laugh. "But I appreciate the offer."

Frank studied him for a long moment, that calculating look back in his eyes. Then he spread his hands in a gesture of acceptance. "Your call. Just trying to be a good neighbor."

"Interesting definition of 'neighbor' these days," James remarked.

"Isn't it?" Frank's smile turned knowing. "Speaking of neighbors, heard from Beth this morning. Seems there was some trouble at Foster's Hardware last night. Some of my boys taking initiative where they shouldn't have. Just reaping what they didn't sow, but a bit too aggressively for my taste." He shook his head with manufactured regret. "Had to discipline them, of course."

The casual way he dropped this information. Acknowledging his men's actions while distancing himself from their methods sent another warning signal through James's mind. Frank was playing games, testing boundaries, seeing what information James already possessed.

"Haven't spoken with Beth yet this morning," James replied truthfully. "Been occupied with our own things. Seems like a rat got in the barn. Had to dispatch that early on. I'm still needing my first cup of the day."

"Of course." Frank nodded as if this confirmed something for him. "Well, if you change your mind about that assistance, you know where to find me. Times like these, communities need to stick together." He turned back toward his truck, then paused. "Oh, and tell young Ethan to be more careful. Children shouldn't play near fence lines these days. All sorts of dangers out there."

The specific mention of Ethan sent a surge of protective fury through James's chest. How could Frank know Ethan had been involved unless he'd been watching—or unless the trespassers had reported directly to him?

"I'll pass that along," James managed, keeping his voice level through sheer force of will.

He watched Frank drive away, dust billowing behind the truck's wheels. Only when the vehicle had disappeared from view did he allow the tension to show in his clenched fists and rigid shoulders.

"Dad?" Daniel appeared beside him, voice low. "What did he want?"

"To let us know he's watching," James replied grimly. "And that he knows about Ethan's encounter. Before he should have known."

Daniel's expression darkened. "You think those men were his?"

"I think Frank's playing both sides of whatever's coming. Building his influence in town while coordinating with outside forces." James turned toward the house. "Double the patrols. I need to update Beth about all of this."

Inside, the farmhouse had transformed from breakfast-time domesticity to strategic command center. The large kitchen table was now covered with maps of the surrounding area, marked with patrol routes and observation points. Sarah moved efficiently between where a pot of coffee percolated on the woodburning stove and the radio station set up in what had once been a breakfast nook.

But their organized response couldn't hide the underlying problems that had been mounting for weeks. James surveyed the food inventory sheet pinned to the wall—numbers dropping steadily as their reserves dwindled. Three more families had left yesterday, taking their share of supplies and significantly reducing the farm's collective strength. The Jackson family with their three children, the Stevensons with their medical expertise, and old Dr. Cooper who'd been helping Emily with the sick. All gone, seeking what they believed would be better conditions further north.

"Any word from the hunting party?" James asked as Sarah handed him a fresh mug of coffee.

Her expression tightened. "Radio call came in just before the incident with Ethan. They were ambushed ten miles west, near Miller's Ridge. Jim Harris took a bullet in the leg. Pete has a concussion from falling down a ravine during their escape." She shook her head. "They're making their way back slowly. No game, obviously."

Another failure. Another blow to their dwindling resources. James absorbed the news with outward stoicism, though internally he added it to the growing tally of setbacks. The hunting expedition had been a calculated risk—sending six of their strongest men deeper into the wooded areas than usual, hoping to bring back enough meat to supplement their diminishing food stores. Now they were returning injured and empty-handed.

"The crops?" he asked, though he already knew the answer.

Sarah's gaze drifted toward the window overlooking their fields. "Struggling. The heat's wilting everything faster than we can water it. We're losing at least thirty percent of what we planted." She hesitated. "James… we need to consider rationing more strictly. Or letting more people leave."

The implied choice hung heavy in the air. Each family that

departed took resources, yes, but also reduced the number of mouths to feed. With resources dwindling and no successful hunting expedition to replenish their stores, difficult decisions loomed.

"We're not forcing anyone out," James said firmly. "Never that."

"Of course not," Sarah agreed. "But if more choose to leave…"

She didn't finish the thought. Didn't need to. If more families departed, the farm's defensive capabilities would be severely compromised—but their food might stretch further for those who remained.

Emily entered from the hallway, medical bag in hand, expression drawn with fatigue. "Ryan's fever's down again. I've changed his IV. We're making progress, but slowly."

James nodded gratefully. "Thank you. Any word on the patients at the funeral home?"

"Katherine Foster's holding steady. Not better, not worse." Emily set her bag on a chair, rubbing her eyes. "James, we need to talk about medical supplies."

Here it was—another critical shortage to manage. "How bad?"

"We're out of IV antibiotics completely. Oral medications will last another week at current usage rates. Pain management…" She shook her head. "Almost nothing left."

"The pharmacy at the mall complex?" James suggested. "We've been avoiding it because of the exposure risk, but—"

"Already picked clean," Emily interrupted. "Beth sent a team three days ago. They found empty shelves and two corpses. Looters got there first."

The walls of their safe world contracted another notch. James absorbed the information, mentally recalculating options, priorities, possibilities.

"We could try the veterinary clinic on Route 5," Daniel suggested, joining the conversation as he entered from outside. "Large animal supplies might be adaptable. Less likely to have been targeted by early looters."

Emily considered this. "Possible. I'd need to research dosage conversions, but in theory…" She nodded slowly. "It's worth exploring."

"I'll organize a team," Daniel volunteered.

"Not today," James countered. "Not with those men in the woods and Frank's sudden interest in our perimeter. Tomorrow, maybe, if things stabilize."

The radio crackled with static, then Beth's voice emerged, tense but controlled. "Thompson farm, this is Martin. Come in."

James crossed to the radio. "Martin, this is Thompson. Go ahead."

"Situation in town is deteriorating," Beth reported without preamble. "Two more families have fallen ill from contaminated water. Maddie Foster is working on filtration systems, but we need more components. And…" She hesitated. "James, there's unrest. People are talking about leaving before winter. Heading south where food might be more plentiful."

The news wasn't unexpected, but it still hit hard. The community they'd worked so carefully to build, to protect, was fracturing under the weight of shortages and fear.

"The council meeting tonight is still on?" James asked.

"Yes. Eight o'clock at town hall." Beth's voice lowered slightly. "James, Frank's people. The Reapers, as folks are calling them now, will be there. Pushing their agenda."

The name struck James like a physical blow. The Reapers. He'd heard it whispered around town, but this was Beth's first official acknowledgment of the nickname for Frank's growing militia.

"We'll be there," he assured her. "With evidence of this morning's incursion."

After signing off, James turned to find Sarah watching him with an intensity that made him uncomfortable. She knew him too well and could see past the composed exterior to the turmoil beneath.

"James," she said quietly. "We need to talk. Privately."

The tone sent warning signals through his mind. This wasn't about tactics or supplies. This was personal. He nodded, following her into what had once been their formal living room, now converted to a sleeping area for two displaced families. Currently empty, it offered the only privacy available in the crowded farmhouse.

Sarah closed the door behind them, then turned to face him directly. In the diffused light filtering through curtained windows, he could see every line that worry had etched into her beloved face. Lines he was responsible for, in ways both direct and indirect.

"You're not sleeping," she said without preamble. "Not eating properly. Pushing yourself beyond reasonable limits."

James sighed. "Sarah, we're all—"

"No." She cut him off firmly. "This isn't about what we're all doing. This is about you specifically. You've lost weight. You pace all night instead of resting. You're making decisions from a place of exhaustion and..." She hesitated before continuing more gently, "...and grief. Unprocessed grief."

The word hit its mark with uncomfortable precision. Grief.

For the world they'd lost. For the friends who'd died. For the grandchildren whose childhoods had been stolen. For the safety and security he'd spent a lifetime building, now revealed as illusory.

"I'm fine," he insisted, the reflexive response of a man who'd never allowed himself the luxury of vulnerability.

"You're not," Sarah countered, stepping closer. "And we need you too much for me to pretend otherwise. The families who left yesterday—they were watching you, James. Watching how you're barely holding together. It scared them."

The observation lanced through his carefully maintained composure. Had he really become so transparent? Had his internal struggles become visible enough to undermine community confidence?

"What would you have me do?" he asked, a rare edge of frustration breaking through. "We're facing food shortages, medical shortages, security threats on multiple fronts. Families are sick, frightened, considering dangerous journeys with winter approaching. Frank's building his own power base while Sherman's forces gather to the south. Should I take a vacation? A mental health day?"

The bitterness in his voice surprised even him. Sarah didn't flinch from it.

"I would have you acknowledge that you're human," she said simply. "That you're carrying too much alone. That you need to delegate more, rest more, and yes—grieve more." Her hand found his, her fingers interlacing with familiar comfort. "The children are watching you, James. Not just Ethan, all of them. They're learning how to survive not just physically, but emotionally, by your example."

The truth of her words settled heavily on his shoulders. He

was modeling more than tactics and resource management. He was showing the next generation how to face catastrophic loss, how to navigate a world stripped of certainties.

"I don't know how to do this, Sarah," he admitted, voice barely above a whisper. "I don't know how to lead people through something I don't understand myself."

The confession—quiet, simple, devastating in its honesty—hung between them. Sarah squeezed his hand.

"None of us do," she said gently. "But we're finding our way together. That's the point. Together. Not you carrying everything alone."

A knock at the door interrupted the moment. Daniel's voice came through the wood. "Dad? Emily needs to talk to you about the supplies for town. And Michael's team has finished the perimeter check."

Back to immediate concerns. Back to the endless logistics of survival.

"We'll continue this," Sarah said, releasing his hand but holding his gaze. "Tonight. After the council meeting."

James nodded, the commitment made despite his discomfort. He opened the door to find Daniel waiting, his expression carefully neutral—though James suspected he'd heard at least part of the conversation. Another blow to the image of strength he'd worked so hard to maintain.

As they returned to the kitchen, James found the children gathered around the table where Sarah had organized an impromptu lesson. Lily, Theo, and even Sophia were listening intently as Sarah demonstrated how to identify edible plants using a field guide salvaged from the local library.

"This one's plantain," she was explaining, holding up a specimen. "Not the banana-like fruit, but the wild plant. The leaves can be eaten raw in salads, cooked like spinach, or used medicinally for insect bites and minor wounds."

Lily raised her hand excitedly. "I saw those by the creek!"

"Good spotting," Sarah praised. "Tomorrow we'll go collect some, learn how to prepare them."

James paused, observing the scene. Despite everything; the shortages, the threats, the departures, life continued. Children learned. Adapting, growing, preparing for whatever came next. Sarah caught his eye from across the room, the message clear. This is what we're fighting for.

Ethan sat slightly apart from the other children, his expression thoughtful as he practiced tying complex knots with a length of paracord. He'd been subdued since the incident at the fence, processing its implications in his own way. James made a mental note to check in with him before leaving for the council meeting, to ensure that the boy understood that mistakes were part of learning, not measures of worth.

Emily approached, clipboard in hand. "I've inventoried what we can spare for the town's medical needs," she said. "It's not much, but it's something."

As they reviewed the list together, James felt the weight of his responsibilities pressing down again. So many needs. So many gaps to fill. So many people counting on decisions he made from insufficient information and dwindling resources.

But Sarah was right. He couldn't carry it all alone. Shouldn't try to.

"Daniel," he said, making a decision. "You'll lead the town hall delegation tonight. Take Michael and two others. I'm staying here."

Surprise registered on Daniel's face. "You sure, Dad? The council will expect you."

"They'll get your perspective instead. Fresh eyes, fresh thinking." James clasped his son's shoulder. "Your mother has informed me that…" He paused to glance at Sarah. "That I need a vacation. I think the children and I need a game night."

Daniel smirked and the kids cheered as Sarah gripped his arm, tipping her head to nuzzle him.

Ethan

Ethan stacked the playing cards carefully, aligning their edges with the precision he'd seen his father use when cleaning his rifle. The living room still echoed with the younger kids' laughter from game night, but that sound felt distant now, belonging to a different world than the one pressing against the farmhouse windows. Through the gap in the curtains, he could see the faint orange glow of Frank's men's patrol beacons moving along the eastern perimeter, methodically sweeping the darkness.

"You don't need to line them up perfectly," Grandpa said, watching him from the rocking chair. "They're just going back in the drawer."

"Dad says details matter now," Ethan replied, not looking up from his task. "Little things can get people killed."

Grandpa's rocking paused, the chair's familiar creak falling silent. In the kitchen, Ethan could hear Grandma Sarah's voice as she herded Lily and Theo upstairs for bed, their protests growing fainter with each step.

"Your dad's right," Grandpa said finally. "But there's a difference between being careful and..." He trailed off, searching for the right words.

"And what?" Ethan prompted, finally looking up from the cards. The lamplight caught the new lines on his grandfather's face, shadows deepening the hollows beneath his eyes.

"And forgetting to live while you're trying to survive." Grandpa leaned forward, elbows on his knees. "You know why I stayed home tonight instead of going to the meeting?"

Ethan shrugged. "Because of what I did at the fence. You wanted to make sure I didn't do something stupid again."

A smile touched the corner of Grandpa's mouth. "Not even close." He gestured for Ethan to join him by the window. "Come here."

Ethan hesitated, then set the cards aside and crossed the room. Together, they looked out at the farm. The darkness transformed the familiar landscape, turning the cornfields into mysterious seas, the barn into a hulking shadow cut against the star-filled sky. The patrol lights flickered between trees, fireflies with purpose and threat.

"See those lights?" Grandpa asked. "Frank's men. Supposedly helping keep us safe."

"But they're not," Ethan said confidently. "Grayson says they're watching us, not protecting us."

Grandpa's eyebrows rose slightly. "Grayson's a perceptive young man." He rested a hand on Ethan's shoulder, the weight of it somehow both comforting and serious. "I stayed home tonight because sometimes being a leader means knowing when to let others lead. And because I needed to talk to you."

Something in his grandfather's tone made Ethan stand straighter. Not the disapproving lecture voice he'd expected after the fence incident, but something different—the voice Grandpa used when discussing supplies with Dad or security with Beth.

"About this morning?" Ethan asked, bracing himself.

"Partly." Grandpa guided him back to the table where they'd played cards earlier. From his pocket, he produced Michael's folding knife—the one Ethan had used to slash the stranger's hand. "I think it's time we talked about this."

Ethan's stomach tightened. "Dad said I shouldn't have taken it."

"He's right." Grandpa turned the knife over, examining its worn handle. "Not because you shouldn't have a knife, but because you took this one without permission and without training." He looked directly at Ethan. "That's not how we do things in this family."

"I just wanted to be ready," Ethan said, the words coming out smaller than intended. "Everyone else has weapons. Even Sophia has that slingshot."

"Being ready isn't just about having tools," Grandpa said. "It's about knowing how to use them. When to use them." He set the knife on the table between them. "And when not to."

Ethan stared at the knife, unexpected tears burning behind his eyes. Not because he was in trouble, but because his grandfather was talking to him like he mattered—like his actions had real weight in the world.

"I could have died this morning, couldn't I?" he asked, the question emerging before he could stop it.

Grandpa didn't flinch from the truth. "Yes. Those men were desperate, armed, and dangerous. You were lucky."

"But I stopped them from cutting the fence," Ethan countered, a flicker of pride warming his chest. "I did something important."

"You did," Grandpa acknowledged. "But at too high a risk. There are other ways you could have helped—ways that wouldn't have put you in direct danger."

"Like what?" Ethan challenged, an edge entering his voice. "Staying in the storm cellar? Watching the little kids? That's not helping, that's just staying out of the way."

To his surprise, Grandpa nodded thoughtfully. "You're right. We've been treating you like something to protect, not someone who can contribute." He leaned back, studying Ethan with new consideration. "That changes tonight."

Ethan blinked, uncertain if he'd heard correctly. "What changes?"

"Your position in our security operations." Grandpa reached for a sheet of paper and a pencil. "Every person on this farm has a role, including the children. But roles have to match skills and judgment." He began sketching what looked like the farm's layout. "What you did this morning showed courage but poor tactical thinking."

"Tactical thinking?" Ethan repeated, leaning forward to see the drawing.

"Strategy. Planning. Considering all options before acting." Grandpa tapped the pencil against the rough map. "If you'd seen those men at the fence and wanted to help, what could you have done besides confronting them directly?"

Ethan frowned, considering the question seriously. "I could have... told Dad right away."

"Good. What else?"

"Maybe watched them longer? To see what they were really doing and if there were more people hiding."

"Excellent." Grandpa nodded approvingly. "Intelligence gathering. Critical before any operation." He added some marks to the map. "What else?"

Ethan sat straighter, mind racing. "I could have used the whistle signal to warn everyone without the men knowing who spotted them."

"Now you're thinking like a tactician." Grandpa's eyes crinkled with a smile. "See the difference? All of those options would have helped protect the farm without putting you in direct danger."

"But none of them would have stopped them from cutting the fence," Ethan pointed out.

"True. But they would have given us time to respond as a coordinated unit." Grandpa's expression grew serious again. "We could replace the fence, but we can't replace you. In this world, Ethan, being brave isn't enough. You have to be smart about how you use that bravery."

A floorboard creaked in the hallway. Ethan turned to see Grayson standing in the doorway, his thin frame tense with hesitation.

"Sorry," Grayson said quickly. "I just—I heard talking and thought..." His eyes darted to the knife on the table, then to the map.

"Come join us, Grayson," Grandpa invited. "We're discussing security."

The older boy moved into the room cautiously, as if expecting to be sent away at any moment. His perpetual wariness reminded Ethan of the half-wild cats that lived in the barn, always poised between approach and flight.

"You're not in trouble for this morning," Grandpa told him directly. "In fact, your warning about the wire cutters was valuable information."

Something in Grayson's posture eased slightly. He took the chair beside Ethan, eyes fixed on the map. "Are those patrol routes?" he asked.

"They will be," Grandpa confirmed. "I'm developing a new security assignment for observers under sixteen."

Ethan exchanged a glance with Grayson, excitement flaring in his chest. "You mean us?"

"You, Grayson, Sophia when she's not helping with the younger children. A proper observation team." Grandpa started marking positions on the crude map. "Not guard duty—I want to be clear about that. You don't engage threats directly. But we need more eyes watching from secure positions."

"Like spotters," Grayson said with unexpected confidence. "In Portland, before everything fell apart, my dad had me watching our street from the attic window. I could see three blocks in each direction."

Ethan looked at the older boy with new respect. Grayson rarely spoke about Portland or his father, the information fragmenting like precious gems dropped into their conversation.

"Exactly like spotters," Grandpa agreed. "Regular observation shifts, proper reporting, specific areas of responsibility." He traced a circle around the farmhouse. "This isn't just busy work. We genuinely need more coverage, especially with Daniel and Michael at the town meeting tonight."

"What about the others?" Ethan asked. "Dad and Mom? Will they agree?"

Grandpa's eyes met his, steady and honest. "Your father will have concerns. He wants to protect you. That's what fathers do. But I'll help him understand that giving you a real role is the best protection we can offer now."

The simple acknowledgment, that keeping children ignorant and idle was more dangerous than teaching them to participate, filled Ethan with unexpected emotion. A tightness built in his throat as he realized his grandfather was seeing him truly. Not as a child to be sheltered, but as a person with value to offer.

"I won't let you down," he promised, the words emerging rough but sincere.

"I know." Grandpa's gaze included both boys now. "But before we implement this new system, I need your complete honesty about something." He leaned forward, voice lowering slightly. "What else have you boys observed that you haven't told the adults?"

The question hung in the air between them. Ethan felt Grayson tense beside him, the older boy's breathing changing subtly. This was the moment—the test of whether adults truly wanted their observations or just their obedience.

"Frank watches the well," Ethan said finally. "Grayson saw him writing in a notebook while everyone was asleep."

"And the men who call themselves Reapers? They change the patrol routes when they think no one's watching," Grayson added, words tumbling out now that the dam had broken. "They don't actually cover the north field at all, even though they report that they do."

Grandpa didn't dismiss their observations or question their accuracy. Instead, he nodded gravely, adding marks to the map. "What else?"

"One of Frank's men…the one with the red hat? He goes into the storage shed every time he's here," Ethan continued. "But he never takes anything out or brings anything in. He just goes in for a few minutes, then leaves."

"And I heard two of them talking about Sherman," Grayson said, voice dropping to a whisper. "They said something about 'when the signal comes' and 'being on the right side when it happens.'"

This information caused Grandpa's pencil to pause, his expression sharpening. "When was this?"

"Yesterday morning," Grayson replied. "When they brought the cornmeal."

Ethan watched his grandfather absorb this information, mentally cataloging it against other evidence. The process was fascinating. He was not dismissing their reports as childish imagination, but incorporating them into a larger assessment.

"This is exactly the kind of intelligence we need," Grandpa said finally. "Details adults might miss because we're focused on the obvious threats." He set the pencil down and regarded them both seriously. "I'm going to show you something, but it needs to remain between us for now."

From a box in the hallway, he withdrew a small device in a ziplock bag that Ethan recognized with a jolt. One of the water contamination units. Just like the one found at the creek.

"We recovered three more of these today," Grandpa said quietly. "All placed at water sources our community uses."

Ethan stared at the device, its innocuous green casing belying its deadly purpose. "Who's doing it?"

"That's what we need to determine." Grandpa turned the device over, revealing markings on the bottom that Ethan couldn't decipher. "These aren't improvised. They're manufactured, which means organization, resources, planning."

"Sherman's people," Grayson stated with cold certainty. "They did the same thing in Portland. Contaminated the reservoir, then offered 'clean' water to those who cooperated."

Grandpa nodded slowly. "That's our working theory. But there's a missing piece." He tapped the map where he'd marked Frank's patrol routes. "How are these devices being placed without our sentries spotting the perpetrators?"

The implication hung in the air, unspoken but clear. Someone inside their security perimeter was involved—someone with access and knowledge of their patrol patterns.

"Frank," Ethan breathed, the pieces connecting in his mind. "That's why he keeps checking the well."

"We can't be certain," Grandpa cautioned. "But it's a possibility we need to consider." He folded the map carefully. "This is why I'm implementing the observer program. We need eyes watching our watchers."

A strange mixture of emotions swirled in Ethan's chest: pride at being trusted with such critical information, fear at the immensity of the threat, and a steely determination that surprised him with its intensity. This wasn't about playing superheroes anymore or proving his bravery. This was about protecting his family from dangers that lurked both outside their fences and possibly within them.

"When do we start?" he asked.

"Tomorrow morning. Early." Grandpa returned the contamination device to the box. "I'll work out the rotation schedule tonight and brief you both before breakfast." He fixed them with a stern look. "This isn't a game. It's not an adventure. It's necessary work that carries real risk."

"We understand," Grayson said, a new steadiness in his voice.

Ethan nodded agreement, feeling something shift within himself. A childish part receding, replaced by something harder and more focused.

Grandpa's expression softened slightly. "I'm proud of both of you. The world changed faster than anyone could have prepared for, and you're rising to meet it." He reached for the knife on the table. "Which brings me back to this."

Ethan tensed, expecting the knife to disappear into his grandfather's pocket. Instead, Grandpa held it out to him, handle first.

"This isn't yours," Grandpa said as Ethan stared in confusion. "It belongs to your father, and you'll return it to him tomorrow with an apology for taking it without permission."

Ethan nodded solemnly, accepting the blade with careful hands.

"But," Grandpa continued, "I'll be speaking with your father about proper training and equipment for both of you. Observers need tools…the right tools, with the right training."

The prospect of official permission, of legitimate inclusion in the farm's security operations, sent a surge of pride through Ethan's chest. Not secret rebellion, but recognized contribution.

"Until then," Grandpa added, "you'll carry this only during your observation shifts, and only after your father approves." He held Ethan's gaze. "Can I trust you to honor that agreement?"

"Yes," he said simply. "I promise."

Grandpa nodded, seemingly satisfied. "Good. Now—" He broke off at the sound of approaching vehicles, headlights sweeping across the living room window as engines growled up the driveway. "That'll be the others returning from town."

Ethan moved to the window, Grayson close behind him. Through the glass, they watched two trucks pull into the farmyard, their headlights cutting sharp beams through the darkness. Daniel emerged from the first vehicle, then Michael and two others Ethan recognized from the morning's patrol. Their body language sent an immediate warning—tense shoulders, quick movements, weapons ready as they scanned the perimeter even within the supposed safety of the farm's boundaries.

"Something's wrong," Grayson murmured.

"Yes," Grandpa agreed, moving toward the door. "Both of you stay inside. Observation begins now—watch from upstairs. Note everyone who enters the property, especially anyone who isn't family."

The swift shift from conversation to command reminded Ethan that his grandfather had been a man of authority long before the world collapsed. Ethan and Grayson exchanged glances, then moved without argument toward the stairs as Grandpa went to meet the returning party.

From the upstairs window, Ethan watched his father emerge from the second truck, rifle cradled in his arms, eyes constantly scanning the darkness beyond the yard lights. Behind him came a figure Ethan didn't immediately recognize—a teenage girl, thin and exhausted-looking, supported by Beth.

"Who's that?" Grayson whispered, pressing close to the glass.

"Don't know," Ethan replied. "Not from town."

They watched as the adults converged in a tight circle, voices too low to hear but body language broadcasting urgency.

The girl swayed on her feet, Beth's arm around her shoulders the only thing keeping her upright.

"They found a survivor," Grayson suggested. "Someone from outside."

"Or a refugee," Ethan countered, remembering Grayson's own arrival days earlier. "Someone running from something."

The girl turned slightly, her face catching the yard light. Despite the distance, Ethan could see the hollow exhaustion in her features, the way her clothes hung on her frame, the wariness in her posture despite her evident fatigue. She clutched something to her chest—a packet of some kind, held with the desperation of someone carrying invaluable cargo.

Below, the adults' conversation grew more animated. His father gestured emphatically toward the road, while Daniel shook his head sharply. Grandpa stood between them, one hand raised in what looked like a call for calm. Whatever news they'd brought from town, it wasn't good.

"What do you think happened?" Grayson asked.

Before Ethan could answer, movement at the edge of the yard caught his attention. A figure slipping through the shadows near the tool shed, moving with deliberate stealth. Not one of the regular farm residents. Not one of the returning council members.

"Look," Ethan hissed, pointing. "By the shed."

Grayson tensed beside him. "One of Frank's men."

The figure paused near the shed door, glancing toward the group of adults still engaged in their urgent conversation. Then, with practiced quickness, he produced something from his pocket. A small object that caught the distant yard light.

"He's putting something in the shed," Ethan whispered, straining to see details through the darkness.

"No," Grayson corrected, voice suddenly hard with recognition. "He's putting something on the shed. Against the wall."

Understanding crashed through Ethan's mind, fragments of overhead conversations suddenly connecting. The secure storage where they kept their remaining fuel. The shed that shared a wall with the rainwater collection barrels that supplemented their well. The mysterious visits by Frank's men that never seemed to include removing or delivering supplies.

The observer program had just yielded its first critical intelligence.

"We need to tell Grandpa," Ethan said, already turning from the window. "Now."

Beth

Blood had dried in the grooves of the town hall's hardwood floor, dark crescents mapping the path of the wounded. Beth Martin crouched beside the largest stain, fingers hovering just above the tacky surface. Pete's blood. The auto shop owner had taken a bullet meant for her, the red blossoming across his shoulder as he shoved her behind the heavy oak table that now lay splintered from gunfire.

"Should've seen their faces when Pete didn't go down," Robbie commented from the doorway, right arm bandaged from wrist to elbow where one of Frank's men had opened him up with a hunting knife. The wound required twenty-three stitches, administered by Emily in the moments after the attack. "Man's built like a damn oak tree."

Beth nodded, not trusting herself to speak yet. Her throat felt tight, constricted by anger that threatened to overwhelm professional detachment. Three of Frank's Reapers sat zip-tied in her holding cells. Two escaped, one leaving a blood trail that had disappeared at the edge of town. And Frank himself? Nowhere to be found, already establishing his alibi at the Thompson farm while his men attempted armed robbery.

"Chief?" Robbie's voice sharpened with concern. "You okay?"

Beth pushed herself upright, her knees protesting the

movement. She winced, hand automatically moving to her side where the knife wound from last week's confrontation at the Pearson homestead was still healing. Four stitches and a cracked rib. A reminder of how quickly routine patrols could turn deadly. She wasn't old, forty-three last spring, but the weeks since the CME had aged everyone in dog years, their bodies consuming themselves to maintain basic function.

"Fine," she said shortly, brushing dust from her cargo pants. "How's Pete doing?"

"Stabilized. Emily gave him the last of the good painkillers." Robbie grimaced. "Says he'll be back up and moving by tomorrow, but she wants him on light duty for at least a week."

A week they didn't have, given the intelligence from earlier today. More scouts at the perimeter. Frank's men making their move in town. The water contamination continuing to claim victims. And somewhere south, Sherman's forces were gathering.

The feed store now all but empty, the occupants moved up to the Thompson farm and word from Old Man Jenkins about issues at the Seabrook Nuclear Power Plant all weighed on her mind and she hadn't even had time to discuss the incident with Sherman's man in the cell yet.

She shook her head to clear her thoughts and focused. "Status on the captured equipment?" she asked, moving toward the table where they'd stacked the water filtration components that had been the raid's target.

"Maddie's on her way to check if anything's damaged or missing." Robbie followed, his injured arm held slightly away from his body. "Kid's been working non-stop on these filters. Taking it personally."

Of course she is, Beth thought. Her father died from the contamination. But she kept the observation to herself. "And our guests?"

"Vocal. Particularly the ringleader. Calls himself Dempsey. Says Frank's going to burn this town to the ground for what we did to his men." Robbie's voice held a bitter edge. "Told him that's going to be difficult from a jail cell."

Beth nodded, mentally reviewing their limited options. The town's judicial system had been informal at best before the collapse. Now, with no functioning government beyond their little council, the meaning of justice became more subjective by the day. Her mind momentarily flashed back to the man she'd shot in the cell. She was just getting ready to tell the tale when Frank's men attempted armed robbery and assault, resulting in serious injuries. In the old world, that meant years in prison. In this world?

"Has anyone checked in on Frank's location?" she asked, already knowing the answer.

"Still at his place according to our last patrol. Acting like it's a normal day. Told Jenkins he had no idea what his 'boys' might have been up to." Robbie's disgust was palpable. "Playing both sides. Always has."

The front door of the town hall swung open, admitting a shaft of setting sunlight along with Daniel Thompson and three farm crew members. All armed, all wearing the grim expressions of men who'd seen too much in too short a time.

"Beth," Daniel acknowledged her with a nod. "We checked the surrounding buildings. No sign of that other guy. I'll wager the bleeder isn't going too far and we'll find his body somewhere in the woods." His gaze swept the room, taking in the bloodstains, the bullet holes in the far wall, the splayed wreckage of what had been their meeting table. They'd only just arrived and didn't wait to assess damage before running after the guys who nearly took them out bolting through the door. His eyes landed on the gleaming white bandaged arm. "Robbie. How bad?"

"Could've been worse," Robbie replied, the standard response of survivors. "Five of them hit during the supply distribution. Maddie had just finished her presentation on the water filters when they came through the back entrance."

"Frank's people." Daniel made it a statement, not a question.

Beth nodded grimly. "Red bands, every single one. Dempsey leading. Frank's right-hand man these days."

"Convenient how Frank himself was heading to our farm right when the attack happened." Daniel's weathered face hardened. "Establishing his alibi."

"My thoughts exactly." Beth gestured toward the clerk's office. "Emily's patching up Pete and checking the other minor injuries. Three of Frank's men in the cells."

"And Frank himself?"

"Still at his compound, last we checked. Acting like he has no knowledge of his men's actions." Beth's jaw tightened. "Playing his usual game."

Daniel moved to the table, examining the water filtration components with a practiced eye. "These were the targets? Not food or medicine?"

"Just the filters and assembly materials." Beth had been puzzling over this detail herself. "They didn't touch the medical supplies or the food distribution packages. Just went straight for Maddie's water filters."

Daniel frowned, the implications clearly troubling him as

much as they troubled her. "Control the water, control the town."

"My thoughts exactly. Especially with the contamination spreading." Beth lowered her voice, though everyone present was trusted. "Daniel, Frank showed up at your farm minutes after your confrontation with those scouts. Now his men try to seize our clean water technology while he establishes an alibi."

"You think he's working with Sherman."

The blunt assessment matched her own suspicions. "I think it's one hell of a coincidence otherwise."

Daniel nodded slowly. "Dad suspected as much. What's the plan for his men?"

The question cut to the heart of their current dilemma. In the old world, there had been clear processes for dealing with criminal acts. In this new reality, those processes had been replaced by necessarily improvised justice.

"Town council meets tonight," Beth replied. "We'll decide then. But my recommendation will be clear. Armed robbery and assault during a community emergency? In the old days, that was twenty years minimum."

"We don't have prisons anymore," Daniel pointed out quietly. "Or the resources to maintain long-term captives."

The unspoken implication hung in the air between them. Their options for dealing with violent offenders had narrowed dramatically since the collapse, trending toward the binary: exile or execution. Neither sat comfortably with Beth's former understanding of justice, but comfort was another luxury abandoned with hot showers and reliable electricity.

"One problem at a time," she said finally. "First, we need to secure the filters and get them to their intended recipients. Then deal with Frank himself."

"He'll deny everything," Robbie predicted. "Say his men were acting without orders. Rogue elements. He's been laying that groundwork for weeks."

Beth knew he was right. Frank had carefully constructed plausible deniability, building his private army while maintaining his public image as community benefactor. His "Reapers" did the dirty work while he kept his hands ostensibly clean.

"Let me talk to the prisoners," Daniel suggested. "My dad's known Dempsey since he was stealing cigarettes behind the high school. Might get more from him than you would."

Beth considered this. Under normal circumstances, she'd have refused—civilian interrogation of prisoners violated every protocol she'd learned at the academy. But these weren't normal circumstances, and Daniel had a way of getting people to talk. The calm authority he'd inherited from James often succeeded where her more direct approach failed.

"Alright," she agreed. "But I'm present for all questions. And we do this by the book, such as it is."

Daniel nodded agreement, and they moved toward the hallway that connected the town hall to the small police station and its three holding cells—originally designed for the town's infrequent drunk and disorderly cases, now repurposed for more serious offenders.

Beth noticed Robbie hanging back, his expression conflicted. "Problem?"

"Just thinking we might want to try a different approach first." He glanced toward the back of the building. "Dempsey's not going to talk easily. But there are other ways to get information."

"What did you have in mind?" Daniel asked.

Robbie hesitated, clearly uncomfortable with whatever he was about to suggest. "Two of Frank's other men are in town. Not involved in the raid, as far as we know. But they might have information. Travis and Connor."

"The hardware store security team." Beth remembered Frank insisting on posting his own men at strategic locations throughout town—"for community protection," he'd claimed. The hardware store, with its valuable tools and supplies, had been among the first locations to receive his unwanted security detail.

"They're at Kristie's Diner now," Robbie continued. "Having lunch like nothing happened. Like their buddies didn't just shoot up town hall."

"You're suggesting we bring them in for questioning?" Beth frowned. "On what grounds? We don't have evidence they were involved."

"Not suggesting we bring them in at all." Robbie's expression darkened. "But Jacob Mercer and his friends might have some questions for them."

The implication was clear, and Beth felt her professional ethics bristle against it. Jacob Mercer—the teacher who'd lost his wife to the water contamination—had formed his own group of grieving, angry citizens. They'd appointed themselves a kind of shadow justice system, operating at the edges of Beth's authority. She'd turned a blind eye to some of their methods, recognizing that formal processes couldn't address every wrong in their current situation. But endorsing their involvement crossed a line she'd been reluctant to approach.

"Vigilante justice isn't the answer," she said firmly.

"Is it vigilante if we know about it and don't interfere?" Robbie countered. "Jacob's people get results."

"And sent those looters to the hospital," Beth reminded him.

"They lived," Robbie said flatly. "Unlike George Miller at the pharmacy or David Foster and the others who died from the contaminated water."

The mention of Maddie's father struck a nerve. Beth had watched the girl cope with her grief by throwing herself into her father's work, trying to save others from his fate. If Frank's men had succeeded today, those efforts would have been severely hampered.

"We do this legally," she insisted, though the concept of legality had become increasingly malleable. "I won't authorize extrajudicial methods."

"No one's asking you to authorize anything," Robbie replied, eyeing her with the raised brow that said what she'd been thinking about her choice of justice the last time someone was in that cell. "Just suggesting you might be busy with the prisoners for the next hour. What happens at Kristie's Diner during that time is beyond your control."

Beth felt Daniel watching her, his expression neutral but attentive. He wouldn't push her either way, she knew. This was her jurisdiction, her decision.

As they reached the holding cells, Beth noticed a small notebook on the floor near the security desk – likely dropped during the chaos of processing the prisoners. She picked it up, flipping it open to find densely packed handwriting. Most entries were mundane patrol notes, but a page marked with a red tab caught her attention.

"Look at this," she said, holding it out to Daniel. "Dates, times, locations. And here – 'S-day confirmed for Thursday dawn. Northern team in position.'"

Daniel examined the page, eyes narrowing. "Thursday. That's two days from now."

"There's more," Beth continued, turning the page. "'Water access points secured before signal. Farm handling coordinated through F.'" She looked up. "F has to be Frank."

"This is one of their planning notebooks," Daniel said. "Must have fallen from a pocket during the fight."

This unexpected intelligence shifted Beth's calculations. The notebook provided what she needed without resorting to Jacob Mercer's methods. Concrete evidence of coordinated planning, a specific timeline, and Frank's involvement.

The police station's holding area consisted of three cells arranged along a short corridor. Simple bars, no solid walls—designed for visibility and temporary detention rather than long-term incarceration. Dempsey occupied the middle cell, his large frame making the small space appear even more confined. The red band that had once adorned his upper arm had been removed during processing, but the tan line marking its habitual presence remained visible on his sun-darkened skin.

He looked up as they approached, expression shifting from boredom to calculated insolence. "Well, if it isn't Chief Martin and Farmer Junior. Come to offer me a plea deal?"

"Came to give you a chance to help yourself," Beth replied, keeping her tone professionally neutral despite the anger simmering beneath. This man had participated in an attack that injured her friends, threatened her community's survival, and potentially collaborated with external enemies. "Your situation isn't good, Dempsey."

"My situation?" He laughed, the sound hollow against the concrete walls. "Lady, you're the one whose situation isn't good. When Frank finds out what happened—"

"Frank already knows," Daniel interrupted calmly. "He was establishing his alibi at our farm when you and your friends decided to shoot up the town hall."

Dempsey's expression flickered. Surprise, quickly masked, but not before Beth caught it. "That's bullshit. Frank wouldn't—"

"Wouldn't what?" Beth pressed. "Wouldn't send you to do his dirty work while maintaining plausible deniability? That's been his strategy from day one."

"You don't know what you're talking about." But Dempsey's conviction seemed to waver, doubt creeping in at the edges.

Beth held up the notebook. "We know about Thursday. We know about S-day, the dawn attack, the northern team already in position."

The blood drained from Dempsey's face so rapidly that Beth actually worried he might faint. "You can't—" he began, then stopped himself, wariness replacing shock. "You're bluffing. Trying to get me to confirm something you only suspect."

"Am I?" Beth opened the notebook to the marked page, showing him his own team's handwriting. "'Northern team in position. Southern approach coordinated through Sherman's people.' It's all here, Dempsey. Your people aren't as careful as they think."

Dempsey's expression cycled through disbelief, fear, and finally a calculating assessment of his options.

"What are you offering?" he asked eventually.

"Depends what you're selling," Beth countered. "We need specifics. Attack vectors. Force strength. Frank's exact role."

Dempsey snorted. "And in exchange, I just walk out of

here? After shooting up your town hall?"

"Not a chance," Beth said flatly. "But cooperation might mean the difference between exile and execution when the town council meets tonight."

The stark options hung in the air between them. Dempsey's eyes moved from Beth to Daniel and back again, weighing their resolve against his loyalty to Frank.

"If I talk," he said slowly, "I'm a dead man anyway. Frank doesn't forgive betrayal."

"Frank won't be in a position to do anything about it," Daniel replied. "Not after we confirm his collaboration with Sherman."

Another calculated risk. Promising an outcome they couldn't guarantee. But Dempsey was wavering, self-preservation beginning to outweigh allegiance.

"What exactly do you want to know?" he asked finally.

Beth maintained her neutral expression, not allowing the flash of victory to show. "Everything. Starting with Frank's arrangement with Sherman. When did it begin? What are the terms?"

Dempsey sighed, seeming to deflate as the decision to cooperate registered fully. "About three weeks ago. Frank was running a patrol south of town, encountered some of Sherman's scouts. Instead of engaging, he negotiated." His lip curled in what might have been admiration or disgust. "That's Frank's genius, you know. Always looking for the angle, the opportunity in chaos."

"The terms," Beth prompted when he fell silent.

"Simple enough. Frank provides intelligence on Cornish defenses, assists with resource control—particularly water—and in exchange, Sherman gives him control of the town afterward. Under Sherman's overall authority, of course."

"And the Thompson farm?" Daniel asked, voice carefully controlled.

"Primary target." Dempsey's gaze shifted to Daniel, something like regret crossing his features. "Nothing personal, Thompson. Farm's too valuable—food production, defendable position, water access. Sherman wants it intact. Means some of your people might survive if they don't resist."

Beth noticed Daniel's hands clench briefly before relaxing with deliberate control. "The contamination devices. Frank's people placed them?"

"Some. Sherman's advance team handled the others." Dempsey shrugged. "Strategy was to weaken resistance through illness, strain medical resources, create dependency on centralized water distribution."

"Which Frank would control," Beth concluded grimly. "Along with who lives and who dies."

"Politics," Dempsey said, as if this explained everything. "Frank understands the new world better than most. Power isn't about badges or elections anymore. It's about who controls the essentials."

The casual way he dismissed the deliberate contamination of their water supply—an act that had already killed multiple people—sent a surge of disgust through Beth's chest. She'd known Frank was ambitious, opportunistic, self-serving. But this level of calculated betrayal surpassed even her worst assessments.

"Attack details," she pressed, keeping her voice level through force of will. "Strength, vectors, timeline."

"Thursday at dawn, like you already know," Dempsey confirmed. "Three-pronged approach. Main force from the south—about thirty fighters, well-armed. Secondary team from the east—smaller, maybe twelve, focused on the town center. Northern team is already embedded, eight men watching the farm, ready to create a diversion."

"Those men at our fence line this morning," Daniel murmured. "Advance scouts."

"Probably," Dempsey agreed. "Timeline accelerated yesterday when Sherman heard about escaped prisoners heading north. Worried they'd bring warning."

Beth's mind catalogued this detail for later examination. Escaped prisoners could mean potential allies, people with inside knowledge of Sherman's operation.

"Frank's role during the attack?" she asked.

"Secure the town hall, police station, and water distribution points. Neutralize you specifically," Dempsey nodded toward Beth. "You're considered the primary local resistance leader. With you eliminated, community response becomes disorganized."

The clinical assessment of her planned murder should have shocked Beth, but she'd almost expected it. She represented legitimate authority—of course she'd be a primary target in any coup attempt.

"And after?" Daniel pressed. "Assuming this plan succeeds?"

Dempsey shrugged again. "Sherman establishes regional control. Frank manages Cornish. Resources get redirected to support Sherman's broader territorial ambitions. The usual warlord progression."

Beth had heard enough. The picture was clear—and more urgent than even their worst projections. Less than forty-eight hours until a coordinated attack from multiple vectors, with internal sabotage from Frank's people. They needed to act immediately.

"One last question," she said, studying Dempsey's face carefully. "Why tell us this? What's your calculation here?"

The man met her gaze directly for the first time, something like grudging respect in his expression. "Frank sold us out. This morning, when he 'established his alibi' at the Thompson farm? That wasn't coincidence. He knew we'd fail. Knew some of us would be captured or killed. All part of his plausible deniability. Right?" Bitterness edged his voice. "I've been loyal. I just wanted to make sure we ended up on the top of the food chain for once. Followed orders, did the dirty work. And he hung us out to dry without a second thought."

Betrayal—the breaking point for even hardened loyalists. Beth filed this away as a potential vulnerability in Frank's organization. His men followed him out of self-interest and a belief that he protected his own. That loyalty was conditional, not absolute.

"Thank you for your cooperation," she said formally. "I'll note it during tonight's council meeting."

Dempsey gave a humorless laugh. "Don't bother with gratitude, Chief. Self-preservation, that's all this is." His expression darkened. "But a word of advice? Don't underestimate Frank. Man's like water—finds every crack, every weakness. And he's been mapping yours for probably years."

Beth stepped back from the cell, gesturing for Daniel to follow her toward the exit. They remained silent until they'd cleared the holding area, entering her small office and closing the door behind them.

"Forty-eight hours," Daniel said immediately. "Not much

time to prepare."

"No." Beth moved to the map of Cornish spread across her desk, mind already shifting to tactical assessment. "Three-pronged attack, advance teams already positioned. And Frank's people embedded throughout town." She glanced up. "We need to move quickly, but carefully. Frank can't know we're onto him."

"Agreed." Daniel studied the map, finger tracing potential defensive positions. "We consolidate at the farm and the funeral home. Defensible positions with water access. Evacuate vulnerable populations from exposed areas."

"And Frank?" Beth asked, though she already suspected Daniel's answer.

"Has to be neutralized before the attack," he stated bluntly. "Him and his closest lieutenants. Otherwise we're fighting on two fronts."

The decision had been forming in Beth's mind since Dempsey began talking. Frank's betrayal went beyond criminal—it was existential. He'd conspired with external forces to overthrow the community, contaminated their water supply causing multiple deaths, and planned her assassination along with anyone else who resisted. In the old world, such actions would constitute treason, terrorism, and multiple counts of murder.

In this new world, the response had to be swift and absolute.

"I'll handle Frank," she said quietly. "Tonight, after the council meeting. With just a few trusted deputies. Officially, we're bringing him in for questioning based on his men's statements."

"And unofficially?" Daniel asked, though his expression

suggested he already knew.

"Justice doesn't always arrive through formal channels anymore." Beth met his gaze steadily. "Frank made his choice when he poisoned our water and allied with Sherman. I won't risk more lives by giving him the opportunity to escape or signal his allies."

Daniel nodded slowly, the gravity of the decision acknowledged between them. "The council will support you. After they hear Dempsey's testimony, there won't be much debate."

"I'll send word once it's done." Beth rolled up the map, mind shifting to immediate practical considerations. "In the meantime, accelerate your farm defenses. Get the children and non-combatants into the storm cellar. Establish fallback positions."

"And Frank's men still at large in town?"

Beth considered this, weighing options and resources. "I'll have Jacob Mercer's people track them quietly. Not to engage, just to monitor. We can't risk tipping our hand too early."

The quiet acknowledgment of the vigilante group's utility marked a significant shift in Beth's position. A pragmatic concession to their new reality. Some principles remained worth defending; others had to adapt to ensure survival.

As they approached the town hall's exit, a commotion outside drew their attention. Maddie Foster was climbing the steps, supporting a young girl who looked ready to collapse. The stranger couldn't have been more than fourteen, her clothes torn and dirty, face gaunt with exhaustion. Angry red marks circled her wrists, and a darkening bruise spread across her left cheekbone. Her split lip had only recently stopped bleeding.

"Found her stumbling down Main Street," Maddie

explained breathlessly. "Says she escaped from Sherman's people early this morning."

Beth moved forward, helping support the girl's other side. "What's your name?"

"Zoe," the girl whispered, clutching what looked like a military map case to her chest. The waterproof canvas container was secured with multiple ties, clearly protecting something of vital importance. "My family and our group were ambushed shortly after dawn. Sherman's scouts took us all."

Beth noticed the girl's fingernails—two were missing completely. Torture marks. She'd seen enough in her career to recognize them.

"They questioned us. About who we'd talked to, if anyone knew about their plans." Zoe swallowed hard, her eyes darting between them with a mixture of wariness and desperate hope. "One of them... he separated me from the others. Said he had 'special questions' for me." Her voice faltered, the implication clear.

"My dad and the others, they fought back when they moved us. Created enough chaos that I could run. I don't know if they made it." Her voice broke. "One of the men came after me, but I remembered what my father taught me. Used his knife against him."

"You're safe now," Beth assured her, recognizing the haunted look of someone who'd been forced to kill to survive. "How did you find your way here?"

Zoe's expression shifted, uncertainty crossing her features. "We met some people yesterday. A girl and her brother. I think he was called Jack or Jake? Something like that. They said they were coming in this direction." She glanced around, her uneasiness amplifying.

"Yes, this is Cornish," Maddie confirmed, leaning closer. "This girl you met—what did she look like?"

"Dark hair. Older than me. Said she was a medical student," Zoe replied. "Had a rifle. Seemed to know what she was doing. They were traveling north, looking for someone. A friend, I think." She frowned, trying to recall. "Hannah. That was her name."

Maddie's face paled, her grip on Zoe tightening. "Hannah? You're sure?"

"Yes. Hannah." Zoe nodded weakly. "They went a separate way from us before the ambush. They were heading this way." Her fingers tightened around the map case. "Before we were attacked, my father found one of Sherman's scouts injured in the woods. We took these from him. Maps showing attack plans."

Beth exchanged a quick glance with Daniel. "These people you met—they didn't say where they were from?"

"South Portland, I think." Zoe winced as if the effort of remembering caused physical pain. "They seemed pretty skittish. Said bad things happened there."

Maddie's expression shifted through shock, hope, and urgent determination. "Hannah," she whispered, more to herself than anyone else. "It has to be her."

Daniel nodded in agreement. He was sure her brother's name was Jake. "Was there anyone else with them?"

"No just the two."

"The maps," Beth prompted gently, refocusing on the immediate threat. "What exactly do they show?"

"Attack plans. Positions. Supply caches." Zoe's voice weakened, her momentary strength waning. "That's why they...why they wanted them back so badly. Why they hurt me."

"Thursday at dawn," Beth said. "That's when they're planning to attack. We just confirmed it from another source."

The girl nodded weakly. "The maps show everything. That's why I came here. I didn't know where else to go when I escaped. Just remembered them talking about Cornish, about hitting it hard."

"You did the right thing," Daniel said, his voice gentle but urgent. "My father will want to see these maps immediately."

Beth made a quick decision. "I'll finish preparations here in town. Daniel, take Maddie and Zoe to the farm immediately, I'll be right behind you. Brief your father on everything from Dempsey's interview." She turned to Maddie, whose face still showed the shock of hearing about Hannah. "And Maddie—if it is your friend Hannah out there, we'll keep an eye out for her."

Maddie nodded, clearly struggling to process this unexpected connection while also supporting the exhausted girl.

Zoe swayed dangerously, her momentary strength flagging completely. "I don't know if I can—"

"You've done enough," Beth assured her, noticing how Zoe's hands trembled from the aftereffects of trauma and exhaustion. "More than enough. Let us take it from here."

As Daniel and Maddie helped Zoe toward the waiting vehicle, Beth couldn't help but admire the girl's resilience. To endure what she had, escape her would-be rapist, and still maintain the presence of mind to protect potentially life-saving intelligence—it showed extraordinary strength of character. Children like Zoe were adapting to this harsh new reality with a determination that both inspired and saddened Beth. No child should have to endure what Zoe clearly had, yet here she was, still fighting. Blood stained the floor. Bullet holes punctured walls that had stood intact since the building's construction in

1888. The mechanisms of democracy—however small and informal—had been attacked directly, deliberately.

But more importantly, their water had been targeted—first through contamination, now through attempted seizure of filtration technology. The most essential element of survival, weaponized against them by one of their own. She headed to give Jacob the green light before following the others up to the farm.

She still had to tell them what happened at the jail and wondered if she'd find herself in one of the cells too.

Maddie

The charcoal crumbled between Maddie's fingers, fine black powder sifting through to dust the hardware store's counter. Not right. Still not right. According to her father's notes, the activated carbon needed to maintain structural integrity while still being porous enough for water to pass through. This batch was either overcooked or ground too fine—the third failed attempt since dawn.

"Damn it," she muttered, wiping her blackened hands on a rag already stained from previous attempts. The leather-bound notebook lay open beside her, pages worn and smudged with her father's precise handwriting detailing a process she still couldn't quite master.

Maddie squinted at a diagram labeled "Carbon Activation Process" with arrows connecting hasty sketches of what looked like a metal drum with holes punched in specific patterns. Her father's shorthand notations crowded the margins: "500°C ideal. Limited O2 for partial combustion. 3-4 hrs minimum."

The words made sense individually. Strung together, they remained frustratingly opaque.

She flipped to the beginning of the notebook again, reading her father's inscription: *For Maddie, when she's ready to learn. Start with the basics.* The words twisted something in her chest—equal parts guilt and determination. He'd prepared this guide specifically for her, somehow knowing she'd eventually need these skills she'd dismissed throughout her childhood.

Sunlight angled through the hardware store's front windows, marking mid-afternoon. She'd been at this for nearly eight hours, breaking only to change out of clothes saturated with charcoal dust. Now she wore an old Cornish High t-shirt and canvas work pants found in the store's back room—employee attire from the before-times.

The camping lantern she'd set up cast additional light over her work area, illuminating her makeshift activation system: a steel drum salvaged from behind the auto shop, punched with air holes using an awl and hammer, filled with chunks of hardwood she'd charred in a controlled burn behind the store. The theory was simple enough—create charcoal, then "activate" it by reheating it in a limited-oxygen environment to increase its surface area and adsorption properties.

The execution was proving maddening.

A knock at the front door jolted her from concentration. Through the window, she recognized Emily Thompson's silhouette. Maddie's stomach immediately tightened. Emily had been monitoring her mother at the funeral home, checking in twice daily as Katherine Foster's condition continued to deteriorate.

Maddie rushed to unlock the door, smudging the knob with charcoal residue. "Is she—?"

"Stable for now," Emily said, stepping inside with her medical bag. Dark circles hung beneath her eyes, the toll of treating multiple patients with limited supplies evident in the new lines etched around her mouth. "But I wanted to give you an update in person."

The careful phrasing told Maddie everything. Not getting

better. Just not dead yet.

"How long?" she asked, the question scraping her throat raw.

Emily hesitated, then sighed. "Hours, maybe. Her kidneys are shutting down. The damage from the toxin is too extensive."

Maddie nodded mechanically, absorbing another blow in a series that had begun with finding her father dieing. "I should be there."

"You will be," Emily assured her, glancing at the charcoal-covered workspace. "But she'd want you doing exactly this. Creating something that might save others." She moved closer, examining the failed carbon batch. "May I?"

"Please. Maybe you can make sense of what I'm missing." Maddie stepped aside, watching as Emily studied the notebook diagrams.

"Hmm. Jessica mentioned you were working on water filters. How's it going?"

"Terribly," Maddie admitted. "I can make basic filters thoat remove sediment, but the activated carbon component keeps failing. We only had three bags of it and now I have to make it. The first one did not go well and I did make two functioning filters with the other two but you need to check the water to be sure it is pure. I'm trying to make more but either it dissolves or clumps or just... doesn't work. And without that, we can't effectively remove the chemical contaminants."

Emily traced her finger along one of David Foster's diagrams. "What temperatures are you reaching?"

"I don't know exactly. The thermometer from the garden section only goes to three hundred degrees."

"That might be your problem. For proper activation, you need much higher heat—closer to five hundred Celsius." Emily glanced around the store. "Do you have any ceramic materials? Kiln bricks, maybe? Something to contain and reflect heat?"

Maddie blinked. "In the masonry supply aisle. I've never—" She stopped, embarrassment flushing her cheeks. "I don't know what they look like."

Emily squeezed her shoulder gently. "It's okay not to know things, Maddie. None of us was prepared for this world. Let's look together."

They moved through the dimly lit aisles, Emily looking at the differences between various masonry products as they went. Checking each label to find something that could stand the heat.

"These firebricks," Emily said, hefting a dense rectangular brick from a lower shelf. "They're designed for fireplace construction, but they'll work for containing heat. We can build a small kiln structure around your drum."

Maddie ran her fingers over the brick's smooth surface. "My dad probably tried to show me these a dozen times. I never paid attention."

"You're paying attention now," Emily pointed out. "That's what matters."

They gathered materials—firebricks, fire cement, metal flashing for a chimney.

As they built the makeshift kiln in the store's back lot, Maddie found herself asking questions she would have dismissed as boring just months ago. Occasionally consulting the notebook when Maddie's father had noted specific details she wasn't sure about.

"He really thought of everything," Emily remarked, examining a detailed cross-section drawing of the activation chamber.

"And a father I didn't appreciate enough," Maddie added quietly, arranging bricks around the metal drum.

Emily paused, meeting Maddie's eyes directly. "You know, when Michael first joined the military, Ethan was only three. For years, he built this idealized image of his father—the hero overseas. When Michael finally came home for good, Ethan was shocked to discover his dad was just a man with flaws, bad moods, and ordinary problems."

"What's your point?" Maddie asked, more sharply than intended.

"Just that we all mythologize what we've lost. Your father wasn't perfect, Maddie. He was wonderful and brilliant, yes, but also stubborn and occasionally overbearing. I remember when he argued with the town council for three straight meetings about the new traffic pattern on Main Street."

A reluctant smile tugged at Maddie's lips. "He said they'd created a 'nightmare of circular logic' and wouldn't stop bringing diagrams to prove it."

"Exactly. The point is, don't burden yourself with guilt over the relationship you had. It was real, imperfect, and entirely normal." Emily helped her position the final bricks. "What you're doing now—that's how you honor him."

The structure they'd created looked surprisingly professional—a square enclosure of firebricks with a small door at the bottom for feeding the fire and a metal chimney rising from the top to vent smoke away from the activation chamber.

"How long will it take?" Maddie asked, stepping back to observe their creation.

"Several hours to reach temperature, then another three or four for proper activation. But let's get a batch started now."

They filled the drum with fresh charcoal pieces, sealed it

with the punched metal lid, and positioned it within the kiln.

As they finished setting it up, Emily checked her watch and frowned. "I should get back to the funeral home. Will you be okay managing this? It needs monitoring, but it doesn't look like it is too complicated once you get the rhythm."

Reality crashed back into Maddie's consciousness. For a brief period, the technical challenge had provided escape. Now her mother's condition reclaimed center stage in her thoughts.

"I'll come with you," she said, already reaching for her jacket.

Emily shook her head. "This needs supervision for the first hour to make sure the temperature stabilizes correctly. After that, you can come to the funeral home." She squeezed Maddie's arm. "Trust me, this is important too. Your mother understands that."

After Emily left, Maddie settled onto an overturned plastic bucket to monitor the kiln, feeding small pieces of wood into the fire chamber at regular intervals. The flames created shifting patterns of light against the brick walls, hypnotic in their dance. Her father's notebook lay open on her lap, his meticulous instructions guiding each adjustment.

The rhythmic work allowed her mind to wander despite her best efforts to stay focused on the technical challenge. Her mother's face swam before her. Not the hollow-cheeked, jaundiced version currently fighting for each breath in the funeral home, but the vibrant woman who had taught third grade for twenty-seven years, who baked perfect chocolate chip cookies every Sunday, who had encouraged Maddie to pursue business school despite David's hopes she would take over the hardware store.

"I'm trying, Mom," she whispered to the flames. "I'm

figuring it out now."

Two hours passed, marked by the gradual change in the kiln's color from black to dull red to the faint orange described in the journal. Maddie maintained the fire, referring constantly to her father's notes, making adjustments based on his guidance. The technical language began to make more sense as she connected theory to practical observation. Words like "thermal decomposition" and "micropore structure" transformed from abstract concepts to meaningful descriptors of what she was witnessing.

When the kiln reached stable temperature, Maddie secured it for the activation phase and hurried toward the funeral home, anticipation and dread forming a leaden weight in her stomach. The sun, high in the sky beat down on Cornish's main street, creating ripples in the air from the pavement. Few people moved about in the heat, staying indoors out of the sun, a new habit formed since the collapse.

Emily met her at the entrance, expression grave. "She's asking for you. Her lucid periods are becoming more scattered, but she's clear right now."

Maddie sat next to her mother, who offered a small smile when she took her hand. "Maddison," she said before a coughing fit interrupted her, flecks of blood appearing on her lips.

Emily moved quickly to elevate Katherine's head, offering a cloth to wipe her mouth. Maddie clutched her mother's hand tighter, terror gripping her chest as the coughing continued.

When it finally subsided, Katherine's voice came weaker but determined. "The store. Make it your home. Your place." Her eyes held Maddie's with surprising intensity. "You are your father's daughter. Carry on for him."

"I will," Maddie promised, understanding dawning. Her mother wasn't just making practical suggestions—she was passing a torch, giving permission for Maddie to fully step into her father's role. "I've started taking notes on everything I learn."

Katherine nodded slightly, satisfaction flickering across her face. "Good girl." Her gaze grew unfocused again, drifting toward the ceiling. "It's getting dark."

"I can light another lamp," Maddie offered quickly, but her mother was already shaking her head.

"No need. Your father has one." Katherine's lips curved in a smile more peaceful than any expression Maddie had seen since finding her parents ill. "He's waiting. Always... so impatient."

Emily placed two fingers against Katherine's neck, checking her pulse with practiced movements. Her expression remained professional, but Maddie caught the flicker of confirmation in her eyes. Not long now.

"I'm not ready," Maddie whispered, the words escaping before she could stop them. "Mom, please. I still need you."

Katherine's focus returned briefly, her fingers tightening around Maddie's with surprising strength. "You're ready. Always were." Her voice faded to barely audible. "So proud... of the woman you've become."

The words pierced Maddie's heart. How could her mother be proud when she'd wasted so much time, ignored so many opportunities to learn from her father, to prepare for this world they now inhabit?

"I've made so many mistakes," she confessed, tears flowing freely now.

"That's... how we learn," Katherine murmured. Her

breathing grew more labored, each inhalation a visible struggle. "Promise me… you'll keep learning."

"I promise," Maddie said fervently. "Every day."

Katherine's eyes closed, exhaustion claiming her. Emily checked her pulse again, face somber.

"It won't be long now," she said softly. "Would you like some privacy?"

Maddie nodded, unable to form words past the ache in her throat. Emily checked the IV one last time—now delivering only morphine for comfort—before slipping quietly from the room.

Alone with her mother, Maddie held Katherine's hand between both of hers, memorizing the feel of it—the calluses from years of gardening, the small scar on her thumb from a childhood accident, the shape of nails always kept practical and short for classroom work. Hands that had guided her through life, now growing cooler by the minute.

"I don't know how to do this without you," Maddie whispered. "Without either of you."

Katherine didn't respond, her breathing growing more shallow with each passing minute.

Maddie talked anyway, words spilling out as if she could anchor her mother to this world through sheer force of communication.

"I moved some things into the store, like you suggested. Set up a cot in Dad's office. Found his old camping stove in the outdoor section. Jessica helped me understand the filtration systems better. I'm going to get it right, Mom. I'm going to make the filters work."

The one-sided conversation continued as dusk fell completely outside. Maddie lit a small oil lamp, its glow casting soft shadows across her mother's face. She told Katherine about the kiln they'd built, about the modifications she planned for the next filtration prototype, about the journal she'd started to document everything she learned.

Katherine's breathing had become almost imperceptible, the rise and fall of her chest barely visible. Maddie ignored it, continuing her gentle monologue, offering what comfort she could through familiar sounds and touch.

"Remember when I was seven and Dad tried to teach me how to fix the leaky faucet in the bathroom? I got frustrated and flooded the entire floor. You weren't even mad, you just handed me more towels and said, 'Now you know one way that doesn't work.'"

A smile ghosted across Maddie's lips at the memory.

"That's what I'm doing now, Mom. Finding all the ways that don't work, so eventually I'll find the one that does."

Katherine's breathing had become almost imperceptible, the rise and fall of her chest barely visible. Maddie squeezed her mother's hand, leaning closer.

"It's okay, Mom. You can go to Dad now. I'll be okay."

Whether her mother heard or simply reached the end of her strength, Maddie couldn't know. But moments later, Katherine Foster drew a final, shallow breath and released it slowly. The hand in Maddie's went slack, the last tension leaving her mother's body.

Maddie sat motionless, still holding the hand that no longer held back. The world narrowed to this single point of devastation—she was now entirely alone. No parents. No family. Just herself in a broken world that demanded skills she was still struggling to master.

Emily returned, quietly checking for vital signs before

gently closing Katherine's eyes.

"Time of death, 8:47 PM," she said quietly, habit more than necessity. She rested a hand on Maddie's shoulder. "I'm so sorry, Maddie."

The familiar words—the same ones Emily had spoken when David Foster died—caused something to crack inside Maddie's chest. A sob escaped, then another, until she was weeping openly, body bent over her mother's still form.

Emily remained beside her, silent support in the face of inconsolable grief. When the most intense waves had passed, leaving Maddie hollow and exhausted, Emily spoke again.

"We need to make arrangements. With the water contamination still active, we can't delay."

The brutal practicality of death in their new world struck Maddie anew. No formal services. No luxury of extended grieving. Bodies needed to be handled quickly to prevent further illness.

"I understand," she managed, voice raw. "What are the options?"

"Burial in the new cemetery by the north woods, or cremation." Emily's tone remained gentle but direct. "Given the contamination concerns, most families are choosing cremation."

Maddie nodded, the decision simple despite its finality. "Cremation, then. Dad too, if he hasn't already been..." She couldn't complete the sentence.

"He's been preserved," Emily assured her. "We were waiting for your mother's..."

"For her to die too," Maddie finished flatly.

In the silence that followed, a knock came at the office

door. Emily answered it, speaking briefly with someone in the hallway before turning back to Maddie.

"Robbie Burns is here. Says he has information you should know." She hesitated. "It can wait if you need more time."

Maddie was about to refuse any interruption to her grieving when she recalled her mother's final request: *Document everything for those who come after.* Her grief wouldn't change anything. Information might save lives.

"I'll speak with him," she decided, wiping her face with her sleeve. "Give me a minute?"

Emily nodded and stepped out, leaving Maddie alone for a final moment with her mother. She bent and pressed a kiss to Katherine's cooling forehead.

"I'll make you both proud," she whispered. "I promise."

When Maddie emerged from the office, she found Robbie Burns waiting in the hallway, his expression grim. The deputy's normally clean-shaven face showed several days' growth, and a fresh bandage wrapped his forearm.

"Maddie," he acknowledged, awkwardness evident in his stance. "Emily told me about your mother. I'm sorry to intrude at such a time."

"It's fine," she said, the words automatic rather than truthful. "Emily said you have information."

Robbie glanced around, then lowered his voice. "Can we speak somewhere private?"

They moved to an empty treatment room, formerly a smaller viewing parlor judging by the ornate molding still visible around the ceiling. Robbie closed the door before turning to face her.

"Two fishing boats came into Casco Bay yesterday," he

began without preamble. "The crews were nearly dead from dehydration, exposure, multiple injuries. Beth had me interview them since I used to work the coast before joining the department."

Maddie struggled to focus, grief making it difficult to track the relevance. "And?"

"They reported organized attacks along the coast. Not just opportunistic raiders—something structured, brutal." Robbie's expression darkened. "The pattern matches what we've been hearing from refugees coming inland. A group hitting coastal communities, taking supplies, people…"

A cold dread settled in Maddie's stomach. "People?"

"Women, mostly. Children sometimes. The ones with useful skills. I couldn't help thinking about Zoe up at the Thompson Farm." Robbie hesitated. "And your friend Hannah. The fishermen described the raids as methodical—not random violence. Said these coastal raiders have a leader who's calculated, strategic."

"Did they say who?" Maddie asked, something uneasy stirring in her memory.

"No names. Just that it's someone who clearly plans ahead." Robbie studied her face. "The fishermen said these raiders contaminate water supplies first, before attacking. Familiar pattern, isn't it?"

The parallel to Sherman's tactics with Cornish sent a chill through Maddie's body. "They're coming here? I thought it was Sherman."

"Eventually, from what we can piece together. But inland, following rivers. Saco River feeds right through Cornish."

The information landed with crushing weight atop her grief. Another threat, another reason why her water filtration work couldn't wait, why every hour spent mourning was an hour lost in preparation. More than that Hannah was on the river last Zoe said.

"Thank you for telling me," she said, rising from the chair with new resolve hardening within her chest. "I need to get back to the hardware store. The activated carbon should be ready soon."

Robbie looked startled by her response. "Maddie, your mother just died. No one expects you to—"

"My mother expected me to," she interrupted firmly. "And whether these coastal raiders are coming or not, people are still dying from contaminated water. My filters might be the difference between survival and more funerals."

She moved past him toward the door, the crushing weight of grief momentarily transformed into purposeful energy. Later, alone, she would collapse under her loss. Now, she had work to do.

"At least let me walk you back to the store," Robbie offered, following her. "It's fully dark now."

Maddie nodded acceptance of his escort, mind already racing ahead to the next steps in the filtration process. The activated carbon would need proper cooling before handling. She tried to focus on it but her thoughts kept drifting back to Hannah.

As they stepped outside into the cool night air, Maddie looked up at the star-filled sky—one of the few improvements in this broken world, the absence of light pollution revealing celestial wonders previously hidden. Somewhere in that vastness, she wanted to believe her parents were together again, watching her figure out, step by stumbling step, how to save what remained of their community.

She squared her shoulders and set off toward the hardware store, toward the kiln that held the key component for more filter, toward the future her parents had tried to prepare her for—a future she was only now learning to navigate without them.

Hannah

Hannah woke to the sound of birds calling in the predawn darkness, their voices carrying across the still water. River fog clung to the Saco's surface, transforming the waterway into something ghostly and ethereal. She'd slept fitfully in the canoe, her body wedged uncomfortably between the wooden thwart and the supply packs, one arm draped protectively over Jake's sleeping form.

They'd made good progress yesterday after leaving Manuel and Neil's group, covering nearly all of the river miles before exhaustion forced them to make camp on a small island in the river's center. The natural defensibility of the location—water on all sides, clear sight lines—had allowed Hannah a few precious hours of rest, though her dreams had been haunted by images of her parents disappearing into darkness.

Hannah eased herself upright, careful not to disturb Jake. Her brother needed every minute of sleep he could get; the strain of the past days had hollowed his cheeks and darkened the skin beneath his eyes. At fourteen, he should have been worrying about school assignments and soccer practice, not how to navigate hostile territory while evading armed pursuers.

The eastern sky had begun to lighten, turning the river fog into a luminous white blanket. Hannah stretched carefully, cataloging the aches in her body—shoulders burning from hours of paddling, hands raw with fresh blisters, legs cramped from confinement in the narrow canoe. She ignored the discomfort, focusing instead on the day ahead.

According to Marcus's map, they had another stretch of river travel before reaching the landing point closest to Cornish. From there, they would need to travel overland for approximately three miles to reach the town. If their pace held and the weather remained clear, they might arrive by evening— barely in time to warn the community about Sherman's planned attack.

Hannah pulled her journal from the waterproof pack, recording their position and observations as she had each morning since their escape. The simple act of documentation grounded her, transformed the chaos of their situation into something quantifiable, manageable. Details mattered. Information kept people alive.

Day 4 post-escape. Position: Small island approximately 15 miles upriver from Marcus's camp. Est. 2-3 miles from Cornish landing point. Jake stable but exhaustion evident. Food supplies adequate (5 days at current consumption). Water purification tablets running low (3 days max).

Note: No signs of pursuit on river yet. Sherman's forces seem focused on road corridors. Maintain water route as long as feasible.

She closed the journal, tucking it carefully back into the pack. The map followed, its waterproof coating crinkling as she traced their route with a fingertip. They would need to navigate a series of small rapids today, followed by a portage around an old dam. Marcus had marked the best approach, but Hannah knew maps could only prepare them so much. Reality rarely matched paper representations.

Jake stirred, his eyes opening with the immediate alertness that had become second nature to them both. No gradual waking, no slow transition from sleep to consciousness. His gaze swept their surroundings, assessing threats before his body had fully awakened.

"Time to move?" he asked, voice rough with sleep.

Hannah nodded. "Dawn soon. Better to clear the island while visibility is still limited."

They worked in practiced silence, packing their minimal camp, checking the canoe for any damage, distributing weight for optimal balance. No fire had been lit overnight—too risky—so breakfast consisted of jerky and dried fruit from their rations, washed down with carefully measured sips of water.

As Hannah secured the last pack, a sound froze her in place—branches breaking on the nearby shore, the unmistakable rustle of movement through underbrush. She dropped into a crouch, pulling Jake down beside her, eyes straining to penetrate the misty half-light.

"Multiple people," Jake whispered, his hearing sharper than hers. "Coming fast. Not trying to be quiet."

Hannah's hand moved to the rifle slung across her back, unslinging it with practiced movements. "Get in the canoe," she ordered quietly. "Be ready to push off."

"I'm not leaving you," Jake protested, though he moved toward the craft as instructed.

"Not asking you to. Just be ready."

The sounds grew louder—definitely multiple people moving with urgency rather than stealth. Either completely untrained or desperate. Hannah positioned herself behind a fallen log, rifle ready but not yet aimed. Shooting would be a last resort; the sound would carry for miles across the water.

Through gaps in the morning mist, shapes emerged on the shore—human figures moving in a ragged line along the riverbank. Four, no, five people, their outlines blurring in the fog. One appeared to be limping, supported by a companion. Their movements suggested flight rather than pursuit.

Hannah remained motionless, watching as the group reached the narrow stretch of water separating the island from shore. The lead figure—a man with what looked like a hunting rifle slung across his back—spotted the island and gestured urgently to the others. The group huddled briefly, then began wading into the shallow water, heading directly toward Hannah's position.

"Hello?" a voice called, pitched low but carrying across the water. "Is someone there? We saw movement."

The voice sounded familiar, though Hannah couldn't immediately place it. She remained silent, evaluating options. If these were Sherman's people setting a trap, announcing her position would be suicide. But if they were refugees like themselves…

"Please," the voice continued, desperation edging the words. "We're not armed. Well, not much. We're running from—"

"Neil?" Hannah said suddenly, recognition clicking into place. "Neil from Deering?"

The figures froze midway across the shallow crossing. Then the lead man pushed back his hood, revealing the weathered face Hannah had spoken with just days ago.

"Hannah? Christ, is that you?"

Relief and wariness warred within her chest. She straightened slightly but kept the rifle ready. "What are you doing here? You were headed northwest to North Conway."

"Plans changed," Neil said grimly as his group continued wading toward the island. "Mind if we come ashore? Zoe's been taken and Manuel is hurt. We've been moving all night."

Hannah hesitated only briefly before nodding. "Come ahead. Slowly."

As the group emerged fully from the mist, Hannah recognized them as the survivors she and Jake had encountered after escaping South Portland—Neil and his wife Carla, their neighbors Manuel, Violet, and Lonny. They looked significantly worse than when she'd last seen them—clothes torn and muddy, faces haggard with exhaustion and fear. Manuel's left arm was wrapped in what appeared to be a makeshift bandage, dark stains seeping through the fabric.

"What happened?" Hannah asked as they staggered onto shore, lowering themselves onto logs and rocks with evident relief.

"Ran into a patrol yesterday afternoon," Neil explained, helping Carla settle Manuel against a tree trunk. "About ten miles northwest of where we met you. Six armed men— organized, well-equipped. They ambushed us while we were resting."

"Sherman's men?" Jake asked, moving to Hannah's side.

Neil exchanged glances with Marcus, something unspoken passing between them. "Not exactly. Or at least, not like the ones we'd encountered before." He rubbed a hand across his face, leaving streaks in the grime. "They had different markings. And they were following orders from someone new."

"Someone they called 'The Queen,'" Manuel added, his deep voice tight with controlled anger. "Kept referring to collecting 'subjects' for her."

Hannah's stomach clenched. "They took people?"

"They took Zoe," Carla said quietly, a sob breaking in her throat.

Neil's expression hardened. "I did what I had to do. One of them won't be taking anyone else but they sped up route 25 and we're following."

The implication was clear. Violence met with violence—the new currency of their world.

"Manuel's wound?" Hannah asked, medical training automatically assessing the visible injury.

"Knife. One of them grabbed him when we tried to run. Cut him before I could—" Neil stopped, swallowing hard. "It's deep, but we controlled the bleeding. He needs antibiotics, proper medical care."

Hannah moved to his side, kneeling to examine the bandage. "May I?"

He nodded, face pale beneath streaks of dirt and dried blood in the corner of his mouth. Hannah gently unwrapped the bandage, revealing a six-inch gash along the man's forearm. The wound had been crudely cleaned and bound, but inflammation was already evident around the edges. Without antibiotics, infection was inevitable.

"I have some antiseptic wipes in my kit," Hannah said, trying to keep her voice matter-of-fact. "And a better bandage. But he needs more than I can provide."

"That's why we changed course," Neil explained. "Manuel remembered you were heading this way. Said there might be medical help where you were going."

Hannah rewrapped the wound with fresh gauze from her medical kit, securing it with the last of her medical tape.

"Emily, Daniel's sister, is a trained nurse. They were going to Cornish. That's were they are." she told them as she worked.

"That's all I know. I don't even know if they made it back."

"If it's still there," Lonny said, his voice hollow with exhaustion and grief. The man had barely spoken since their arrival, his eyes fixed on the middle distance, seeing something none of the rest could. "If this 'Queen' hasn't taken it too."

Hannah glanced at him sharply. "What exactly did you hear about Cornish?"

Neil and Manuel exchanged another look before Manuel spoke. "They were talking while they searched our packs. Not bothering to keep their voices down. One of them said Sherman's forces had 'bent the knee' to the Queen already. That she was—" he paused, searching for the exact words, "—'consolidating her territory before moving inland.'"

"They specifically mentioned Thursday," Jen added. "Said the Cornish operation was still scheduled for dawn Thursday, but under new command."

Jake moved closer to Hannah, alarm evident in his expression. "That's the same timeline. Sherman's attack is still happening, just with this new leader?"

Hannah nodded grimly. "Sounds that way." She turned back to Neil. "Did they say anything else about this 'Queen'? Who she is? Where she came from?"

"Not much," Neil admitted. "Just that she'd appeared on the coast about three weeks ago with a small but heavily armed group. Took control of fishing villages first, then moved inland. Absorbed Sherman's operation somehow." He shook his head. "They seemed almost afraid when they talked about her. One of them said she 'makes examples' of people who fail her."

The description sent a chill down Hannah's spine. Not just another opportunistic raider, but someone with strategy, with vision. Someone who was building something amid the collapse.

"They're collecting people with skills," Carla said quietly. "That's why they took Amelia and Sara. Amelia was a nurse. Sara's only twelve, but she's smart, adaptable. That's why they wanted Zoe too. Young, trainable."

Hannah processed this information, the implications twisting in her gut. Sherman had been dangerous enough—ex-military, organized, ruthless. This new leader taking control of his operation suggested someone even more formidable.

"We need to move," she decided, rising to her feet. "If the attack timeline is still Thursday dawn, we have less than two days to reach Cornish and warn them."

"The canoe won't hold all of us," Jake pointed out.

"We'll travel together along the riverbank," Hannah said. "Faster than you could manage on your own," she added, noting Neil's skeptical expression. "Jake and I know the route, and the canoe can carry supplies when the terrain allows, or we can just hide it somewhere and go on foot."

Neil hesitated, then nodded agreement. "We don't have better options. And strength in numbers might help if we encounter another patrol."

They redistributed supplies, and the expanded group moved out as the sun finally breached the horizon, burning off the river fog and revealing a landscape of stunning beauty that belied the dangers it contained. Jake and Hannah took the lead, with Neil and Manuel flanking the group and the others in between. Carla walked in the middle keeping eyes on either side of them with Violet,

As they walked, Hannah extracted more details about their encounter with the patrol. The attack had been precise, coordinated—not random violence but a specific operation with clear objectives. The patrol had sorted through captives based on apparent criteria with one man taking undue interest in Zoe.

"They had a list," Marcus revealed as they paused to navigate a fallen tree blocking the path. "Actually, checked names against it. Like they knew exactly who they might encounter out here."

"Hunting us," Lonny said bitterly. "Like animals."

No one disputed his assessment.

The morning wore on, the group making steady if slower progress than Hannah had hoped. By midday, dark clouds had gathered on the horizon, promising afternoon rain. They reached the first set of rapids just as thunder rumbled in the distance.

"We need to portage here," Hannah announced, studying the churning water with a critical eye.

"There's a sheltered area just past the rapids," Neil said, consulting the map Hannah had shared. "Old campsite, according to these markings. We could wait out the worst of the storm there."

Hannah weighed the options, calculating risks against necessity. Stopping meant lost time, but pushing through a thunderstorm carried its own dangers. Rain-slicked rocks, poor visibility, lightning strikes—all potentially deadly.

"One hour," she decided. "Just until the lightning passes."

The campsite proved to be a slight hollow beneath an overhanging rock face, offering reasonable protection from the intensifying rainfall. They crowded beneath it, using an outstretched tarp as additional shelter. Manuel's condition had worsened, fever flushing his cheeks while he shivered beneath a thin emergency blanket.

"He needs those antibiotics sooner rather than later," Carla said quietly to Hannah, fear evident in her voice.

Hannah nodded, the weight of responsibility settling heavier on her shoulders. Every hour of delay diminished his chances—and potentially the chances of everyone in Cornish who remained unaware of the approaching threat.

As the rain hammered down outside their shelter, conversation turned inevitably to what awaited them at their destination.

"What kind of defenses does Cornish have?" Manuel asked. "If this Queen is taking over Sherman's operation, they'll be facing a significant force."

Hannah hesitated. She had never been to Cornish and her information came primarily from Maddie's occasional comments about home and what she'd overheard from Sherman's men.

"I don't know much about Cornish's defenses," she admitted. "I only know my friend Maddie was heading there after we separated in Portsmouth. She mentioned it at school.

"And this friend of yours—Maddie—she'll vouch for us?" Violet asked, huddled close to Manuel for warmth.

"If she's still alive," Hannah said, the possibility sending a fresh wave of anxiety through her chest. She hadn't allowed herself to dwell on it, but the reality remained stark: she had no confirmation that Maddie had ever reached Cornish safely. "But even if—" she caught herself. "When we find her, the community will need to be convinced quickly. We'll have less than a day to prepare once we arrive."

"Prepare how?" Lonny asked, breaking his long silence. "Run? Fight? Against this 'Queen' who's apparently powerful enough to make Sherman bow down?" Bitterness edged his words, the loss of his family corroding hope.

"We give them information," Hannah said firmly. "Attack vectors, force strength, timeline. Knowledge is power." She believed this with the conviction—that understanding threats was the first step toward countering them.

"And if they don't believe us?" Lonny pressed. "If they think we're just spreading panic?"

Neil answered before Hannah could. "Then we do what we've all been doing since this started. We adapt. Survive. Find another way."

The simple determination in his voice silenced further argument. They had come too far, sacrificed too much, to surrender to despair now and they needed help to find Zoe.

The storm passed as quickly as it had arrived, summer thunderheads rolling eastward toward the coast. They emerged from their shelter to find the river swollen with rainwater, its current stronger and more treacherous.

Neil and Lonny propped Manuel up between them, following the river path that wound through increasingly dense forest.

By mid-afternoon, Hannah estimated they had covered perhaps three miles since morning and they should be reaching the point where they would change direction into town. The terrain had begun to change, forest giving way occasionally to clearings where abandoned farms stood silent testimony to the world before collapse. They avoided these open spaces when possible, keeping to tree cover, but Hannah noted potential resources for future reference.

As evening approached, fatigue began taking a serious toll. Muscles accustomed to regular exertion were pushed beyond endurance, and even Neil—the strongest among them—showed signs of flagging. They needed rest, real rest, not just a brief pause beneath a storm shelter.

"There's a hunting cabin marked on the map about a mile ahead," Hannah said, checking their position against landmarks. "We'll stop there for the night."

Relief visibly washed over the group. Neil and Carla scouted ahead while the others continued at a slower pace, Manuel struggling with each step as Lonny and Jake tried to steady him. Without antibiotics, the infection would continue spreading, potentially becoming systemic. They needed to reach Cornish by tomorrow evening at the latest.

The hunting cabin proved to be little more than a three-sided shelter with a partially collapsed roof, but it offered better protection than they'd had in days. They arranged their meager bedding, established a watch rotation, and rationed the remaining food supplies.

"We should reach Cornish by mid-afternoon tomorrow if we push hard," Hannah told the group as they huddled around a tiny, carefully shielded fire—their first hot meal since the escape.

"What's our approach strategy?" Neil asked, "We can't just wander into an unfamiliar community, not with Sherman's people potentially watching."

Hannah had been considering this problem throughout the day. "Maddie mentioned a creek that runs near Cornish in her letters before all this happened. If we can find that waterway, we might approach from a less monitored direction."

"And if we're spotted before we reach friendly territory?" Neil pressed.

Hannah met his gaze steadily. "We'll send Jake ahead with the core information. He's fast, knows how to move unseen. The rest of us will create a diversion if necessary."

Jake straightened, surprise and determination warring on his young face. "I can do it," he said, though his voice betrayed uncertainty.

"Let's hope it doesn't come to that," Carla said, casting a worried glance at him. "We need to stay together if possible."

Night fell fully, stars emerging in brilliant clarity through breaks in the forest canopy. Hannah took first watch, positioning herself at the cabin's open side where she could observe the approach trail and the river beyond. The others fell into exhausted sleep almost immediately, the day's exertions claiming even the most vigilant among them.

Alone with her thoughts, Hannah found her mind returning to the fragments of information about this new threat—the "Queen" who had somehow subjugated Sherman's forces and was now extending her control northward. The methodical collection of skilled individuals, particularly women and adaptable children. The apparent fear she inspired even in hardened fighters.

Hannah pulled her journal from her pack, recording these details by the fire's dying light. Information kept people alive. Understanding threats was the first step toward countering them. Her father's principles, applied to a world he hadn't survived to see.

Something rustled in the undergrowth beyond the cabin's perimeter. Hannah froze, pen poised above paper, every sense suddenly alert. The sound came again—deliberate movement, not the random stirrings of nocturnal wildlife.

She set the journal aside silently, reaching for the rifle that never left her side. Whoever—or whatever—approached was taking no care to disguise their presence. Either supremely confident or untrained.

Hannah eased to her feet, moving to position herself between the approaching sound and the sleeping forms of her companions. The darkness beyond the cabin's opening seemed absolute, the forest swallowing even starlight. She strained to pinpoint the direction of movement, finger resting lightly against the rifle's trigger guard.

A figure emerged suddenly from the tree line, stumbling rather than walking, clearly at the limits of endurance. Female, from the silhouette. Alone and unarmed, or at least not visibly carrying weapons.

The woman took two more faltering steps toward the cabin before her legs buckled. She collapsed to her knees, then pitched forward onto the damp earth of the clearing.

Hannah maintained her position, rifle ready, watching for others who might be using this apparent victim as bait for an ambush. When no further movement came from the forest, she advanced cautiously toward the fallen figure, keeping low and using available cover.

The woman lay face-down, her clothing torn and muddied, hair matted with what appeared to be dried blood. Hannah approached from an angle, rifle trained on the motionless form, ready for any sudden movement. When none came, she reached out cautiously with her boot, nudging the woman's shoulder.

No response.

Hannah kneeled, keeping the rifle ready with one hand while checking for a pulse with the other. Beneath her fingertips, a heartbeat fluttered—rapid but present. Still alive, then.

She rolled the woman onto her back, needing to assess injuries and determine threat level. The face that appeared in the faint starlight stopped Hannah's breath in her throat, recognition hitting her with physical force.

"Oh my God," she whispered, rifle lowering unconsciously. "Mrs. Henderson?"

It was indeed Julia Henderson—her neighbor from South Portland whose screams Hannah had heard during their escape, whom Sherman's men had taken while Hannah and her family fled into the night. The woman was nearly unrecognizable—face gaunt with exhaustion and streaked with dirt and blood, clothes hanging in tatters from her thin frame. But the delicate gold cross still hanging from her neck confirmed her identity beyond doubt.

"Jake," Hannah called softly over her shoulder, not taking her eyes from Mrs. Henderson's unconscious form. "Jake, wake up."

Her brother appeared at her side moments later, sleep forgotten as he registered the situation. His sharp intake of breath confirmed he recognized their neighbor as well.

"Is she—?"

"Alive," Hannah confirmed. "Help me get her inside."

Together, they carefully lifted the unconscious woman, carrying her into the relative shelter of the cabin. The movement woke Neil, who reached instinctively for his weapon before recognizing Hannah.

"Found her at the perimeter," Hannah explained quickly as they settled Mrs. Henderson onto an empty bedroll. "She's one of our neighbors from South Portland. Taken by Sherman's men during the attack."

Neil was immediately alert, moving to secure the cabin's entrance. "Could be pursued," he said, voicing Hannah's own concern.

"Or escaped," she countered, already checking the woman

for injuries. "She will have information we need."

Mrs. Henderson's physical condition told a grim story. Bruises in various stages of healing marked her arms and neck. Her wrists bore raw abrasions from restraints. A poorly treated gash ran along her hairline, explaining the matted blood. Most concerning was her severely dehydrated state, skin tenting when Hannah pinched it between her fingers.

"Water," Hannah instructed Jake. "Just a few drops at first. We don't want to shock her system."

As Jake complied, the others gradually woke, the quiet activity impossible to ignore in the confined space. Carla immediately moved to assist, her maternal instincts overriding caution.

"Who is she?" she asked softly, helping Hannah elevate Mrs. Henderson's feet to improve blood flow.

"Julia Henderson. Lived three houses down from us in South Portland. Elementary school teacher." Hannah didn't elaborate on the circumstances of their last encounter—the woman's screams as Sherman's men dragged her from her home still haunted Hannah's dreams.

Mrs. Henderson stirred as drops of water touched her cracked lips, eyelids fluttering. Hannah motioned for everyone to give her space, knowing the disorientation that would accompany consciousness.

"Mrs. Henderson? Julia? It's Hannah Mitchell. You're safe now."

The woman's eyes opened fully, confusion giving way to recognition and then immediate terror. She thrashed weakly, trying to push herself away from the perceived threat.

"No! Don't take me back!" Her voice was a harsh rasp, damaged from dehydration or screaming—or both.

"You're safe," Hannah repeated firmly, not touching her but maintaining eye contact. "Sherman's men aren't here. You're with friends."

Mrs. Henderson's panicked gaze darted around the cabin, taking in the unfamiliar faces before settling back on Hannah. "Mitchell," she whispered. "Rebecca's daughter?"

Hannah nodded, relief flooding her chest. The woman's cognitive functions seemed intact despite her ordeal. "Yes. My brother Jake is here too. We escaped during the attack. We thought you were—" She stopped herself. "We didn't know what happened to you."

Mrs. Henderson's eyes filled with tears. "They took so many of us. Separated us. The men—some were killed immediately. Some were kept for labor. Women were sorted, like cattle at auction." Her voice broke on the last word.

"Here," Hannah offered more water, which Mrs. Henderson accepted gratefully. "Small sips. Then rest. You don't have to talk now."

"I do," the woman insisted, struggling to sit up despite her evident weakness. "There's no time. They'll be looking for me. She'll want me back."

"She?" Hannah asked, the pronoun catching her attention immediately.

Mrs. Henderson's expression changed, something beyond fear darkening her features. "The one they call the Queen." A shudder ran through her body. "She's—there's something wrong with her. The way she talks, the things she does. Like it's all some kind of game to her."

Hannah exchanged glances with Neil, the confirmation of the "Queen's" existence sending a cold wave through the group. Manuel and Lonny moved closer, eager to hear more details about the force that had taken their family members.

"What's her real name?" Hannah asked gently. "Where did she come from?"

Mrs. Henderson shook her head. "No one uses her real name. Just 'the Queen' or 'Her Majesty' when addressing her directly.

"Something else. The men who guarded me said she knew things she couldn't possibly know. About Sherman. About his men. Their pasts, their secrets." Another shudder ran through her. "They said she broke him in an hour. Just talking."

Hannah felt the hairs rise on the back of her neck. This description matched nothing in her experience since the collapse. Most power shifts had been brutally straightforward— superior firepower, better organization, more resources. What Mrs. Henderson described suggested something more insidious.

"How did you escape?" Neil asked, voicing the question Hannah had been considering.

Mrs. Henderson's eyes darted to the cabin entrance, as if expecting pursuers to materialize at any moment. "Transport vehicle broke down about five miles south of here. They were moving a group of us north. To Cornish. For the operation."

"Thursday's attack," Hannah confirmed.

The woman nodded. "During the confusion, I managed to slip away. Had to hide in a drainage culvert for hours until they moved on."

Jake returned with more water and a few strips of dried meat from their rations. Mrs. Henderson accepted both gr

"We need to move at first light," Hannah decided, the urgency of their mission intensifying with each new detail. "Mrs. Henderson needs medical attention, and we have to warn Cornish."

Neil nodded agreement. "I'll take first watch for the remainder of the night. Everyone else should rest while they can. Tomorrow will test us all."

As the group settled back into uneasy sleep, Hannah remained beside Mrs. Henderson, monitoring her condition and recording every detail of her account in the journal. The woman drifted between consciousness and exhausted slumber, occasionally murmuring fragments that revealed more about her ordeal and captors.

"She talks to herself," Mrs. Henderson whispered during one lucid moment. "To people who aren't there."

"The Queen?" Hannah clarified, pen poised above paper.

Mrs. Henderson nodded weakly. "Sometimes laughs at nothing." Her eyes, fever-bright in the darkness, fixed on Hannah's face. "I taught school for twenty-six years. I know broken minds when I see them. And hers is shattered in a very dangerous way."

The assessment sent another chill through Hannah's core. Physical threats could be countered with sufficient preparation. Tactical advantages could be neutralized with proper strategy. But this—a leader operating from a fractured reality, unbound by rational constraints—presented a different category of danger altogether.

Mrs. Henderson's eyes drifted closed again, exhaustion claiming her despite evident fear. Hannah tucked the emergency blanket more securely around her thin shoulders before returning to her journal.

Unknown female leader ("The Queen") now commanding Sherman's forces. Appears mentally unstable but tactically effective. Demonstrates knowledge that gives her psychological advantage over subordinates. Targets individuals with specific skills. Attack on Cornish remains scheduled for Thursday dawn, with advance teams already in position.

Water contamination confirmed. Need to warn Cornish immediately.

She closed the journal, tucking it into her pack before checking the time. Just past midnight. A few hours until dawn, when they would make their final push toward Cornish. Hannah leaned back against the rough cabin wall, rifle across her knees, gaze fixed on the darkness beyond the entrance.

The silence in Foster's Hardware pressed against Maddie's ears like water. She sat cross-legged on the floor behind the counter where she'd spent countless childhood hours, surrounded by the detritus of her failed attempts at processing her mother's death. Tissues scattered like fallen leaves. An untouched mug of coffee, now cold. The leather-bound journal Hannah had given her, still open to the page where she'd tried to write about loss and found no words adequate.

In her hands was the handkerchief Martha had given her back in Boston. Hers and Harold's wisdom and kindness stuck with her, although it felt like a lifetime had passed since that day. She wiped the tears with that small square and clutched it to her chest, and wondering if they'd survived all of this.

Her mother had been dead for six hours. The funeral pyre still smoldered behind the funeral home, thin smoke rising into the July heat. No ceremony, no gathered mourners, just necessity dressed up as closure. Another adaptation to their broken world.

Maddie's fingers traced the worn groove in the wooden counter where her father had sharpened his pocket knife thousands of times. The familiar texture anchored her, connected her to something solid when everything else felt like it was dissolving. She remembered perching on this exact spot as a five-year-old, watching him sort inventory while she colored in the margins of his order forms. He'd never scolded her for the unauthorized artwork, just smiled and said she was "adding value."

The memory brought fresh tears, hot and unexpected. She thought she was all cried out, wrung dry by the successive losses. But grief, she was learning, didn't follow logical patterns. It ambushed her in moments of quiet reflection, in the spaces between urgent tasks where her mind wandered to what she'd lost.

Foster's Hardware had been her playground, her after-school refuge, her introduction to the adult world of commerce and responsibility. Every aisle held memories layered like sediment—her first successful sale at age eight, confidently explaining the differences between Phillips and flathead screwdrivers to Mrs. Patterson. The summer she'd convinced her father to let her reorganize the entire fastener section by size and function. The countless times she'd hidden behind these very shelves when customers asked questions she couldn't answer, leaving her father to smooth over her adolescent embarrassment with patient explanations.

She'd taken it all for granted. The knowledge offered freely, the patient lessons, the assumption that this world would always exist for her, always the same and steadfast. Now she sat alone among tools she still couldn't fully identify, surrounded by solutions to problems she was only beginning to understand.

A soft scuffing sound from the front of the store pulled her from reverie. Maddie went still, listening. The front door was locked, had been since she'd returned from the pyre. But sound traveled strangely through the old building, echoing off high ceilings and bouncing between aisles.

The sound came again—deliberate movement, someone

trying to be quiet but not quite succeeding. Maddie rose slowly, her bare feet silent on the worn linoleum. Her father would have understood. He'd often worked in his stocking feet during inventory days, claiming he could feel problems with the floor that way.

Peering through the gap between shelving units, Maddie spotted them near the front window. Two men, both wearing the red fabric strips that had become Frank Wilson's calling card. They moved with the casual confidence of people who believed themselves unobserved, examining her filtration equipment with proprietary interest.

"This the setup?" one asked, his voice carrying clearly in the store's acoustic.

"Has to be," the second replied, lifting one of her water filter prototypes. "He said she's been working on this stuff since her old man died."

Maddie's chest tightened. They were discussing her work, as if it belonged to them. As if her grief and effort were commodities to be evaluated and claimed.

"Frank wants her cooperation," the first man continued, setting down a PVC fitting with careless handling that made Maddie wince. "Says it's better if she comes willingly. Less messy."

"And if she don't?"

A pause that stretched long enough to carry implications. "Frank's got plans for this place either way. Town needs clean water, and he's gonna be the one providing it. We're gonna be the heroes."

"And why does Frank get to be King? This is bullshit!"

"He says that Queen of Likes wants it that way. Now shaddup and find the girl."

Maddie felt something harden in her chest, crystallizing around the core of loss that had been consuming her since dawn. These men—Frank's men—were discussing her life, her work, her father's store as if she had no say in the matter. As if her cooperation was inevitable, her resistance was merely a temporary inconvenience.

Something quiet but unyielding was crystallizing inside her—a line drawn in bedrock that wouldn't be moved by pressure or convenience.

Her father's hunting rifle hung on pegs behind the sporting goods counter, unloaded but accessible. The ammunition sat in a locked case three feet away. She could arm herself, confront them from a position of strength. But something deeper than tactical calculation was stirring in her chest—a quiet fury that demanded personal confrontation.

Maddie walked deliberately toward the front of the store, her footsteps loud enough to announce her presence without suggesting stealth. The men turned, expressions shifting from casual exploration to alert assessment.

"Store's closed," she said, voice steady despite the adrenaline flooding her system.

The larger of the two men, she recognized him now as Tommy Grover, who'd fixed her car's transmission last winter, smiled with manufactured warmth. "Hey there, Maddie. Sorry for your loss. Your mom was a good woman."

The casual sympathy, delivered while standing uninvited in her store, examining her property without permission, felt like a slap. "Thank you," she replied flatly. "But you still need to leave."

"Actually," the second man said, "we were hoping to talk to you. Frank sent us with a proposition."

"I'm not interested in Frank's propositions right now. I am still trying to handle my parents' burial arrangements. Another time."

Tommy's smile tightened slightly. "Now, don't be hasty. You haven't heard what he's offering yet."

"I don't need to." Maddie crossed her arms, positioning herself between the men and her workstation. "Whatever it is, the answer is no."

"Protection," the second man said anyway, as if her refusal had been merely conversational. "Frank's building something here in Cornish. A real community, with real security. People who contribute get taken care of. People who don't..." He shrugged eloquently.

The threat was implicit but unmistakable. Maddie felt her jaw clench. "My father built something here too. This store, this business, these relationships. I don't need Frank's protection to continue his work."

"Your father's dead," Tommy said, his manufactured warmth evaporating. "So's your mother. You're alone now, girl. Alone people make mistakes. Dangerous mistakes."

Maddie's jaw clenched. A quiet stubbornness was emerging, refusing to be moved by threat or intimidation. Something fundamental that wouldn't bend when pushed past tolerance.

"I'm not alone," she said, voice dropping to something harder than she'd known she possessed. "I have this store. I have customers who depend on me. I have work to do that matters."

"Water filters," the second man said dismissively. "Frank's got better systems. Professional equipment. You're playing with toys here."

Another miscalculation. She moved to her workstation,

lifting one of the completed filtration units with careful precision.

"This 'toy' can process twenty gallons of contaminated water per hour," she said evenly. "It removes bacteria, parasites, heavy metals, and most chemical contaminants. I built it with components available in any hardware store, using techniques any competent technician can master." She set it down with deliberate care. "How many people has Frank's 'professional equipment' saved this week?"

Tommy's expression hardened. "You're making this difficult, Maddie. Frank's trying to be reasonable here."

"No," she replied, something shifting inside her like tectonic plates finding new alignment. "Frank's trying to steal what my father built. He's trying to use my grief and my fear to make me complicit in my own robbery." Her voice gained strength with each word. "I won't be reasonable about that."

The second man moved closer, trying to use his height advantage for intimidation. "You sure you want to be unreasonable? In times like these?"

Maddie held her ground, though her heart hammered against her ribs. Something had shifted inside her. It wasn't courage exactly, but clarity. A quiet determination that found strength not in the absence of fear, but in the presence of something more important than fear.

"I'm sure," she said simply.

Tommy sighed with theatrical disappointment. "Frank's not gonna like this answer."

"Frank can take his answer and choke on it."

The crude defiance surprised even her, but it felt right. The two men exchanged glances, some silent communication passing between them.

"You got until tomorrow to reconsider," Tommy said finally. "After that, things are gonna change and Frank makes his own arrangements."

"I'll save him the trouble," Maddie replied. "My answer won't change."

They left without further argument, but their casual confidence remained unshaken. They knew something they thought she didn't. They seemed sure they possessed some advantage that made her defiance merely temporary. The realization sent a chill through her newfound resolution.

After they'd gone, Maddie locked the front door, placing a shelf in front of it to add a kind of alarm.

She returned to her workstation, hands shaking slightly from the adrenaline crash. The confrontation had lasted perhaps ten minutes, but it had changed something fundamental inside her. The girl who'd been paralyzed by grief this morning was gone, replaced by someone harder, more focused. Someone who understood that survival meant more than simply staying alive—it meant protecting what mattered.

But protection required allies. Frank's confidence suggested he had resources, support, and plans that extended beyond simple intimidation. There was something in the reference to this Queen of Likes that felt ominous. She needed to warn Beth, needed to understand the scope of the threat Frank represented. Her water filters were valuable, but they were also a target now. Knowledge that could save lives, but only if she lived long enough to share it.

Maddie gathered her most critical notes, sealed them in a waterproof container, and tucked them into her jacket. The hunting rifle came down from its pegs, ammunition loaded with steady hands that surprised her with their competence. Her father had insisted on firearms training, another preparation she'd resented at the time.

The back door of Foster's Hardware opened onto the alley that connected to Main Street. Shadows stretched long between buildings in the setting sunlight, providing concealment as she moved toward the town hall where Beth maintained her headquarters. Time to find out just how alone she really was, and how much fight was left in Cornish when the reasonable people stopped being reasonable.

Hannah

The makeshift stretcher scraped against rocks and roots, each jarring impact sending a fresh wave of agony across Mrs. Henderson's bruised face. Hannah gripped the front handles, fashioned from torn strips of tarp and tree branches, her shoulders screaming in protest as she pulled the unconscious woman through the forest undergrowth. Behind her, Neil and Lonny practically carried Manuel between them, his fevered weight growing heavier with each stumbling step.

"I can't," Jake gasped, his end of Mrs. Henderson's stretcher wavering as his fourteen-year-old frame reached its limit. "Hannah, I can't do this anymore."

The admission hit Hannah like a physical blow. Dark circles ringed his eyes, his clothes hung loose on his shrinking frame, and his hands shook from exhaustion that went bone-deep.

"We're almost there," she lied, though the map showed at least another mile or so through increasingly difficult terrain. "Just a little further."

Mrs. Henderson stirred, a low moan escaping her cracked lips. The burns on her wrists had begun to fester, angry red lines spreading up her forearms. Without proper medical care, infection would claim her within days. The same infection that was already claiming Manuel, whose delirious muttering had grown more frequent as his fever spiked.

Hannah adjusted her grip on the stretcher handles, feeling blisters burst and reform on her palms. The forest floor was a maze of fallen logs, exposed roots, and hidden holes that threatened to snap ankles or send them tumbling into ravines. Every hundred yards became a tactical puzzle—finding paths wide enough for the stretcher while avoiding the open areas where Sherman's patrols might spot them.

"Water," Manuel whispered, his voice barely audible. "Please, just a sip."

Carla pressed their last bottle to his lips, tilting it carefully. Three swallows remained, maybe four. After that, if they didn't reach help, they'd be drinking from streams without purification tablets, risking the same contamination that had killed so many back in Portland.

"Route 25," Neil said suddenly, stopping so abruptly that Lonny nearly dropped Manuel's legs. "We need to get to the road."

Hannah stared at him. "Are you insane? That's where they'll be watching. We'll be sitting ducks."

"Look around," Neil gestured at the dense forest, at Mrs. Henderson's still form, at Manuel's fevered face. "We're dying by inches out here. Manuel needs a hospital. Mrs. Henderson needs a doctor. We need help, and we need it in hours, not days."

"If Sherman's people see us—"

"If we stay in these woods, we're dead anyway," Neil cut her off. "At least on the road, we can make time. Maybe flag down someone who can help."

Hannah's medical training warred with her survival instincts. Neil was right about their condition. Manuel's infection was spreading, Mrs. Henderson was slipping into deeper unconsciousness, and their group was reaching the point of complete physical breakdown. They didn't have enough supplies now with the larger group to sustain them even another night. But the road meant exposure, meant trusting their lives to the hope that whoever found them would be friendly.

"How far to Route 25?" she asked, defeat creeping into her voice.

Neil consulted the compass, squinting at landmarks through the canopy. "Maybe a quarter mile northeast. There's a service road that connects to the main highway."

Jake's shoulders sagged with relief. Even half a mile sounded insurmountable when dragged through forest, but manageable on flat pavement. Hannah looked at Mrs. Henderson's unconscious face, at the blood seeping through Manuel's bandages, at her brother's exhausted features.

"We take the road," she decided. "But the moment we see vehicles, we hide. No unnecessary risks."

They struggled through the remaining forest, every step a small agony. Hannah's legs had gone into a numbing kind of pain hours ago, operating on muscle memory and desperate will. The stretcher's improvised handles cut into her palms, leaving bloody marks that matched Jake's. Behind them, Neil and Lonny moved in the mechanical rhythm of men beyond exhaustion, carrying Manuel's dead weight between them, while Carla and Violet carried all of what was left of their supplies. They were exhausted and out of options.

When Route 25 finally appeared through the trees like a beacon of hope they all let out a collective sigh. The ribbon of cracked asphalt stretched before them, north toward Cornish. Hannah nearly wept with relief. The road surface, though pitted with potholes and scattered debris, looked like paradise compared to the root-tangled forest floor.

They emerged from the tree line like survivors of a shipwreck, blinking in the afternoon sunlight. Hannah set down her end of the stretcher, flexing her cramped fingers as circulation returned in painful waves. While the others took a short rest, she and Neil crept to the edge of the tree line to scout before they committed to it. The road stretched empty in both directions, no sign of patrols or traffic.

"Which way?" Jake asked from behind them, though they all knew the answer. North toward Cornish, toward, hopefully, whatever remained of civilization, toward the increasingly slim hope of finding Maddie… alive.

Hannah gripped the handles of the stretcher, gritting through the pain, saying, "Stay close. Single file. If anyone sees vehicles, we dive for the ditch."

The first mile passed without incident. The road's surface made carrying the stretcher easier, though Mrs. Henderson's weight seemed to increase with every step. Her breathing had grown shallow, rapid. The breathing of someone whose body was shutting down. Hannah had seen it before, in emergency rooms during her clinical rotations. The look of someone running out of time.

Manuel had stopped talking entirely, his head lolling against Lonny's shoulder. The infection was winning, spreading through his bloodstream faster than his depleted immune system could fight it. Without IV antibiotics, he had maybe twelve hours. Less if his fever continued climbing.

"Hannah," Jake's voice cracked. "I don't think I can make it to Cornish."

She turned to look at her brother—really look at him—and

her heart clenched. Jake had lost at least ten pounds since she'd made it home from Boston, his clothes hanging loose on his diminished frame. His eyes had sunken into his skull, and his movements carried the careful deliberation of someone conserving energy they no longer possessed.

"You can make it," she said, though the words felt hollow. "You're stronger than you know."

"I'm not," he replied with devastating honesty. "I'm done, Hannah. I've got nothing left."

The admission shattered something inside her chest. Jake, her little brother she promised her parents she'd look out for, her reason for continuing when everything else seemed hopeless, was giving up. Without him, she'd be truly alone, carrying the weight of their parents' sacrifice and her own impossible mission to warn Cornish.

"Then we'll rest," she said, though they couldn't afford to stop. "Just for a few minutes."

They lowered Mrs. Henderson's stretcher beside the road, in the meager shade of an abandoned guardrail. Manuel lay still, his breathing so shallow Hannah had to watch his chest carefully to confirm he was still alive. The group sat in exhausted silence, staring at the empty road that stretched endlessly ahead.

"I'm sorry," Jake whispered. "About Mom and Dad. About not being stronger."

Hannah felt tears burning behind her eyes—the first she'd allowed herself since their parents' capture. "You have nothing to apologize for. You've been braver than anyone should have to be."

"Have I?" Jake's laugh held no humor. "Because I feel like I've been terrified every single day since we left home."

"Being scared doesn't make you weak," Hannah said, echoing words their mother had spoken during Jake's nightmares as a child. "It makes you human."

A sound in the distance froze them all—the rumble of approaching engines. Hannah's hand moved instinctively to her rifle, though she knew it would be useless against multiple vehicles. They'd chosen the road for speed, accepting the risk of exposure. Now that risk was bearing down on them at sixty miles per hour.

"Into the ditch," she ordered, but even as she spoke, she knew it was too late. Mrs. Henderson couldn't be moved quickly, and Manuel was barely conscious. They were caught in the open, helpless as newborns.

The vehicles appeared around a curve—two pickup trucks and what looked like a converted school bus, all bearing the scars of months without proper maintenance. Hannah's finger tightened on the rifle's trigger as the convoy slowed, engines rumbling to idle as armed figures emerged from the vehicles.

But instead of the tactical gear and red bandanas she'd expected from Sherman's forces, these people wore mismatched civilian clothing. A woman with graying hair stepped forward, hands raised in a gesture of peace.

"Easy there," the woman called. "We're not looking for trouble. Just saw you folks might need help."

Hannah kept the rifle raised, though her arms shook with exhaustion. "Who are you?"

"Beth Martin. Police chief of Cornish." The woman's eyes moved to Mrs. Henderson's still form, to Manuel's fevered face. "Looks like you've had a rough time of it."

"We're trying to reach Cornish," Hannah said, not lowering the weapon. "We have information about an attack. Tomorrow morning."

Beth's expression sharpened. "What kind of information?"

Before Hannah could answer, a commotion erupted from the direction of town. Another vehicle approached at high speed—a figure running alongside it, rifle in hand. As the runner drew closer, Hannah's breath caught in her throat.

The face was thinner than she remembered, marked by grief and hardship, but unmistakable. Dark hair pulled back in a practical ponytail, determined jaw set in an expression of fierce resolve. The girl from her dorm room, from late-night study sessions, from tearful goodbyes in Portsmouth.

"Maddie?" Hannah whispered, scarcely believing her eyes.

The other girl stopped running, staring across the distance between them. Recognition dawned slowly, then blazed into something approaching joy.

"Hannah? Hannah!" Maddie's voice cracked as she broke into a sprint, covering the remaining distance in seconds. She crashed into Hannah's arms with enough force to stagger them both, rifle clattering to the pavement as Hannah's defenses finally completely collapsed.

"I thought you were dead," Maddie sobbed against Hannah's shoulder. "I thought everyone was dead."

Hannah held her friend with desperate strength, feeling the first genuine hope she'd experienced since South Portland burned. They were alive. Against impossible odds, through unimaginable hardship, they'd found each other again.

"We made it," she whispered, her voice breaking on the words. "We actually made it."

Ethan

The morning sun cast long shadows across the garden when Ethan first spotted the two men climbing through the hole in the north fence. His focus on them shifted to find what they were going after. From his position in the watchtower, he could see Elena kneeling between the squash rows, her dark hair catching the light as she worked as Marianne moved slowly among the tomato plants, her arthritic hands gentle with the ripening fruit.

He looked back at the men and panic rose in his chest. They weren't after some tomatoes. They were headed straight for Elena and Marianne.

Ethan's radio crackled. "Movement on the north perimeter," Grayson's voice reported from the eastern tower. "Two men, armed."

"I see them," Ethan whispered back, his finger finding the radio's transmit button. The men were moving with casual confidence, rifles slung across their backs, talking loudly enough that their voices carried across the morning air.

They were not bothered by any worry about who might see them and this made Ethan almost panic. He glanced back toward the house. Grandpa wasn't there and Dad was in the barn. Frantic his head snapped from side to side. Where was uncle Daniel?

"Look at that," one of the men called out loudly, his gaze

fixed on Elena. "Been a long time since we seen something that pretty."

The other man laughed, crude and hungry. "Old woman won't be much trouble. Girl looks like she might be fun."

Ice formed in Ethan's stomach. He keyed the radio again. "They're heading for the garden. Elena and Marianne are in danger."

"Stay in position," Grayson warned. "I'll go get your dad."

But the men were already at the garden's edge, and Grayson was too far away. Ethan could see Elena looking up from the squash plants, confusion flickering across her face as she registered the strangers. Marianne had straightened, her weathered hands still clutching a tomato, recognition dawning in her expression.

"Well, hello there, sweetheart," the first man called out, his hand sliding down to the handgun in his belt. "Don't be scared. We just want to get acquainted."

Elena struggled to her feet, one hand pressed to her still-tender abdomen. The miscarriage scare had left her weak, unsteady on her feet. She took a step backward, toward Marianne, but the older woman was already moving.

"You need to leave," Marianne said, her voice carrying the authority of someone accustomed to being obeyed. "This is private property."

The second man snorted. "Private property. That's rich." He stepped closer, and Ethan could see the hunger in his movements, the predatory focus. "Everything's public now, grandma. Especially the pretty things."

Ethan's hands shook as he gripped his small pocket knife. The decision was already forming in his mind, now he just had to make his feet comply.

"Run, Elena," Marianne said quietly, but her voice carried clearly in the morning stillness. "Run to the house."

Elena turned to flee, but her weakened condition betrayed her. She stumbled, crying out as she fell to her knees among the large leafy squash plants that tangled around her feet. The sound seemed to galvanize the two men, who moved forward with quickening steps.

"That's the spirit," the first man said. "On your knees is perfect."

Marianne stepped between Elena and the approaching men, her slight frame trembling but determined. "You leave her alone. She's been sick. She's pregnant."

"Not for long," the second man said with vicious humor. "We'll fix that real quick."

Ethan was moving before conscious thought took hold, scrambling down from the watchtower with reckless speed. His small pocket knife felt pathetic in his sweating palm, but it was all he had. Elena was trying to crawl away, sobs tearing from her throat as the men closed in. Marianne positioned herself directly in their path, arms spread wide despite her obvious terror.

"Get out of the way, old woman," the first man snarled, reaching for Marianne's shoulder.

She grabbed his wrist with surprising strength, her fingernails digging into his skin. "I said leave her alone!"

The man backhanded Marianne with casual violence, sending her sprawling among the tomato plants. She hit the ground hard, her thin frame no match for his bulk, but she immediately began crawling back toward Elena.

"Persistent old bitch," the second man observed. He drew back his foot and kicked Marianne in the ribs, the impact audible across the garden. She gasped, curling around her injured side, but still she tried to position herself between the men and Elena.

"Stop!" Ethan's voice cracked as he burst into the garden, his small knife raised but shaking in his grip. "Get away from them!"

Both men turned, their expressions shifting from predatory focus to amused contempt. Ethan stood twenty feet away, his slight frame holding nothing but a three-inch pocket knife. His face was flushed with terror and rage, but his weapon looked like a child's toy against grown men with guns.

"Well, look what we got here," the first man said, laughing outright. "Little boy with a butter knife."

"Put that away, kid," the second man added, not even bothering to unsling his own weapon. "Before you cut yourself."

Ethan's grip tightened on the knife handle, but his hands were shaking so badly he could barely hold it steady. "I said get away from them!"

"Or what?" The first man took a step toward Ethan, grinning. "You gonna stab us, little man? That toothpick ain't gonna do much damage."

Elena was still crawling away, leaving bloody handprints on the dirt as something warm and wet spread between her legs. The sight of her pain, her terror, her desperate attempts to escape, sent a spike of fury through Ethan's chest.

"I know how to use it," he said, though his voice betrayed his terror.

"Your daddy ain't here now," the second man observed, raising the handgun in his direction with lazy confidence. "Just you and us and, of course, these pretty ladies."

Marianne had managed to pull herself upright, blood trickling from her mouth. One arm hung at an odd angle, probably broken from her fall. But she was still moving, still trying to reach Elena.

"Such a sweet old grandma," the first man said mockingly. "Maybe we'll let you watch what happens next."

"Your little knife ain't gonna save nobody," the second man observed as he looked away dismissively and started moving toward the women.

The casual cruelty, the complete dismissal of his threat, the way they spoke about Elena and Marianne as if they were objects to be used and discarded caused something desperate and wild to erupt inside Ethan's chest. He wasn't strong enough, wasn't big enough, wasn't old enough, but Elena was bleeding and Marianne was broken and no one else was close enough to help.

He charged.

The first man was still laughing when Ethan crashed into him, the small knife slashing wildly. Pure desperation guided his movements as the blade caught the man's gun arm, dragging deep across the forearm. The man screamed, his pistol clattering to the ground as blood poured from the gash.

"You little bastard!" The man's free hand caught Ethan across the jaw with brutal force, sending him sprawling backward into the dirt. Stars exploded behind his eyes as he hit the ground hard, the knife spinning away from his numbed fingers.

A gunshot cracked across the garden. The second man— the one who'd been advancing on Elena—jerked and looked down in surprise at the spreading red stain on his chest. He took a step forward, then toppled face-first into the squash vines.

Jessica stood on the farmhouse porch, her rifle still smoking. "Get away from them," she called across the garden, her voice deadly calm.

The wounded man spun toward this new threat, reaching for his fallen pistol with his uninjured hand, but Ethan was closer. His fingers closed around the weapon's grip just as the man lunged for it.

Stunned for a moment the man stared at him as he raised the gun toward him. He smirked in a vicious sneer. Glaring at Ethan with hatred, a fire that brokered no mercy. His good hand moved to slide the rifle from behind. And terror rose like bile in Ethan's throat.

His small finger shifted, poised on the trigger as he raised the pistol's muzzle toward the man's chest. Ethan looked into eyes filled with rage and disbelief—a grown man's fury at being thwarted by a child. Time seemed suspended, balanced on the edge of a decision that would change everything.

"Please," Elena whispered from somewhere behind him, her voice weak with pain and terror. "Please help me."

Ethan pulled the trigger, his eyes never leaving that malicious stare and smirk.

The sound, like a loud crack rang in Ethan's ears and the eyes full of contempt widened in surprise when the man registered what happened. The man's body went limp and crumpled to the ground next to him. His eyes still wide with surprise stared into the sky, the life now gone from them and with it the evil that threatened. Blood spread across his shirt and Ethan rolled away from the corpse, crab walking away as he skittered backward, the pistol still clutched in his trembling hand.

"Elena," he gasped, stumbling toward her. She was lying

curled on her side, her face pale with pain and shock, hands and legs covered in blood.

"I'm here," he said, though his own voice sounded strange to his ears. "You're safe now. They can't hurt you."

Marianne crawled over, her broken arm cradled against her chest. "Good boy," she whispered, tears streaming down her dirt-stained face. "You saved us. You saved her."

Ethan looked at the two dead men, at the blood on his hands, at Elena's anguished face. The victory felt hollow, tainted by the cost. He'd saved them, but the weight of taking human life settled on his shoulders like a physical burden and tears sprang forth rolling down his cheeks.

Shouts echoed from across the farm as Michael and the others finally reached the garden. But Ethan barely heard them. He sat in the dirt beside Elena, holding her hand as she wept for the lost child, both of them forever changed by the morning's violence.

The boy who had climbed down from the watchtower was gone, replaced by someone harder, older, marked by choices no child should have to make.

James

The static on Old Man Jenkins' ham radio crackled like a fire consuming dry leaves. James hunched forward in the cramped shed behind Jenkins' house, adjusting the frequency dial with practiced movements while the elderly operator fine-tuned the antenna connections. The radio setup was impressive for amateur equipment—three different receivers, a powerful transmitter, and enough wire strung between trees to contact operators across New England.

Sweat beaded on James's forehead despite the shed's shade. The July heat was oppressive, but the tension radiating from the radio equipment made the small space feel like a furnace. Every transmission could bring news that would change everything, and James found himself holding his breath between bursts of static.

"There it is," Jenkins muttered, his weathered fingers dancing across the controls. "Emergency frequency. Been monitoring it since dawn."

The voice that emerged from the speakers carried the flat professionalism of someone reporting a catastrophe as routine. "...reactor cooling systems offline for approximately eighteen hours. Backup generators failed at 0300. Current status unknown, but radiation readings at the perimeter are climbing."

James felt ice form in his stomach, the cold spreading

through his chest like a physical presence. Seabrook Nuclear Station sat barely sixty miles southeast of Cornish, close enough that if the prevailing winds shifted, they could carry contamination directly over their community. He'd worked construction at the plant during its expansion in the nineties, knew the layout, understood the implications of cooling system failure. The reactor cores, without cooling, would begin to melt. The containment systems, stressed beyond design limits, could fail catastrophically.

"How bad?" he asked, though he already suspected the answer would redefine their understanding of catastrophe.

Jenkins adjusted his headset, leaning closer to the microphone. His hands shook slightly—whether from age or fear, James couldn't tell. "This is KC1GHT requesting an update on Seabrook Station status, over."

Static filled the shed for long moments, the electronic noise seeming to swallow their words and spit back only uncertainty. When a different voice finally responded, it carried the weight of someone delivering a death sentence. "KC1GHT, this is emergency coordination. Seabrook evacuation zone... prior operations to contain are straining. Advise cautionary measures."

Twenty miles. The formal evacuation zone now reached within thirty miles of Cornish. James's mind automatically calculated wind patterns, rainfall, the dozen variables that would determine whether radioactive fallout drifted toward their community or dispersed harmlessly over the Atlantic. His engineering background provided the knowledge, but no comfort. Radiation was invisible, tasteless, odorless. It could be drifting toward them right now, and they'd never know until people started dying.

"Jesus Christ," he whispered, the profanity escaping before

he could stop it.

"There's more," Jenkins said, his voice grim as he switched to another frequency. "Been tracking communications from Portland all morning. That new leader everyone's talking about? She's moving faster than anyone expected."

The next transmission carried a different kind of urgency— field reports from survivors fleeing the coast. The voice was breathless, desperate, describing horrors in clipped phrases. "...took Biddeford completely. No resistance. Reports of organized columns moving inland along Route 25. Estimate two hundred combatants, heavy weapons. They're not taking prisoners."

Route 25 ran directly through Cornish.

James felt his chest tighten, breathing becoming more difficult as the implications cascaded through his mind. Nuclear contamination from the southeast. Armed invasion from the south. His community caught between radioactive death and human violence, with nowhere to run and limited resources to fight.

"Timeline?" James asked, though his handheld radio was already crackling with an incoming transmission from the farm.

"Dad, this is Daniel. We've got a situation here. Over."

The controlled tension in his son's voice sent alarm bells through James's nervous system. Daniel was unflappable, had inherited the Thompson steadiness that had carried their family through three generations of Maine hardships. If Daniel sounded stressed, the situation was beyond serious.

James keyed his radio with hands that had begun to shake. "Go ahead, Daniel."

"Two men breached the north perimeter. Attacked Elena and Marianne in the garden." Daniel's voice carried controlled tension, but James could hear something else underneath—a father's rage barely held in check. "Dad, Ethan... Ethan had to defend them."

James's chest fell and he was instantly filled with dread that seemed to hollow out his bones. His thirteen-year-old grandson, forced into violence. The boy who still collected beetles and read adventure stories, suddenly thrust into the kind of situation that broke grown men. "Ethan? Is he—?"

"He's okay. The attackers are dead."

The words hit James like physical blows, each one a hammer strike to his solar plexus. His grandson—his gentle, curious, innocent grandson—had killed men. The boy who cried when they had to put down a sick calf had been forced to take human lives. Elena, already fragile from her recent pregnancy scare, traumatized further. Marianne, who'd survived seven decades only to face assault in what should have been a safe garden.

James gripped the radio so tightly his knuckles went white. "Casualties?" he asked, dreading the answer but needing to know the full scope of the horror.

"Elena's hurt." A long pause followed, filled with static that seemed to echo the emptiness in James's chest before Daniel returned. "She lost the baby."

James choked, holding in a sob as the news hit him. Elena's child—Matthew's child—gone. Another life stolen by this broken world, another dream crushed under the weight of survival. He pressed his free hand against his mouth, fighting the urge to scream his rage at a universe that demanded such sacrifices from innocent people.

Daniel finished his report in the clinical tone of someone forcing emotion aside to deliver necessary information.

"Marianne has a broken arm, possible internal injuries. But they're alive. Ethan..." Daniel paused, and in that silence James heard a father's anguish. "He's in shock. Michael's with him now."

James closed his eyes, feeling the weight of leadership pressing down like a physical force. Every decision rippled outward, affecting people he loved more than his own life. The intelligence from Jenkins' radio painted a picture of coordinated assault approaching from multiple vectors. The farm attack suggested advance teams were already probing their defenses—either that, or it was more of Frank's people testing their resolve. But more than tactical concerns, his grandson was now dealing with trauma that would mark him forever.

The boy who'd asked endless questions about how things worked, who'd wanted to understand every tool in the shed, every mechanical process on the farm, had been forced to understand the mechanics of death. The weight of that knowledge would change him in ways that made James's heart break.

"I'm coming home," James said into the radio, his voice rough with suppressed emotion.

"Negative." Daniel's response was immediate and firm. "Farm is secure. We've got medical support, defensive positions established. Beth needs you in town. There's new arrivals—they've got intelligence about the attack we've been getting bits of intelligence on."

Jenkins looked up from his radio adjustments, his weathered face creased with concern. "What new arrivals?"

Before James could answer, both his handheld and Jenkins' ham radio erupted simultaneously. Multiple voices overlapping, urgent reports flooding the airwaves like a dam burst of catastrophic information. The cacophony was overwhelming—desperate voices reporting disasters, calling for help, sharing fragments of intelligence that painted a picture of coordinated collapse.

"Thompson farm, this is Martin. Convoy approaching from the south—"

"—medical emergency at the funeral home, need all available—"

"—armed group moving north on 25, estimate forty vehicles—"

"—radiation readings climbing, wind shift predicted—"

James sorted through the chaos, his mind automatically prioritizing threats and cataloging information even as his heart hammered against his ribs. He identified Beth's voice among the overlapping transmissions, her professional calm an anchor point in the storm of panic.

"James, we've got survivors from South Portland. They confirm a coordinated attack planned for tomorrow dawn. Three-pronged assault, Sherman's forces under new command."

"New command?" James asked, his hand going to his forehead, trying to process all the incoming reports while maintaining some semblance of calm leadership. Something cold was already settling in his chest, a premonition that the worst news was yet to come.

"Some kind of coastal raider calling herself the Queen. Took over Sherman's operation, moving inland with significant force." Beth's transmission crackled with static, but her words came through clearly enough to send another chill through James's blood. "These survivors have intelligence we need. Can you meet us at the funeral home?"

James looked at Jenkins, who was frantically adjusting

frequencies, trying to track multiple emergency channels simultaneously. Sweat poured down the old man's face as he worked, his hands moving with desperate precision across controls that connected them to a world falling apart in real time. Through the shed's single window, James could see the main road leading north out of town. No traffic, but dust hanging in the air suggested a recent passage—someone moving fast, with purpose.

"Daniel," James keyed his radio again, fighting to keep his voice steady. "Status on the farm defenses?"

"Perimeter secure. We've moved everyone to predetermined positions. Ryan's fever broke, he's mobile. Elena's stable, Marianne will get treatment from Emily when she returns from town but is stable for the moment. Mom is looking after them." Daniel's voice steadied, and James heard the competence that had made him proud of his son countless times. "Dad, they can handle this. We're needed elsewhere."

The decision tore at James's chest like a physical wound. His family—his blood—dealing with trauma and threat while he coordinated community response. Ethan, probably curled in some corner trying to process what he'd been forced to do. Elena and Matthew, grieving a child they'd never hold. Marianne, her elderly body broken by violence that should never have touched their peaceful farm.

But that was leadership—carrying responsibilities that demanded personal sacrifice, making choices that carved pieces from your soul.

"I'll head to the funeral home," he decided, each word feeling like another step away from his family when they needed him most. "Daniel, as soon as Michael has Ethan settled, I need you in town. We're going to need all hands."

"Roger that. I'm on my way. Daniel out."

James stood to leave, his knees protesting the movement. Age and stress were taking their toll, making every action feel labored. But Jenkins grabbed his arm with surprising strength, weathered fingers digging into muscle.

"Wait. There's something else." The old man's expression was grim as he switched to yet another frequency, his face pale in the shed's dim light. "Been monitoring military channels. There's chatter about coordinated attacks across multiple towns."

Static filled the shed as Jenkins fine-tuned the signal, the electronic noise seeming to whisper of disasters beyond their immediate comprehension. When a new voice emerged, it carried the official and controlled tone of someone coordinating catastrophe on a regional scale.

"...pattern suggests organized campaign. Coastal raiders have established supply lines, communication networks. Recommend all surviving communities implement immediate defensive protocols. This is not random violence—repeat, this is coordinated territorial acquisition."

"It's not random," James realized aloud, the pieces clicking together in his mind with horrible clarity. "This Queen, whoever she is, she's building something. Territory. Infrastructure."

"She's building an empire," Jenkins corrected grimly, his fingers still working the radio controls as more reports filtered through. "And Cornish is her next acquisition."

James headed for the door, his mind racing through tactical considerations that seemed woefully inadequate for what they were facing. Three-pronged attack, superior numbers, coordinated timing. Nuclear contamination potentially drifting their way. Their community's survival would depend on intelligence, preparation, and the kind of desperate courage his grandson had already been forced to display in the garden.

He stepped outside Jenkins' shed just as a convoy of vehicles roared past on the main road—pickup trucks and a converted school bus, all bearing the red fabric strips that marked Frank Wilson's followers. The vehicles moved with obvious urgency, kicking up dust clouds that obscured their exact numbers. James counted at least twelve men, all armed, all moving north with the purposefulness of people who knew exactly where they were going and why.

Frank himself sat in the lead truck's passenger seat, and when he spotted James, their eyes met across fifty yards of dusty road. Time seemed to slow as Frank's expression shifted from surprise to calculation to something approaching vicious satisfaction. The man who'd been positioning himself as Cornish's savior was abandoning them at their hour of greatest need.

Frank said something to his driver, and the truck slowed.

James reached for his sidearm, instinct and training overriding conscious thought, but Frank was faster. The rifle appeared in the truck's window, muzzle flash bright in the afternoon sun. The bullet whined past James's head, close enough to feel the air displacement, close enough to singe hair. A second shot shattered Jenkins' mailbox, sending wood splinters flying like shrapnel.

"Next time!" Frank shouted over the engine noise as the convoy accelerated again, his voice carrying a promise of violence that made James's blood run cold. "Next time, old man!"

James drew his pistol, muscle memory guiding the smooth motion, but the vehicles were already pulling away, dust clouds marking their passage toward whatever rendezvous Frank had planned. Pursuing them would mean abandoning the intelligence gathering, leaving Beth without backup, failing his community when coordination was most critical.

The rational part of his mind knew this, but every fiber of his being screamed for revenge. Frank—the man who'd eaten at their table, who'd accepted their hospitality, who'd positioned himself as their protector—had just tried to kill him. The betrayal burned in his chest like acid.

He holstered the weapon, frustration and rage burning in his chest like molten metal. Frank was escaping, probably to coordinate with the incoming assault. The man knew their defenses, their capabilities, their weaknesses. He could provide intelligence that would make the attack devastatingly effective.

But the immediate choice was clear—they needed to prepare more than he needed vengeance.

His radio crackled again, Daniel's voice cutting through his churning emotions. "Dad, this is Daniel. I'm leaving the farm now. ETA to town fifteen minutes."

Relief flooded through James like cool water on burned skin. His son—competent, steady, unshakable Daniel—would help shoulder the burden of what was coming. Together, they could coordinate the defense Cornish would need to survive the next twenty-four hours. They could transform their scattered community into something capable of standing against whatever darkness was moving toward them.

"Meet me at the funeral home," James replied, his voice steadier now with purpose. "We've got intelligence to review and very little time to prepare."

As he walked toward his vehicle, Jenkins emerged from the shed, a handheld radio in his arthritic grip. The old man looked haggard, aged years in the span of hours, but his voice was firm with resolve.

"I'll monitor all frequencies," the old man promised. "Any changes in the situation, I'll relay immediately. You go do what needs doing."

James nodded his thanks, then paused as something caught his attention. In the distance, barely audible over the wind and the lingering echo of Frank's convoy, came the sound of voices. Singing. Not the rough harmony of men preparing for battle, but something else—children's voices, carrying a melody that seemed to drift from another world entirely.

The sound was incongruous, almost surreal against the backdrop of approaching war and nuclear disaster. Yet it drew him forward, a reminder of what they were fighting to preserve. He followed the sound, walking toward the funeral home where smoke rose from Emily's medical preparations.

As he drew closer, the voices became clearer. Children, singing an old song about peace and hope, their voices rising above the smell of antiseptic and the low murmur of adult conversation. The lyrics spoke of better days, of faith in the face of adversity, of love that endured beyond understanding.

At the funeral home's entrance, James paused to observe the scene inside through the windows. Strangers—obviously refugees—receiving medical attention from Emily and her volunteer assistants. Their clothes were torn and dirty, their faces marked by exhaustion and trauma, but they were alive. They had survived whatever horrors had driven them from their homes, and now they sought shelter in Cornish's embrace.

Beth was coordinating security arrangements, her movements efficient and purposeful. She'd transformed from small-town police chief to military commander with remarkable grace, adapting to leadership demands that would have broken lesser people.

And there, in the corner, a young woman with dark hair holding hands with Maddie. She was about the same age, and both had the hollow-eyed look of people who'd seen too much, endured too much, yet somehow survived. The connection between them was obvious—these weren't strangers brought together by circumstance, but friends reunited against impossible odds.

The singing stopped as James entered, replaced by the urgent whispers of people sharing intelligence that could mean life or death for everyone in their small town. The transition was jarring, beautiful innocence giving way to harsh necessity. Tomorrow would bring the storm they'd all been preparing for, whether they knew it or not.

James squared his shoulders and stepped inside, ready to hear what these survivors had learned. Daniel stepped up beside him and clamped a hand on his shoulder. As they entered the gasp from Daniel made him pause and turn.

"What? What is it?"

Daniel hurried over to where Maddie sat with the other girl and began speaking animatedly. James approached and glanced from Maddie to the other girl and a young boy before speaking. "Hi, I'm James."

Daniel turned to him saying, "Dad, this is the family I told you about that helped us in Portland." He paused looking around and asked, "Where's your parents?"

Hannah looked at the floor before she broke. Great sobs racked her body as Maddie tried to console her. She didn't need to say anything, James knew.

Outside, the wind had picked up, rattling windows and

carrying the scent of distant smoke. Whether from fires or worse, James couldn't tell. But change was coming, riding on that wind, and all they could do was stand ready to meet it.

Grace

The convoy stretched along Route 25 like a steel serpent, forty-three vehicles strong, each one a testament to Grace's divine vision. She stood in the back of her command truck, a modified F-350 with armor plating and a raised platform, filming herself with a cracked iPhone that hadn't worked since *the day*.

"Good morning, my beautiful followers!" Grace beamed at the dead screen, her voice carrying that familiar bright enthusiasm. "Today is going to be absolutely EPIC! We're about to drop the most amazing content, and I literally cannot wait to share this journey with you all!"

Derek Santos, her newly appointed lieutenant, shifted uncomfortably in the driver's seat and glanced back at her through the wide open segment where the roof and back window had been cut off to accommodate her throne. The man had witnessed what happened to Grace's previous commanders when they disappointed her. Sherman's skull still decorated the grille of her truck, after all. Polished white bone bleached and polished looked classic as she said.

"Grace," Derek said carefully, his voice tight with barely controlled fear, "maybe we should consider stopping soon. The men are getting tired, and we've been pushing hard for—"

The transformation was instantaneous. Grace's bright smile twisted into something feral, her eyes going flat and cold like a shark's. The phone clattered to the truck bed as she spun toward Derek with predatory grace.

"Excuse me?" Her voice dropped to a whisper that somehow carried more menace than screaming. "Did you just interrupt me while I was creating content?"

Derek's face went pale. "I just thought—"

"You thought?" Grace laughed, the sound bright and musical and completely devoid of humanity. "That's adorable. Really. You thought you knew better than the Queen of Likes herself."

She pulled a chrome-plated .45 from her designer holster, custom pink grips that matched her nail polish, and pressed the barrel against the back of Derek's head. Around them, the convoy ground to a halt as drivers witnessed their leader's mood shift.

"Here's the thing about thinking, Derek," Grace said conversationally, as if discussing weekend plans. "It's really overrated. Especially when you're thinking about questioning my creative process."

Derek's hands shook as he gripped the steering wheel. Sweat poured down his face despite the morning chill. "Grace, please, I wasn't—"

The gunshot was deafeningly loud, shattering the momentary silence as the others watched. Derek's body slumped forward, blood and brain matter splattering across the windshield in an abstract pattern that Grace found aesthetically interesting.

"Oops!" She giggled, wiping blood spatter from her cheek with the back of her hand. "Sorry about that, followers.

Sometimes you have to deal with negative engagement in real time."

She holstered the weapon and retrieved her phone, resuming her bright smile as if nothing had happened. Around the convoy, hardened fighters who'd survived coastal raids and inland battles watched with the kind of careful attention that kept them alive around their unstable leader.

"Where were we? Oh right! Today's amazing content schedule." Grace stepped over Derek's corpse with practiced ease, shoving his limp body into the passenger seat pushing into a crumpled heap beside her as she settled into the driver's seat with the casual confidence of someone who'd made this transition dozens of times before. "Production meetings can be so tedious, but that's handled now."

The dead man's blood dripping off the dashboard pooled around her designer combat boots. A pair of limited edition tactical wear that had cost more than most people's cars in the before-times. Grace said she always believed in investing in quality accessories, even during the apocalypse.

"Timothy!" she called to a scared veteran in the truck behind her. "You're my new assistant director. Try not to disappoint me like Derek did."

Timothy nodded quickly, his face professionally neutral despite the fear in his eyes. He'd seen Grace's "creative differences" with previous staff members. The smart ones learned to agree with enthusiasm and save their suggestions for later, much later.

Grace put the truck in drive, humming softly as the convoy resumed its northward crawl. She reached out and smeared Derek's remains across the glass in rhythmic arcs, creating patterns that reminded her of abstract art installations she'd seen in gallery showings.

"The thing about authentic content," she said to her phone, "is that it requires absolute creative control. No committee decisions, no focus groups, no beta males trying to mansplain production schedules."

She paused at the crest of a hill, surveying the landscape ahead with the satisfaction of a film director scouting locations. In the distance, smoke columns rose from what might have been a town or perhaps forest fires. Either way, it would make excellent atmospheric footage.

At the head of the convoy, the prize that made this entire expedition so much more interesting rattled in its cage. Rebecca Mitchell huddled behind reinforced bars welded to the bed of the lead truck, her will beaten out of her by psychological torture. Grace had been so pleased when they'd captured the woman during the South Portland raids.

Grace climbed onto her platform, phone in hand, ready to document the next phase of her masterpiece. The blood on her boots was already drying in the morning sun.

"Sometimes," she said to her invisible audience, "you have to make hard choices to protect your artistic vision. But that's what separates real influencers from wannabe content creators."

She smiled at the camera, her expression bright and enthusiastic and completely divorced from the corpse cooling in the seat beside her. Around the convoy, her followers checked their weapons and tried not to think about what would happen if they ever gave her a reason to turn that smile in their direction.

Grace parked the convoy in a semicircle among the abandoned vehicles that littered this stretch of Route 25, creating what she cataloged as a perfect amphitheater setting.

The other drivers followed her lead without question. They'd learned that creativity flowed better when the Queen had proper staging.

"Location scouting is so important for content creation," she told her phone, panning across the automotive graveyard that stretched for miles. Rusted cars and trucks sat abandoned where they'd died during the CME, their owners long since scattered to the winds or feeding the crows. "You need the right aesthetic to tell your story effectively."

She hopped down from the truck bed with practiced grace, her designer boots crunching on broken glass and scattered debris. The afternoon sun caught the pink grips of her holster, creating what she knew would be excellent lighting for her eventual edit.

"Time for a special segment, my gorgeous followers," Grace announced, skipping toward the lead truck where Rebecca Mitchell's cage sat like a medieval pillory. "I want to introduce you to someone very special who's been helping with today's production."

Rebecca pressed herself against the far corner of the cage as Grace approached. The time in captivity had taught her that Grace's moods could shift like weather patterns, bright sunshine followed by devastating storms.

"This beautiful lady is going to help us create the most authentic emotional content you've ever seen," Grace said, producing the cage key from around her neck with theatrical flair. "Rebecca, sweetie, wave to my followers!"

Rebecca remained motionless, her eyes fixed on some middle distance where hope might once have lived. The calculated non-response sent a flicker of annoyance across Grace's features, like a crack in perfect porcelain.

"She's just being shy because she knows how much this means to her daughter," Grace explained to the camera, her voice taking on that patient, condescending tone she'd perfected for dealing with difficult guests. "Hannah is probably somewhere nearby, thinking she's so smart with her little survival skills. But what she doesn't realize is that Mommy Dearest is going to be the star of today's show!"

Grace unlocked the cage with a flourish, the metal door swinging open with a rusty screech that echoed across the automotive wasteland. Rebecca didn't try to run. She found out quickly that escape attempts only made things worse. Much worse.

"Come on out, sweetie," Grace cooed, her voice sickeningly maternal. "We need to get you camera-ready for your big scene."

Rebecca stumbled from the cage on unsteady legs, her body weak from confinement and irregular feeding. Grace immediately began circling her with the phone, filming from different angles like a predator studying wounded prey.

"The thing about authentic content," Grace explained to her invisible audience, "is that real emotion can't be faked. Studio lighting and professional makeup can only do so much. But genuine terror? Authentic despair? That translates beautifully on any platform."

Timothy approached cautiously from the perimeter, his scarred face carefully neutral. He'd survived three different raider groups before joining Grace's operation, and he'd already learned to read the subtle signs of impending violence. The Queen's shoulders were too rigid, her smile too wide, her movements too precise.

"Status report on the northern approach," he said carefully, keeping his voice professional and deferential.

"Oh, that's so boring," Grace replied without looking away from Rebecca. "We're having a creative moment here. Can't you see I'm working?"

Timothy retreated quickly, recognizing the warning signs. Around the convoy, other fighters found sudden interest in equipment maintenance or perimeter security. Anything that kept them out of Grace's immediate attention span.

Grace grabbed Rebecca's chin with manicured fingers, forcing the woman to look into the dead camera. Her grip was gentle but implacable, like a steel trap wrapped in silk.

"Tell Hannah how much you've missed her," Grace commanded, her voice bright with artificial enthusiasm. "Tell her how excited you are for your reunion."

"Please," Rebecca whispered, the word barely audible. " She's never done anything to you."

Grace's expression shifted instantly, storm clouds gathering behind her bright facade. The hand on Rebecca's chin tightened until the woman winced.

"Never done anything?" Grace's voice dropped to that whisper that made hardened fighters check their weapons. "She tried to cancel me. She and her little friend Maddie thought they could silence the Queen of Likes herself."

The rage built in her voice like pressure in a kettle, but her smile never wavered. That was the most unsettling thing about Grace's madness. The way her expressions remained perfectly curated even as she described unspeakable horrors.

"They thought they were the heroes of the story," Grace continued, releasing Rebecca's face to gesture expansively at her army, her weapons, her perfect amphitheater of destruction. "But here's what they never understood about narrative structure. Sometimes the most interesting character is the one everyone calls the villain."

She spun back toward the phone, her energy ramping up to manic levels as the mood shift completed its cycle.

"Which brings us to today's special episode!" Grace announced with genuine excitement. "We're going to create content that breaks all the engagement metrics. The kind of authentic emotional storytelling that defines entire generations."

Around the convoy, her followers continued their careful pantomime of productivity while monitoring their leader's psychological weather patterns. They all knew what came next… the brittle laughter, the rapid topic changes, the way her hands moved to her weapons when she felt contradicted.

Grace walked to the edge of the road, surveying the landscape ahead with the satisfaction of a director who'd found the perfect location. Cornish lay somewhere beyond the next ridge, unsuspecting and unprepared for what was coming. But first, she had content to create.

"The thing about influence, Rebecca," Grace said conversationally, not bothering to turn around, "is that it's not about followers or likes or any of that surface-level bullshit. Real influence is about making people do things they never thought they'd do."

She gestured toward her assembled forces, former coastal raiders, survivors who'd bent the knee, desperate souls who'd traded their humanity for the promise of safety under the Queen's protection.

"Like my beautiful army here. A few months ago, they were separate groups fighting over scraps. Now look at them— perfectly coordinated, absolutely loyal, ready to die for content they'll never even see."

Grace's laugh was bright and musical and completely devoid of sanity. In the distance, crows circled something that might once have been human, their cries mixing with the wind to create a soundtrack that would have been perfect for her eventual edit.

The sun continued its arc across the sky as Grace prepared for the next phase of her masterpiece. Soon, very soon, she would give her followers the content they deserved—the kind of authentic storytelling that would be remembered long after the last phone had died and the final server had gone dark.

But first, she had a reunion to orchestrate.

Grace stood at the edge of the automotive graveyard, her phone held at arm's length as she filmed herself against the backdrop of rusted metal and scattered bones. The afternoon light was perfect—golden hour approaching, dramatic shadows creating natural contrast that would translate beautifully in post-production.

"Okay, my gorgeous followers, we're about to pivot to the main event," she announced with the breathless excitement of someone unveiling a surprise gift. "But first, I want to show you something that's going to make today's content extra special."

She gestured toward Rebecca, who sat huddled against the wheel of an abandoned semi-truck, still trying to process the casual violence she'd witnessed. Derek's execution had been swift and efficient, but the psychological impact lingered like smoke.

"This amazing lady is going to help us create the most authentic emotional content you've ever seen," Grace continued, her voice taking on that warm, inclusive tone. "Real family drama, genuine reactions—the kind of storytelling that goes viral because it touches something fundamental in the human experience."

Timothy kept his distance, monitoring radio chatter from the northern teams while trying to avoid drawing attention to himself. Grace's mood had stabilized somewhat after the impromptu execution, but stability was relative when dealing with the Queen of Likes.

"The production value here is absolutely incredible," Grace narrated, panning the phone across the wasteland of abandoned vehicles. "Post-apocalyptic aesthetic with authentic decay. You literally could not hire set designers to create anything this realistic."

She skipped between the rusted hulks, her energy infectious despite the circumstances. Several of her fighters found themselves unconsciously smiling at her enthusiasm—a testament to the charisma that had built her empire from the ashes of civilization.

"Visual storytelling 101," Grace explained, climbing onto the hood of a destroyed pickup truck to get a better angle, "is all about creating environments that support your narrative. And this place? It's perfect for what we're planning."

She jumped down with practiced grace, landing near Rebecca with the predatory confidence of someone who'd turned violence into performance art. The older woman flinched, instantly hyper-aware of Grace's proximity.

"The thing about authentic content," Grace said, her voice dropping to something more intimate, "is that it requires absolute creative control. No committee decisions, no beta male input, no focus groups trying to sanitize the vision."

She pulled Rebecca to her feet with deceptive gentleness, positioning her for better camera angles while keeping up the cheerful commentary.

Around the convoy, her followers continued their equipment checks with the kind of focused attention that came from understanding the stakes. Grace's content creation sessions had a way of escalating, and smart fighters made sure their gear was ready for whatever artistic vision might emerge.

The thing is, they all knew she was bat shit crazy and it wasn't just her. She had an inner circle that enjoyed the delights of torture and the worst that humanity could conjure, and Grace gave them that freedom to rape and torture all they liked while she stood on a pedestal with her dead phone.

Grace's phone buzzed with a notification, or would have, if it had actually been functional. She glanced at the blank screen with the satisfied expression of someone receiving exactly the validation they expected.

"Look at that engagement!" she squealed, showing the dead phone to Rebecca as if the woman could see the invisible metrics. "The algorithm is already picking up on our content strategy. This is going to break the internet when we finally upload to all the platforms."

She tucked the phone into her tactical vest and produced a small mirror from her equipment pack, checking her appearance with the professional attention of someone who understood that presentation was everything. Her platinum blonde hair remained perfect despite the road dust, her makeup flawless even after hours of travel.

"Appearance consistency is so important for brand recognition," Grace explained to Rebecca, who watched with the hollow-eyed attention of someone who'd learned that ignoring the Queen led to immediate consequences. "Your audience needs to know they're getting the same quality experience every time."

Timothy approached carefully, his radio crackling with updates from the advance teams. "Grace, we're getting reports from the northern approach. Cornish has defensive positions, but nothing we can't handle."

Grace's smile brightened, genuine excitement replacing the performed enthusiasm. "Perfect! Everything is falling into place exactly like I visualized." She squeed with excitement. "The resistance element is going to add so much dramatic tension to the final act."

She grabbed Rebecca's arm, pulling the woman toward the command truck with renewed energy. The cage had been cleaned and repositioned for maximum visibility. Just another prop in Grace's elaborate stage production.

"Time for places, everyone!" Grace called out, her voice carrying across the convoy with theatrical authority. "Lights, camera, apocalypse!"

As the sun began its descent toward the horizon, painting the sky in shades of orange and crimson, Rebecca Mitchell huddled in her mobile prison, watching the landscape roll past and the Queen of Likes had promised her followers the ultimate content drop, and Grace always delivered on her promises—though never in the way her victims expected.

"It is impossible to show why certain things should not utterly destroy and end the human race and story..."

- H.G. Wells

Thank you for reading. Please consider leaving a review.

Also by DJ Cooper

<u>Dystopia Series</u>

Beginning of the End

Long Road

Revelations

Dark Days

<u>Apocalypse Fire Series</u>

Endure the Chaos

Survive the Chaos

Beyond the Chaos

<u>Cincinnati Fall Series</u>

Cincinnati Fall 1

Cincinnati Fall 2

Cincinnati Fall 3

<u>Nine Meals From Anarchy Series</u>

Sun's Fury

Terminus State

<u>Insurrection Series</u>

Deception

Evasion

Abolition

<u>WordPeddler Magazines</u>

COMING SOON

https://fire-n-ash.com

Acknowledgements

Decayed World is a story of not just survival but of human desire to persevere. In book one *Wasted World*, the separate journeys through areas mired with challenges around every corner. Now they face challenges they never thought would come to them.

What's next for our group in Cornish and what of Hannah? Find these answers and more questions in the next book *Altered World*.

If you would like to stay updated on this and other emerging stories in my new Fire & Ash World, visit my website at https://authoroftheapocalypse.com

I am incredibly grateful to all who read this and my other stories. A passion I never knew existed until I sat down one day to write and now, I try harder with each book, chapter, paragraph and sentence to make it better than the one before. If it were not for the amazing readers who give up their time to walk these tales along with me, I would not be able to do so. It is for you I try to make each one more than the last. I love hearing from readers even if you don't like it. Without feedback I can't do better next time.

I need to express my deepest gratitude to those who were stuck reading this in its early stages. Nancy (N.A.)

Broadley is an author friend who is always willing to tell me like it is. Wendy Durison Editor who painstakingly checked that I dotted all my I's and crossed all my T's and didn't use the same word twelve times in a sentence. And I am thankful for Dan Uebel who offers the best insights on many forms of work and is the hard work behind the Book Asylum Podcast. I couldn't do it without your help.